OPERATION: SAPPHIRE

LEXI GRAVES MYSTERIES

Camilla Chafer

Visit the author online at www.camillachafer.com

ALSO BY CAMILLA CHAFER

CHAPTER ONE

"They're definitely up to something," said Lily. She lowered her binoculars and fixed me with a look that said she was certain she'd positively identified criminals in the midst of a nefarious act.

"They're getting coffee," I said before sipping mine, a small puff of foam erupting from the cup and threatening to stick to the tip of my nose.

"They're *shifty*."

"You said that about four different guys yesterday. These ladies have the combined age of two hundred and fifty. They couldn't look shifty if they tried." I watched the trio of elderly ladies shuffling out of the jewelry store across the street, chattering away, and queue at the sidewalk coffee cart before shaking my head.

"And that's why they're definitely up to no good," Lily decided. "They might have fooled you, but they haven't fooled me." She pushed back her blonde curls with one hand and lifted her binoculars again.

"Do you have to use those things in the coffee

shop?" I asked.

Lily lowered the binoculars and frowned. "Would a telescope be less conspicuous?" She began to reach for her purse as I sighed. There was no telling what Lily might have stashed in there although a telescope seemed the most reasonable item I could think of. Plus, I had to harbor the hope she wouldn't upgrade a simple tool like that to an actual weapon. That would be scary. I took another look at her purse. Was that *my* purse? "It's not your purse," said Lily. "They look the same but yours has the skinny handles. This one has wider handles."

"I never said it was!"

"You were thinking it! I know you!"

"I would nev…"

"They're on the move," Lily cut in, the binoculars firmly pressed to her eyes.

I followed her gaze as the elderly ladies shuffled towards a bus stop, the coffee cart now abandoned, and not a single takeout cup in sight. "Are you sure they're moving?" I asked. I did a mental calculation and estimated they might reach the bus stop in three to four business days at that speed.

Lily tracked their epically slow movements. "We should follow."

"Absolutely not."

"Why not?"

"Because there's no reason to. They're just three nice, old ladies enjoying a day out…"

"In an upscale jewelry shop?"

"Maybe they wanted some jewelry appraised? Or possibly buying a gift? Or perhaps one of them is treating herself to a big purchase? We don't know," I said.

"Exactly! *We don't know.* They could have been casing the joint."

"I don't think their joints allow for anything that exciting."

"But we followed them this far!"

"We happened to be going in the same direction, and I wanted a coffee. I still have no idea why you wanted to follow *them*, of all people!"

"I told you already! They were acting suspiciously. They were being furtive. *And* they were in the jewelry store a weird amount of time. Too short to get an appraisal, and too long to buy a gift."

"Maybe one of them was indecisive. Maybe it was a joint gift and they were all arguing?" I reasoned, although I wasn't sure why I was bothering. Lily was as determined as me, only we were heading in different directions mentally. Lily thought she had a trio of geriatric thieves in her sights. I thought the three old ladies needed to be left alone by me, Private Investigator Lexi Graves and her nutso best friend, and much-loved sister-in-law, Lily Shuler-Graves.

A bus glided to a stop. Nearly a minute later, the three ladies shuffled down the aisle, flopping into seats near the back. "They're getting away," wailed Lily.

It was the slowest, most inefficient getaway I'd ever seen if that were the case. I countered, "They're going back to their homes for an afternoon nap."

"That does sound a good idea," said Lily. Then she gasped. "What have I become?"

"A mom."

"You'd think I'd be used to it by now." Lily stifled a yawn. "Well, those master criminals..."

"Elderly, law-abiding ladies," I corrected her.

Lily shot me a withering look. "Those master

criminals have gotten away this time but mark my words, that won't be the last we'll see of them."

"Ooo-kaaay," I said, dragging the syllables out far longer than necessary as I made my point.

Lily peered at me. "Did you just have a stroke?"

"No," I said as my phone beeped. I pulled it from my pocket and checked my screen.

"Is it your man wanting to play the baby-making game again? If so you're excused," said Lily. "And maybe order a shot of espresso to go."

I shook my head. "It's my cousin, Tara. She says she's looking forward to dinner later and it's a shame you can't make it. She says we should do a spa day soon. Just us girls."

"Pick a date and I'll find a babysitter. I'm sad I can't make dinner tonight but with Jord on night shift and your mom and dad already having plans, I'm a babysitter short. Jord says we should try a babysitting service so we don't over-rely on family."

"That sounds like a good idea. Although maybe next time we could do lunch and take Poppy too?"

"And miss out on child-free time? No thank you! Much as I love my precious girl, I'm determined to enjoy life occasionally as someone who doesn't spend their personal life eternally covered in applesauce and spit, or at work splashed in beer and tears. I'm not even going to feel guilty about wanting some me time. No matter what society tells me."

"What does society know?" I asked with a shrug.

"You'll find out when it happens to you," said Lily. "The minute you're pregnant, suddenly your body belongs to everyone else, and then you give birth and everyone has an opinion on how you raise your kid and live your life. Stay-at-home mom? Bad. Working mom?

Bad. Hobbies? You should have them or you're pathetic. But spend time on them? Bad! Unlike men. Men hobbies are *oooooh so amazing, look at him, he's so strong*! Also, unlike men, no one slaps us on the back and thinks we're great for doing the bare minimum. Jord changed a diaper in the park once and five women offered to help him. I changed all the diapers the day before and three women told me I was doing it wrong. Don't get me started on breastfeeding."

I crossed my legs. "I'm rethinking the whole getting pregnant thing."

"Sensible."

"But I kind of like the doing the bare minimum and getting praise for it thing."

"Hence your job," said Lily.

"I am not doing the bare minimum," I pointed out. "I'm doing absolutely nothing and not getting praise for it either."

"You'd think someone would thank you for you not getting into trouble at least. Think of all the mayhem you could be causing."

"I barely ever cause mayhem!" I wasn't usually the *cause* but that was probably semantics since I definitely got involved in more than my reasonable share of strange events. The mayhem definitely wasn't my fault. Most of the time, anyway.

"That's going on your epitaph." Lily checked her watch, placed the binoculars on the table and hoisted her bag onto her knee. "I really should get going. I need to go over the bar's alcohol order with Ruby. I think we've over-ordered but she thinks we've under-ordered given the recent uptick in happy hour sales. I can fit that meeting in before picking up Poppy from daycare if I go now."

"Are you really leaving so you can follow the bus?" I asked, my eyes narrowing at Lily's suspicious slide from determined amateur sleuth into being a responsible adult who wanted to conduct a logistics meeting.

"No!" Lily scoffed. "There's no way I'd catch that bus now! Plus, you're probably right. They're probably not up to anything truly dangerous. Just little, old ladies on a day out from their nursing home. Minding their own business. Shuffling along. Waiting to die." Lily gathered her purse, hugged me, and grabbed her coffee. She was already out the door by the time I realized she'd left her binoculars. I grabbed them and my coffee, and hurried after her.

As I stepped onto the sidewalk, Lily sped past me in her car and hung a right, just as the bus had done minutes earlier, only she sailed through the light change. "Not following indeed," I snorted. Well, let Lily have her wild goose chase. I had other fish to fry, and other idioms to try.

Tara had picked a Greek place downtown for an early dinner with our respective partners and I was looking forward to hanging out with her. Since the restaurant was near the agency's office, I headed there first and parked in the underground lot. Bypassing the office entirely, I walked up the exit ramp and called Solomon. He didn't answer but a moment later, I got a text: *Might be late. Start without me.*

That was disappointing. I'd looked forward all day to the four of us enjoying dinner together but I knew Solomon was working on a case that was sucking up a lot of his time. If he couldn't make it, it was for a reasonable cause.

I headed to the restaurant, unsurprised that I

arrived first. My office was closest. Tara, like numerous members of my family was a police officer who worked at the Montgomery Police Department where she would be finishing her shift. Her boyfriend, Sadiq Farid, was an FBI agent and their building was a little further away.

The restaurant was wedged between a fancy juice bar and a no-packaging foodstuffs shop. The interior had been decorated in what I assumed a Greek taverna looked like, never having been lucky enough to travel to the country nor its many islands: whitewashed walls picked out with blue accents and a pretty sea mural covering the back wall. Plants hung from the ceiling and trailed over shelves displaying Greek tchotchkes. The tables had pristine white tablecloths, each with a pink posy in a small glass vase, and the chairs were pale wood. Several families already occupied some of the tables, myriad small dishes and baskets of bread covering the surfaces, while their chatter and softly piped music filled the air.

After being shown to a table in the window facing the street, I settled in to wait and nibble on the fresh pita bread and oil deposited in front of me. Only minutes later, Tara and Sadiq strolled past the window, hand-in-hand, before entering the restaurant.

"Isn't this nice?" said Tara, hugging me before slipping off her light summer jacket. "Can you believe this restaurant has been here decades, and in the same family, and I never knew? I'm glad I saw the review in *The Gazette*."

"Me neither," I said, "but it is tucked away on a backstreet."

"A real word-of-mouth type place," said Sadiq, leaning in to hug me too before taking the seat opposite, while Tara sat between us. "Is Solomon on his way?"

"He said he'll be late and not to wait."

"Good. I'm hungry!" said Tara.

"If we order now, either the food will arrive by the time he gets here, or the food will have arrived and we'll have the opportunity to eat some before he vacuums up the rest," I added.

"Big guy gotta eat," said Sadiq with a broad, jovial grin.

"I'll tell him you'll share yours," I said.

"Not a chance!"

"Don't tell me you're turning into a food hoarder," said Tara as she reached for the bread basket.

I shrugged. "More like a 'defender of my plate'. Although Solomon might suggest that it's the other way around. He's getting territorial about his fries."

"A worthy cause," said Sadiq. "I can get behind that."

"Does that mean you're not going to pick at my plate?" asked Tara, her eyebrows raised.

Sadiq grinned, his dark brown eyes sparkling. "Heck, no. What's yours is mine, honey."

"I'm sure Solomon was more flexible on his sides ownership pre-marriage," I said, enjoying their banter. "Now he's got me, he doesn't want to share." I pulled a face and they laughed.

The waitress deposited a carafe of iced water, handed us menus, and ran through the day's specials before she left the three of us to make our choices from the mezze options. Making a decision wouldn't take me long; I wanted one of everything.

"So how's work?" asked Tara, glancing up from the menu. "Any wild cases?"

"I wish," I said. "It's been quiet these past two weeks since we wrapped up that cold case from my parents' street. A little surveillance work. I followed a guy last week whose wife thought he was stepping out on her."

"Was he?"

"Yeah, but to an actual step class. Turned out he was trying to get fitter because he thought she didn't find him attractive anymore."

"Awww," said Tara.

"She cried, he cried, then there was a huge outburst of *love yous*. It was sweet. I recommended they turn the class into something they could share together or actually designate a date night so they could get those romantic moments. Case closed."

"A positive outcome."

"And the week before that was another husband surveillance case."

"Tell me it was a cute story too!"

"Nope. This one actually was stepping out on his fiancée. Only he was stepping out with his wife… and also his girlfriend."

"Oh, boy," said Sadiq as he blew out a breath.

"I'm not sure if that's devastating or a lucky escape," said Tara.

"Both," I said.

"I wonder if he was ever going to marry the fiancée. That would be bigamy," said Sadiq.

"I doubt it. From what she showed me, it sounded like he was stringing her along with a bunch of false promises. I'm not surprised she was suspicious," I explained, "despite his top-notch time management skills."

"I'm surprised Solomon put you on those nickel

and dime cases," said Sadiq. "He doesn't have any more pressing cases?"

"I don't mind. It's nice to have easy wins between the big cases and they're not as arduous as going undercover or tracking down leads. Plus, Solomon always says you never know when small clients will remember us and recommend us for a big money case."

"I saw two of your guys, Fletcher and Flaherty, hunkered down outside one of the warehouses out of town last week," said Sadiq.

"That must be because of all the break-ins over there. The new owners wanted peace of mind with a visible security presence before they moved in and had to make any more repairs. It ended up being bored kids stirring up trouble."

"We need more facilities for youths so they don't go making their own fun," said Tara. "It's a shame they have nowhere to go. I'm sure it wasn't so bad when we were kids."

"Now I feel old." I laughed. "But these kids rolled up in their beamers looking for trouble so I don't think they were suffering from lack of options, just poor judgment."

"I bet they don't even get slapped on the hand for getting caught either," said Tara with a shake of her head. "I wish I could say life was more exciting in the police force but it's not. I'm stuck on paperwork for a string of thefts over in Frederickstown."

"There're always thefts in that neighborhood," said Sadiq.

"Hence the paperwork. Actually, there's talk of new initiatives going on over there. More police, more investment into the neighborhood. Better lighting, improved public transport, a gardening initiative. It could be a nice area if it's done right. I've been asked to go along to the community session to listen to what the residents want. It could be an exciting project," said Tara. Her eyes lit up as she spoke. "I was involved in something similar in Chicago so I have a lot of knowledge to bring to the table."

"That sounds great!"

"It's all dependent on money, of course. Isn't everything? Hey, did Sadiq tell you he's going to Europe next week with work?"

"Germany is back on," clarified Sadiq. "Maddox and I are working a case with a strong lead in Berlin."

"Why do you get all the fancy jobs?" I wondered. "Why don't I ever get a job in Berlin?"

"It compensates for federal pay," said Sadiq.

"Have you ever thought of moving to the private sector?" I asked.

"Do you get jobs in Berlin?"

"No."

"Then no. Plus, I want to move up the ranks and serve my country."

"I tried serving my country once," I remembered, thinking back to my brief and not very shining Army days. Well, I attended boot camp before I was served an unceremonious return home. I'd like to say I gave it my best shot, but that would be lying.

"What happened?"

"Turns out I was better serving at a bar."

"A true service to your countrymen and women," said Tara. "Let's order."

We ordered several sharing plates and spent the time chatting while we waited for the food to be delivered.

"Does the Berlin case have anything to do with your mysterious, brilliant thief?" I asked. Only a couple of weeks ago, we'd been foiled from returning a priceless ruby, missing for years, to the small European state that claimed it. While the common line was our expert had simply misidentified the jewel, I was certain an audacious thief named Cass Temple had broken into MPD's evidence locker and stolen it right out from under their noses. MPD, meanwhile, had swept the embarrassing incident under the rug. I figured Cass could be anywhere in the world now and given that Maddox was determined to catch her, Berlin sparked my curiosity.

"Maybe," said Sadiq and winked.

"You're not going to tell me?"

"I can't discuss ongoing cases," he said.

"Can you talk about the Cass Temple case?" I asked.

"Like I said." Sadiq grinned and I knew I didn't have to press further. Cass Temple had been sighted in Berlin!

"Have you heard anything about the Queen's Ruby?" I wondered.

"It seems to have disappeared."

I shook my head, not at all surprised. The ruby was subject to a diplomatic clash and I suspected it would never officially turn up.

Just as the plates were placed on the table, my phone rang.

"Sorry," I said as I reached for it, noting Solomon's name flashing on the screen.

"I'm not going to make it," he said.

For a moment, my heart stopped and the restaurant receded into the background. "You're... dying?" I gasped.

CHAPTER TWO

"No! I'm alive and well. I'm stuck with the client going through the particulars of the security detail they want. It's more complicated than I thought. I just stepped out to call you but I can't take long. I won't make dinner tonight."

"We'll miss you," I said, my racing heart returning to normal. "Do you want me to bring leftovers home?"

"Yes, and don't eat them on the way."

"I'll do my best," I said, primly, and disconnected. "Solomon can't make it," I explained to Tara and Sadiq even though I was sure they caught the gist of our conversation as they waited patiently for the call to finish.

"Then we'll have to do this again another night. How are you fixed for…" said Tara, trailing off. She squinted and I followed her gaze out the window. "Is that Maddox?" she asked.

"Waving frantically to us?" I replied, following her gaze. Maddox was across the street, collar undone, shirt sleeves rolled up, and smiling. His usually unruly brown hair was freshly cut and he had a smattering of stubble.

"Yeah."

Sadiq twisted in his seat and waved. "I thought he had a hot date tonight," he said.

"He had a date?" I asked, my mind immediately whirring. "Who? Where? What?"

Maddox jogged across the street and burst through the doors, grinning as he approached the table. "You ordered without me!" he said.

"No one invited you," I replied.

"And yet there's an unoccupied chair with silverware and a plate." Maddox dropped into the chair and reached for a napkin. "Hey, gang. This is nice."

Tara poured water into the glass at the now occupied setting, apparently not at all bothered at Maddox's self-invite. "Sadiq said you were supposed to be on a date," she said.

"You had a date?" I asked, again.

Maddox flashed a smile at me, his blue eyes sparkling. "I have dates most nights, babe."

I raised my eyebrows. "Babe?"

"Trying it out, darling."

"Darling?"

"Sweetheart?" He winked at me.

I rolled my eyes. The man was incorrigible. Not only that, but perpetually sweet. I couldn't be mad at his teasing... not if I was going to get my own back.

"Sadiq says you're going to Berlin next week," said Tara, holding back a laugh.

Maddox nodded. "Let me make a note that Sadiq tells you everything. Did he tell you we're working with Interpol too?"

"He didn't."

"I didn't tell them we're in spitting distance of catching our thief either. We've been after this woman for a long time," said Sadiq. "But she's so damn slippery. Nothing sticks to her."

"We'll get her," said Maddox. "One way or another."

"Maybe you should hire Lexi," said Tara.

"Actually, getting a woman on the team might be a good idea," said Sadiq. "A woman might get nearer than we can, although we've come pretty close."

"I like the idea of seeing Lexi and our target squaring up." Maddox grinned and I knew he wasn't thinking entirely professional thoughts.

"You have the hots for her," I said decidedly.

"I do not!"

"You do too."

"Babe."

"Do you?" asked Sadiq. "She is reportedly beautiful, although I'm not entirely sure what she actually looks like since her appearance changes every three minutes. Interpol's not even absolutely sure it's her in Berlin. Their case seems mostly based on supposition and rumor."

"Then why are you going?" I wondered.

"Just in case. If she's in Berlin, something is about to be stolen, and whatever it is will be worth a fortune."

"Is there a reason we're not saying her name?" I asked.

"I'm afraid of summoning her," said Maddox.

"Cass. Temple," I said her name slowly.

Maddox made the sign of the cross over his chest. "Don't say her name three times or when facing a mirror!"

"She's not the bogeyman," I said with a roll of my

eyes.

"I'm also not confirming that's who we're talking about." Maddox shoved a piece of bread into oil, then into his mouth.

"Shouldn't you leave this minute?" asked Tara. "Won't she be gone by next week?"

"That's what I said, but the powers-that-be, meaning our bosses, want positive confirmation before we get on a flight as well as a reasonable idea of what she's up to. Temple's already cost the bureau a lot of money in chasing around after her. If catching her wouldn't be such a big win, I'm sure they would have given up by now," explained Sadiq.

"Aha!" I said, on hearing her name.

"Damn it," said Sadiq, not at all sadly, and pulled a face.

"She sounds like a dream criminal to catch," said Tara. "A real career boost. Could an arrest like that lead to a promotion?"

"More like a nightmare and an office in the basement," countered Maddox as the server began to set sharing plates on the table. "You ordered squid! Great! Can we get another dish of this, and another bread basket?" he asked the server and she nodded.

"What are you doing in the neighborhood anyway?" I asked. "Shouldn't you be on this date?"

Maddox shrugged. "Maybe I already got it over with and just happened to be passing and here you all are, all my favorite people, except your mom. I call it serendipity, especially since I was getting hungry. Where's your lesser half?"

"Huh? Me? If you mean Solomon, he's held up at work." I did my best not to rise to Maddox's teasing but I was fairly sure if I pressed my heel just a few inches to my left, I might cause him to hobble home.

"Bank robbery gone wrong? Again?" he quipped. "Good thing I'm here to eat Solomon's share. Isn't this the best night for everyone?" And with that, my three companions dove into the food, so after a deep sigh, I figured I better get on with the eating too.

An hour later, our stomachs full, and several fresh dishes ordered to go for Solomon, we said our goodbyes, hugging outside the restaurant.

"Where are you parked?" asked Maddox.

"At the agency."

"I'll walk you there. I'm parked a block beyond."

"It's nice to hear you're dating," I said.

"I don't remember saying I ever stopped," he replied, strolling along beside me, his hands in his pockets.

"Well, I'm just glad you are."

"Oh, stop fishing," he said. "I know you're dying for all the details."

"I am not!"

"My sex life is not your business."

"I didn't ask!"

"We both know that's what you were thinking. You're a married woman, Lexi, you've got to leave us bachelors alone!"

"I am!"

"You can look but you can't touch!"

"I wasn't—"

"Jealousy isn't becoming."

"I'm no—oh, I see! You're winding me up." I contemplated thwacking him with the takeout bag but I didn't want to risk the taramasalata exploding on impact and coating the other packages in pink sauce.

"You'll always have a place in my heart," said

Maddox, sliding an arm around my shoulders and giving me a warm squeeze. Then he dropped his arm and continued, "But I'm afraid it's just not going to happen between us, no matter how much you beg."

"I didn't b—"

"I have too much respect for both of us," he carried on, apparently oblivious to my protestations. "And there's also a lot of beautiful and crazy women out there. It's only fair I date them all while you sit at home, on your couch, eating your ice cream, wondering where your husband is, and contemplating how life got you there."

"I don't—" I started, then I stopped. Eating ice cream alone on the couch had been on tonight's plans before Tara suggested dinner.

"While I jetset around the world," he continued.

"You're flying coach, aren't you?"

Maddox ignored that. "—Champagne in hand."

"Expenses won't even pay for sparkling water."

"—Staying in glamorous hotels."

"Not on the Fed's budget."

"—Chasing the international criminal elite."

I had to admit that did sound fun. But before I could say anything else, my phone rang. I reached for it, hoping it was Solomon with news of a case so wild that I wouldn't have any choice but to rub it in Maddox's face.

Instead, it was my mom.

"Are you home?" she wanted to know.

"Not yet. I'm just walking to my car at the agency."

"Can you drop by on your way home?"

"Hi, Mrs. G," called Maddox.

"Adam Maddox, is that you? Oh, he's such a nice young man," said my mom. "You really missed out there."

Maddox gave me a smug look. "Thanks for the muffins," he spoke into my phone.

"Tell him he's welcome. Such a nice boy. I'll miss him when he's in Germany but he always brings such nice treats home from his trips. It's very exciting."

"You bring my mom treats?" I mouthed and Maddox's grin got wider. "How do you know he's going to Germany? Where else has he brought you gifts from?" I asked.

"Make sure you drive in from the south side," said Mom, ignoring my question. "The Dugans are landscaping. It's going to be so nice now they know for sure there're no more dead bodies under their yard. I told your father he needs to cut the lawn or we'll tarnish the whole neighborhood. You have to take a look."

"I'll make sure I do."

"And bring Adam with you. I won't take no for an answer!"

"You can drive," said Maddox, his grin so wide I could probably fit the whole takeout bag inside.

By the time I turned onto my mom's street, I'd almost forgotten about the landscaping she wanted me to see and was approaching from the opposite direction.

"I'm not comfortable with letting your mom down. Keep driving to the Dugans' place," said Maddox when I slowed near my parents' house as I searched for a space big enough to fit my car. Unfortunately, everyone parking on the street today seemed to have zero spatial awareness, and I wasn't prepared to park nose in, trunk hanging out in the street. That kind of parking was strictly for emergencies.

"I have no idea why I let you come along," I said, but I kept driving.

"My sparkling personality."

"Nope. It's not that."

"I'm the only thing to stop you from eating the doggy bag."

I glanced at the bag lodged in the rear footwell. He had a point.

Maddox followed my gaze. "Damn. I really thought it was my sparkling personality."

I flipped on the blinker and turned, parking across the street from the corner house, and peered out the window. "Wow. Mom wasn't kidding when she said how much work they were doing. This might end up being the best house on the street," I said.

The Dugans' front fencing had been ripped out and replaced with new white pickets. A camellia tree had been dug into the center of what would be the lawn and ringed with a bed of lavender. The dirt had been turned over, ready for the rolls of new turf stacked to the side of the path. Flower beds had been planted under the first-floor windows and a gloriously stuffed hanging basket flanked the front door. A Bobcat mini digger was parked in the back yard, just visible through the gates.

I'd met the homeowners and knew they deserved a lovely home after the fright they'd endured recently.

Maddox leaned forward to get a better look. "I like that they've kept the original porch and the woodwork rather than try and turn it into a dwarf McMansion. Plus, I really want to drive that Bobcat."

I held back a laugh. Of course he did. I wanted to too.

"Where would you drive it?" I asked.

"Into the backyard and then I'd dig stuff up." He sighed happily.

"You sound like a four-year-old."

"Thank you."

"It wasn't a compliment."

"I took it as one." He nudged me. "What if they had two Bobcats? We could team up to dig stuff. Winner takes all!"

"All the dirt?" I gave him skeptically raised eyebrows.

"Maybe there's more treasure."

"I'm pretty sure they've turned over every inch of their yard just in case."

"Stranger things have happened."

I thought about all the strange things that had happened since that fateful day I'd walked into an insurance agency as an unenthusiastic temp and met Maddox in his undercover role while he was amassing evidence for a huge fraud. If I'd made a list of all the crazy events that had happened since that day, it would look like pure fiction.

"The Dugans did the right thing in buying a house they could extend and grow into. That's exactly what I would do."

I glanced at him. "Are you in the market for a house?"

"No, I like my apartment. Besides, I'm not at home often enough to justify wanting a bigger place or a yard to manage. Plus, there's only me and I have plenty of space for me. Also, it would be nice to pay off my mortgage this decade rather than be enslaved to the bank forever."

"I wonder what they'll do with the remodeled garage," I said.

"Playroom? Home office? A den just for the adults? Oh! A games room!"

"Don't tell me you'd put a bar in there too."

Maddox grinned. "Okay."

"They have a nice sized lot," I said. "They could have a great swing set for the kids, an ample seating area, and still have plenty of lawn in the back."

"You sound almost wistful."

"No, just curious about what they'll do with the land. I'm sure Mom will keep me updated." She'd probably send surveillance photos, exact dimensions, and a vision board too. For once, I was in full agreement with that.

"I'm sure she'll keep the whole town updated. Has she succeeded in making fast friends with the owners?"

"Yes," I said. "Mostly through not giving them a choice." I turned the engine back on and pulled a U-turn, then headed back along the street before pulling up in a recently vacated space in front of my parents' pretty, white-and-yellow-painted house that resembled an egg more than it did a daisy. Mom was right; the lawn was looking a little overgrown and it lacked the whimsical charm of the Dugans' decorative planting. So much for my Dad's relaxed gardening years during retirement; it didn't look like he'd maintained it in weeks.

As we walked along the path to the door, I became more puzzled by the lack of tending. Dad was usually as house proud as Mom, so the unkempt borders were particularly unusual. And was that peeling paint by the windows?

"Hey," I called as we walked in. "Where are you? Is everything okay?"

"Kitchen," called Mom.

We headed into the kitchen and found my mother at the long table, a variety of magazines spread around her and a large cork pinboard in front of her. Several glossy cut-outs had been arranged on the pinboard. "I'm making a vision board for the Dugans," she said, looking up. "They said they weren't sure what they wanted to do in the backyard so I figured I'd be a good neighbor and help them out. I'll take it over to them later. Plus, I can use it as credit for my garden design course at the Adult Education Center."

"You're studying garden design?"

"One can only love a square lawn for so long without getting bored of it. Hello, Adam. That's a lovely shirt you're wearing. That shade of blue really brings out your eyes."

"Thanks," Maddox beamed. "I'll make sure to wear it when I take you out to dinner after my trip."

"You're going out to dinner?" I frowned. "Together?"

"How else should I thank your mom for all the sweet things she does? Dinner is the least I can do."

"I don't know. A text message?"

"Lexi's a grouch because we didn't invite her," said Maddox, clearly enjoying this.

"She won't get an invitation with that attitude," said Mom right before she reached for her black-handled scissors and snipped an image of a floral border from an open magazine. She added it to the vision board with a triumphant flash of her hands.

"You've got the knack," said Maddox as he moved to look over my mother's shoulder. "That's a beautiful color scheme and I like all the texture."

"Oh, get a room, you two," I huffed under my breath.

"Are you two working a case together?" asked Mom.

"No, we just went out for dinner with Tara and Sadiq," said Maddox.

"And you're upset we're going out to dinner when you've just been to dinner?" asked Mom, giving me a quizzical look.

"She is," said Maddox promptly. "And she has leftovers in the car!"

"I am not! And Maddox gate-crashed. Solomon couldn't make it so the leftovers are for him."

"He works too hard. How are you ever going to have a baby when he works those hours?" Mom's attention returned to the vision board. "I need more foliage."

"You're having a baby?" asked Maddox, his gaze moving to my stomach.

"No," I said without adding *not for lack of trying*. It had been a few months and still nothing. Then I tried to hold in my stomach.

"The world remains relatively safe from a tiny, chaos-causing Mini Lexi," said Maddox, still staring. I wished he would stop; I needed to breathe. I could only suck it in for so long before I popped.

"You'll make a wonderful father one day," said Mom, beaming at him.

"If Solomon doesn't step it up, I'm happy to step in," he said and Mom laughed and batted his arm with her hand while I tried not to scowl at them. I didn't know what had gotten into me today. My family were so warm and welcoming, and Maddox's own family were aloof. Why should I mind that he was so ingrained with mine? After all, they'd practically adopted Lily as their own too, and that was long before she married my brother. Maybe it was because Maddox was my ex. Maybe it was because of the relentless teasing my brothers subjected him to back when he was my boyfriend and on the force, although they all loved him now. Maybe it was because it almost seemed like my family preferred Maddox to me? I gulped down the horrible thought and shook it away. Of course they didn't prefer him! They just liked him. Everyone did. I did!

Maddox was a great guy.

He was also a butthead, but two truths could co-exist.

"You just missed Daniel," said Mom. "He's a changed man since leaving the police force."

"I helped him organize his garage only last weekend," said Maddox. "You should see it. New pegboard for tools, not that he has many, but now they all have a place. And spaces for all kinds of garden equipment and a new area for Alice to organize her nursing equipment. We had a barbecue after."

"Daniel mentioned how pleased he was to tackle another house chore now that he has the time," said Mom. "And he mentioned how much he's looking forward to the FBI academy. Do you think they'll post him here when he graduates?"

"I have no idea but it's likely. He has an excellent working knowledge of the area and its lowlifes."

"Imagine if you'll be working together. You, Daniel and Sadiq. Won't that be wonderful? Don't you think, Lexi?"

"Wonderful," I agreed, mostly meaning it.

"Lexi just wants more people to do her dirty work with federal computers," said Maddox.

"I hardly ever!" I protested although the idea was

pleasing. "Anyway, what did you want me to stop by for, Mom?"

"I need you to cheer up your father."

"Why does he need cheering? What's wrong?"

"Ever since I said I'd take over the yard work as part of my course, he's been moping around the house like a lost soul. He needs something to keep him busy."

"Can't you give him back the yard work?" I asked, thinking about the unmown lawn.

"Not for the next six weeks. Instead, I'm giving your father to you."

"Why me?"

"Garrett and Jord are busy with work. Daniel's leaving for the academy soon. You're the only one that's left."

"What about Serena?" I asked, thinking of my uptight sister.

"I don't like to bother her. She's always so busy."

"Well, as much as I'd love to entertain Dad, I'm also busy."

"No, you're not," snorted Maddox.

"Perhaps your father can help you on a case? He does so love to be involved, and it would be nice for you two to spend more time together," said Mom.

I contemplated it. My dad was hugely knowledgeable and nice to be around. Yet he was retired and I'd assumed he was enjoying it. "I suppose it would be nice," I said. At the very least, he and I could go for lunch while Maddox entertained my mom.

"Plus, if you don't get him out from under my feet, there will be a new crime for you to solve," added Mom.

I sucked a breath in through my teeth. "I'll ask Solomon," I said. "He is my boss. He might say no."

I thought I heard my mom say *not if he knows what's good for him* but it was so soft under her breath, I couldn't be sure.

"Where's Dad now?" I asked.

"Upstairs, watching YouTube videos on his laptop."

"I could probably swing a ride-along with us," said Maddox. "We can pitch it as information-sharing from a senior detective with decades of state and area knowledge. His years of experience will be a boon to us."

Mom brightened. "He would love that. Did you hear that, Lexi?"

"I'm right next to you!"

"But it won't be until we're back from the Berlin trip," Maddox added. The edges of his mouth frowning, clearly disappointed to let my mother down.

Mom turned to me and fixed me with a stare. At that moment, my phone rang. Saved by the Solomon!

"Where are you?" he asked.

"At my parents'. I have your food in the car. I'll leave soon."

"Can you bring it to the agency? A case just came in and I might want you on it."

"Can I bring my dad?" I asked, leaping on the idea.

"Please do. His city knowledge might come in useful for the case."

"Great! What's the case?" I asked, hardly believing my stroke of luck in getting my mom off my back, potentially cheering up my dad, and scoring points off Maddox. Triple whammy!

"I'll have more details when you get here."

"I'll drive as fast as I can!"

"Please don't," said Solomon before disconnecting.

"Solomon says yes," I said. "So you're welcome." Turning to Maddox, I added, "We have to go. I'll drop you at your car."

"Terrific. This turned out to be an unexpectedly fun evening."

"You could stay and help me with this if you like?" suggested Mom.

"Garden design isn't my forte, plus, we came in Lexi's car and I need her to return me to mine. I need to buy some groceries on the way home and get gas too. Maybe I'll do some recycling. Who said being an adult wouldn't be fun?" Maddox grinned. Mom hugged him first, then me, but mine was extra long so take that, Maddox.

I called down a sweats-wearing Dad and his excitement at being liberated was palpable after I explained there was a case and, while I didn't know the particulars, could he join me? He told me he'd be ready in five minutes, and returned downstairs in two, wearing smart jeans and a navy polo, looking every inch the retired police detective.

Dad called shotgun, which was his right as the co-creator of my life, and we all hopped in. I returned Maddox to his car, and all the while, he deftly avoided answering any questions about his forthcoming trip or how they had tailed Cass Temple this far. The latter caught Dad's attention and he fired myriad questions that Maddox batted away like they were plastic bullets. When he hopped out, he leaned back in and said, "I'll send you a postcard from Germany."

"Thanks! Are you sending my mom one?"

"I always do."

"Do you send your mom a postcard?" asked Dad.

"I'm not sure my mom knows what a postcard is.

29

Good luck with the new case, guys. Let me know if there should be any federal interest in it," said Maddox.

"Absolutely," I said, covering the "not" with a shallow cough.

"Do you think he'd steal your case?" asked Dad, looking after Maddox as he strolled away, apparently without a care in the world. It was almost like he was too chill about his international case, which made me suspicious. What was Maddox really up to? And just how personally interested in Cass Temple was he for him to act this nonchalant?

"Probably, if it's interesting enough, but the client came to us for a reason. Let's go find out what that reason is."

CHAPTER THREE

Since it was late evening, and the agency's caseload was light, there wasn't a lot of noise coming from any of the three floors the agency occupied. I figured most of my colleagues were taking advantage of the opportunity to have an evening off. Even though I'd done the same, I wasn't at all perturbed about returning to the agency on short notice. It was simply the nature of the job.

My dad and I headed to the middle floor where the PIs' shared office was situated and aimed directly for the boardroom. Solomon occupied his usual seat at the head of the table but there were two other people, a man and a woman, with their backs to us. I deposited the bag of food on my desk and indicated to my dad that he should follow me.

"Here's my investigator now," said Solomon, standing as we entered. "This is Lexi Graves-Solomon and our consultant, Steve Graves. Steve is a decorated police detective."

The two people pushed back their chairs to stand

and when they turned, I smiled.

"Laura! Hi! This is a nice surprise!" I said, extending my hand towards her.

Laura Reynolds shook my hand, then Dad's. "I wish we were here for a social visit but unfortunately not," she said. "This is my brother, Alan."

"Laura and Alan own Reynolds' Fine Jewelry and Theia downtown," said Solomon to my dad.

"And Laura consulted for us on the Queen's Ruby case," I added.

"That was a fascinating case. Is Theia a jewelry store too?" asked Dad. "I know Reynolds', of course. I've bought items from there for my wife, my kids' graduation gifts, and so forth when something special was called for."

"That's right," said Alan Reynolds. "And thanks for your patronage. It's repeat customers like you who are our bread and butter."

"Reynolds' Fine Jewelry has been in our family for three generations," continued Laura. "We opened Theia a few years ago to cater to a slightly different market. We're opening a third store soon too. Most of our customers don't know the stores are connected and we like to keep it that way."

"Why's that?" I asked.

Laura pursed her lips, but it seemed less a snobby action and more resigned. "Reynolds' customers pay for exclusivity and premium items. Yet it's our mid-priced store that has a bigger client base and a larger turnover. We figured we could pool resources for both of them, without advertising the connection."

"Sensible," said Dad as we all took our seats. "I know your security is tight. I remember an attempted smash-and-grab at Reynolds', oh, twenty years ago."

"Twenty-five, I think. That would have been when our father was in charge," said Alan. "I was around fifteen years old, and Laura would have been twelve, so we didn't have much to do with the business back then. I remember the attempt though."

"Our parents tried not to talk about it at home. The thieves didn't get anything from what I recall, but I know our parents were alarmed," said Laura, "and you're right, our security has always been extremely good. Our parents didn't scrimp on it but perhaps it is due for an upgrade."

"I didn't work the case but I recall the would-be thieves were indicated in several other robberies in the area over a few months," said Dad. "They weren't jewel robbers, just opportunists."

Solomon reached for the water jug, refreshing the Reynolds' glasses and then pouring for my dad and me. "The Reynolds' would like our assistance," he said as I gulped the cool water.

"We've had a suspected theft today," said Alan.

"Today?" I asked, surprised that they were already calling in investigators and not talking to the police.

He nodded. "That's right. We take inventory at the end of every day and when we did so today, a ring was missing. A very expensive one." He paused, scratching his head. "Only I can't work out how it was stolen."

"Did you do a recount?" I asked. "Could you have made a mistake?"

"That's what I thought initially, so I did do a recount. Then my assistant manager did. Then we called Laura and she came over and counted too. The ring's definitely missing and it was included in our inventory the day before and that morning."

"Did you call the police?" asked Dad.

"No, we didn't, and I'm not sure I plan to. We pride ourselves on our exclusivity and our security. If it gets out we can be robbed, it might become open house for every other thief in the state who thinks we're now fair game."

"Plus, our insurers have been just dying to increase our premiums," said Laura. "The jewelry business isn't what it used to be. We're doing okay but we're not pulling in the cash like the business did in our father's day."

"That must stay strictly between us," added Alan, glancing at all of us, a spark of worry in his eyes. "After taking on the third store, we're slightly overextended on every front at present and we don't want to put the shops in anyone's crosshairs."

"Everything you say here is confidential," Solomon assured them. "What would you like us to do for you?"

"Finding the ring would be great, although I suspect it's long gone," said Alan.

"I know it's only been a few hours, but it's most likely already broken apart, the metals melted down, and the stones separated for resale," said Laura.

"That's what you would do?" asked Solomon. "You wouldn't try to sell it?"

She nodded. "I would. It's one of a kind, vintage, so it's easily recognizable and would be hard to sell as it is, especially if it's registered as stolen. The thief couldn't expect to get the full sale value for it."

"Of course, there will always be some unscrupulous people who just don't care. Or it could end up overseas where neither the buyers nor the sellers will look too closely at its provenance," added Alan.

"We can scour sales pages and online auction sites

but it would be arduous and unlikely to pay off," said Laura.

"What else would you like from us?" asked Solomon.

"Finding the ring is important. It's worth a great deal. In addition, we want to know who stole the ring and how. We want to adjust our security protocols and make sure it never happens again," said Alan. "Does that sound reasonable?"

"It does." Solomon relaxed in his seat, steepling his fingers together. "How do you feel about having someone undercover in the store?"

"Do you think they'll come back?" asked Alan. He and Laura exchanged a worried look, telling me that was exactly what they were afraid of.

Solomon cocked his head. "It's possible. Stealing the ring could be a warmup for a bigger theft. They might be wondering if you noticed this theft, and if so, what you would do about it. That could determine their next moves. Placing an undercover investigator in the store would help us in that event."

"We didn't do anything different today after we discovered the theft," said Laura. "Only the three of us at the shop know about it. Alan and I talked about it a little before locking up and we decided to call the agency."

"There's another reason," I said, taking point. "The thief might have never left the store."

"I'm confident there's nowhere for a person to hide. We don't allow clients beyond the shop floor unless it's a private appointment."

"Lexi means we should take a look at your employees," said Solomon. He held a hand up when both of them started to protest. "It's just a precaution to rule them out as fast as possible. The more avenues we can eliminate from our inquiries swiftly, the sooner we can pursue other avenues."

"I guess," said Alan as he exchanged a disappointed look with his sister. "But the only people in the store that day were me, my assistant manager, Jonathan, and our shop clerk, Tansy. Both have worked for us for years. Our cleaner was in this morning but she's worked for us for years too."

"And me," added Laura. "I was there too, at the end of the day for the final recount."

"You wouldn't have stolen from us!" scoffed Alan.

Laura glanced at me, then Solomon. "All the same, I think you should work to eliminate both of us from your suspect list too."

"Oh, goodness, Laura, that seems like a waste of their time!" Alan sighed.

"I'd like it done for my own peace of mind," said Laura, a touch stiffly. "If we're going to scrutinize our employees, we should be accountable under the same lens."

"Of course," said Solomon. "That's prudent."

"I agree," said Dad. "It would be remiss not to rule everyone out."

"We agreed to come for help, not put ourselves in the spotlight," said Alan. Then he sighed and threw his hands in the air in defeat. "All right, fine. Investigate us too. I wouldn't want to be accused of not being thorough."

"Will you take our case?" asked Laura. "Can you find the ring?"

Solomon nodded, after an almost imperceptible glance at me where I wondered if he could read my mind. A theft and a potential jewelry heist to foil? And the theft was recent, meaning our chance of leads was high? Of course I wanted in on that! It sounded impossibly glamorous and I was keen on the idea of working undercover around so many precious jewels. Plus, it crossed my mind that the last time I'd worked on a case involving stolen jewels, I hadn't exactly come out on top. This could be my chance to redeem myself.

"We'll try," I said.

"Let's get the paperwork drawn up," said Solomon.

~

"I wonder if they have tiaras," I said wistfully, thinking how cute I'd look in a little diamond-encrusted number. We were in the car, having dropped Dad off at his house, and now we were almost home, the bag of food in my lap still untouched. That just went to show how much I was thinking about the new case, and how much Solomon was finicky about people eating in his car.

"Is there much call for tiaras on the east coast?" asked Solomon.

"There should be."

"I don't recall seeing anyone wear one. Ever."

"You'd hardly wear a tiara to the grocery store. Tiaras are for special occasions."

"What kind of special occasion?"

That was easy. "Friday and Saturday nights," I said.

"They're not special occasions. They're every week."

"They should be special. You wouldn't have a tiara and only wear it once a year."

"You would if you were stupendously rich. You would have a whole range of tiaras to choose from."

"I'd like a range, as well as a range of occasions," I decided.

"I'll get you dangly earrings for your birthday," said Solomon. "How does that sound?"

"Lovely." There was nothing like the offer of some glitz to put me in a good mood. Not that I wasn't already. The evening had been plentiful in terms of food and activity, and now there was a tempting case to get stuck into tomorrow.

Solomon pulled over in front of our house and hopped out. He moved around the car and opened my door before I even had a chance to snatch my purse and reach for the handle. "Thank you," I said as he gently removed the takeout bag from me. Now I thought about it, the food did seem to be currently more interesting to him than me. This was why I needed a statement tiara! To be noticed!

"I thought I'd start the evening on a few good notes," said Solomon, offering me a hand.

"The lure of jewelry, and the gentlemanly behavior. It's almost like you want your wicked way with me."

"It's absolutely like that," said Solomon, a devilish smile playing on his lips. "But I have to eat first. I need my energy if tonight's going to be the night."

My eyes widened. "You really think it could be?"

"I want to hedge my bets in case it wasn't last night or the night before. If neither of those, then definitely tonight. But just to be sure, we'll try tomorrow too. Then I might need a nap. Baby-making attempts are exhausting despite being immense fun."

"Fair," I agreed. "Should I check my ovulation app to see if any of these nights hold promise or should we just go for it anyway?"

Solomon stopped, frowned. "You didn't check already?"

"No, I thought we needed practice regardless of

whether it was a promising evening for my internal organs."

Solomon shrugged. "Let's go for it regardless, but tomorrow might be less planned just to keep excitement high."

"Consider me excited."

"While I eat, you can give me your thoughts on the Reynoldses. I noticed you were quiet during the meeting."

"Not deliberately. I figured you knew more about the case from what they told you before Dad and I arrived and you'd catch us up once they were gone," I said as Solomon shut the car door behind me and beeped it locked. "Dad is thrilled, by the way. He can't wait to be involved."

"I noticed that by the way he tried to keep his face impassive. That's his tell when he's overexcited."

"You should have seen him do that face at Christmas when we were kids," I said. "We would all be asking him stuff about Santa and his reindeer and the North Pole and what we might find under the tree. Dad would be so stony-faced, we thought he had enough of us pestering him, but really he was just excited about keeping secrets so we would be surprised on Christmas morning." Now I thought about it, perhaps my older siblings had been just as in on the secret magic as my parents were. There was no way teenage Garrett would have believed that next to toddler me. Well, damn. If that hadn't taken my entire adult life to occur to me!

"Plus, he was very nonchalant on the way home. *Sure, he just happens to be free*, he says. *If we really need the help*, he says," continued Solomon.

"You're going to make his year," I said. "Thank you

for letting him sit in and consult."

"I'm not just being nice. I'd like his input on other crimes in town, be they jewelry or high-end store thefts. I figured he probably covered things like that in his time on the force, along with homicides, and he'll be tapped into the police network to know what's going on in town since. I'd like to know if he notices any correlations between this case and another."

"So you don't think the theft is isolated?" I asked as I stuck my key in the lock and pushed the door open. I flicked on the lights and Solomon followed me into the kitchen. He removed the insulated boxes from the bag and opened them, peering inside before starting to pick at the contents with his fingers.

"I think it's unlikely an opportunistic thief picks a high-end, security-conscious jewelry store as their first target, although I'll admit stealing one ring is conservative and strange."

"Did Laura or Alan say how much it was worth?"

"Fifty thousand dollars."

I grabbed the edge of the kitchen island to steady myself. "Did I hear that correctly? Fifty thousand bucks? For a single ring? And you call that conservative?"

"You did, and I do. The thief could have tried for a bigger haul, even a handful of items would be worth a few hundred thousand dollars, but instead, the thief stole a single item. They weren't trying to draw attention with a big heist. The Reynoldses didn't know the ring was gone until they took inventory. I think the thief is relying on confusion as cover while they get away with it. It worked initially. If the Reynoldses weren't so diligent, it could have taken days to notice the theft, if not longer."

"Could the ring have been targeted?" I asked.

"As in, stolen to order?"

"Yes, or the theft commissioned by someone else?"

"The middleman theory is a good one. A commissioned theft was my first thought and it's a possibility, although it would be risky to knowingly wear stolen goods even if there were a middleman to separate the final destination from the crime."

"Or unknowingly," I pointed out. "What if someone really wanted to gift a ring they couldn't afford and stole it specifically for that purpose?"

"Also a possibility. Although if it were stolen to order, it would retain far less value. The thief could never sell it through legitimate channels. It would attract attention. Giving it as a gift would rely on the gifter being assured the recipient would never resort to selling it or having it appraised. I'm not sure anyone could be one hundred percent certain of that."

"It would have to be for someone they're very close to. It's a woman's ring, right? So, a wife or fiancée? Perhaps their mother? Or a daughter? You wouldn't give a ring that expensive to just anyone."

"They couldn't insure it either," said Solomon. He reached for rice wrapped in a vine leaf and chewed, then reached for another. "Good food. We should go again."

"Why not? I mean, yes to the restaurant, but why can't the ring be insured?"

"Well, for one, an item like that would have to be appraised or the receipt provided. If it's significantly beyond the owner's means, that could raise questions as to how they acquired it. Many jewel appraisers are tapped into the wider jewel market. They might recognize a stolen item from the description."

"Laura told me most jewels these days have an inscription mark invisible to the naked eye, rendering it impossible to sell or insure once it's registered stolen," I said, recalling her advice in our previous case. "Of course, could the thief want to keep it for himself… or herself? To wear or admire alone?" I frowned, wondering what kind of person would do that. Then I decided *me*. That's who! I'd wear what I loved even if no one else was around to admire it.

"It's possible. A lot of high-value art is kept in private viewing rooms, or even in freeports away from tax inspectors and detectives. It makes sense someone might enjoy stolen jewels in a similar fashion."

"What's a freeport?" I asked.

"It's a special economic zone, usually situated in, or near, ports or airports. Tax and customs are different in those zones than to the countries they're situated in."

"I'd find it too tempting, wear it outside, and get caught pronto," I decided with a resigned sigh. At least my mugshot would be fashionable.

"And that's why you're on the right side of the law," said Solomon and blew me a kiss.

"Finders keepers?" I asked, growing hopeful.

"The Reynoldses offered a small finder's fee on top of what we'll bill. It's not enough for a big diamond, but you could probably get a small one."

"In a small tiara?"

"This is what I love about you. Always so optimistic."

"Any food left in those containers?" I asked, even more hopefully.

"All gone." Solomon crushed the containers and walked them over to the recycling can as I spun on my stool to watch. Years ago, I wouldn't have found that kind of domestication sexy, but now that I was in my thirties, home cleanliness rated high on my hot or not scale. Yet above that was consistency and emotional availability. Solomon had it all in spades... and his butt was a great view too. In my twenties, a great butt had been enough. I was glad I'd learned since then that there were far better attributes in a mate.

"I have the biggest crush on you," I said when he walked back. The man was so handsome he took my breath away. His skin had deepened brown under the summer sun and his eyes resembled molten chocolate. With the added domestication, it was all I could do not to drool.

"Ditto," he said, coming to a stop in front of me and leaning to kiss me. "I don't even need to know why you made that statement, but I assume it's because you're all heated up about my lack of weaponized incompetence, also known as I used the trash can like a normal adult human and loaded my breakfast things into the dishwasher this morning rather than leaving them next to the sink. The bar is low but it's working for me."

I tugged at my neckline, feeling increasingly hot. Was it possible to get pregnant from those words alone? "I thought you wanted to talk about the particulars of the case?" I asked breathily.

"I did. You just changed the topic."

I pushed my thumbs into his belt loops and gave his hips a small push so that he had to take a step backwards. "Let's get back to the topic before I forget all about it," I said, already regretting it. "Let's talk about the case."

Solomon circled the island and resumed his

position on the opposite stool, out of reach. Well, that's what he thought. I was pretty sure I could launch myself like a torpedo across the kitchen island. The only thing stopping me was that I might give off more of a sea lion vibe than a gliding siren of the sea. "Do you like sea lions?" I asked.

"Love them," he said. "Although I'm not sure I want to know why you asked. Give me your thoughts on the Reynoldses. You've met Laura before but I'm not sure if you met Alan."

"Laura was very helpful and I'm pleased she came to us now, especially as Garrett's superiors at the MPD tried to shift the blame on her over the ruby disappearing," I said, still feeling bad about it. "She's been very gracious despite that. I didn't meet Alan before and I can't say I disliked anything about either of them tonight. They appeared to get on well. I didn't pick up any animosity between them, except a touch of exasperation from Alan when Laura suggested they should be investigated too."

"What did you think of that?"

"It's sensible to rule them out and she knows it. Either that or it's an elaborate ruse to cover up wrongdoing by one of them." Even as I said it, it didn't feel right.

"Not both?" asked Solomon.

"If it were both, or even one of them, I'd have thought they would have gone to the police and called their insurers, not come to us for extra special assistance."

"I agree."

"But that's not to say one did it and the other trusts them enough to believe they didn't. Laura is correct. We should check them out so that they can be definitively ruled out by a third party for their benefit as well as ours."

"I think that was her point."

I nodded. "Aside from that, they seem like pleasant, earnest people. There was nothing flashy or exorbitantly expensive about the way either of them dressed. I don't know much about jewelry but I did notice Alan wore a Rolex and Laura had a Cartier bracelet. They could have bought them at a discount through the business, not that it matters. It's just neither of those items are out of place for their industry or what I'm guessing is their income bracket."

"I noticed the watch. I didn't notice the bracelet. I don't know enough about either to assess the retail value, other than they're high-end, sought-after brands."

"Me neither, but I'd guess the Rolex is worth more than the bracelet. I think it depends on the year, how many were made, its age, and quality."

"Worth more than the missing ring?"

"A lot more. The best ever sale price for a Rolex watch so far was close to eighteen million dollars."

Solomon blinked. "I don't think I heard you correctly. Eighteen million dollars for a watch?" he asked.

I nodded. "It was owned by Paul Newman."

"I suppose being owned by a Hollywood icon does come with extra cachet, yet it's still just a portable clock on a strap." Solomon glanced at his own watch, a rugged sports model. He held it up. "Does Alan Reynolds' watch tell you his heart rate?"

I reached for his hand and noticed a small quickening of his heart rate. With any luck, I'd make it beep a cardiac arrest warning sound later. "Nope," I said.

"What do you think about their claim that they've never suffered a theft?" said Solomon.

I considered that. "It seems implausible, given the decades Reynolds' has been in business, but not entirely impossible. We should still consider that a question mark given that the family might not have chosen to involve the police in any thefts in the past either. Officially, that would make them never stolen from. Unofficially, might be another matter." I thought about it a moment more. "Would they have mentioned a two decade-old failed smash-and-grab if that were the case?"

"Your dad mentioned it but they were happy to talk about it. I'm inclined to think they stayed a step ahead of the times with their security. Hence, why an actual theft is so troubling to them now."

"Especially if they can't figure out how it happened," I added. "What's the next step?"

"Tomorrow, we review their security tapes and background check everyone who was in Reynolds' this week. Everyone from the cleaner to the manager to the client. It should be a short list. It may have been an opportunistic theft, but I think it's most likely someone cased the place prior to the theft and formulated an effective plan."

"We should divide the tasks," I said.

"That would be most efficient. Now, for other matters..." Solomon rose and circled the island, closing in on me like I was easy prey. Which I was. I was *not* going to make this tough for him.

I was just going to enjoy it.

Lucky me.

CHAPTER FOUR

Solomon had responded to a very early call out and I'd awoken to an empty bed and a text message saying he would meet me at Reynolds' as soon as he could get away.

Since there was no point lingering at home, I headed directly to the office, texting my dad when I got there to let him know to meet us at the jewelers' later. His thumbs up emoji response was probably the fastest he'd ever returned for a text, indicating his enthusiasm. A second later, another text appeared: *I think that means okay.*

Then: *Your mom says a thumbs up is passive aggressive.*

As the text bubble displayed on the screen, I fired back: *Great!* and added my own thumbs up.

I started up the stairs from the parking garage, calling Solomon as I ascended. "How's it going?" I asked.

"I'm going to be tied up for the next hour. There've been a few developments and I can't get away until then. The Reynoldses aren't expecting us until midmorning so I should make it. Hold on," he said, and the line became muffled. "Sorry about that. Last night, I asked them to email both of us a list of people who'd been in the store this week. I just checked my email and it's there. Like I hoped, it's a short list although there are some customers they didn't know, which is to be expected."

"I'll look into it now."

"Can you handle the case alone if necessary?"

"Are you anticipating problems?" I countered.

"Yes."

"Then yes, and I won't be alone. Dad is helping."

"We'll go through the security tapes together when we get to Reynolds'. I figured if your dad's going to help out, he should see everything we see." Loud voices sounded down the line, angry and muffled. "Gotta go," said Solomon and disconnected.

The office was empty but there was a lukewarm, half-filled coffee pot and an abandoned cup, only the dregs remaining. I figured Delgado, Solomon's right hand man, was most likely with him. So that meant the other two PIs I shared the office with, Steve Fletcher and Matt Flaherty, had come and gone. The office felt empty without the two seasoned, ex-law enforcement guys here to tease and jest and discuss their cases, and it struck me that maybe that lonely feeling was a big reason why our tech guy, Lucas, had moved his desk to the floor above. Perhaps it wasn't just the lure of a bank of monitors and more space for his other high-tech equipment; it was the gentle thrum of other people around him.

I flopped into my desk chair, trying to ignore the quiet, and pulled out my laptop. As promised, Laura Reynolds' email was waiting in my inbox.

Her list of names focused solely on their employees, comprising her and her brother, their assistant manager, Jonathan Mazzina, their shop clerk, Tansy McDonald, and their cleaner, Monika Balint. According to Laura, she'd checked with Alan and he'd confirmed no one else they employed had been in the building that week and they hadn't taken any deliveries or conducted any maintenance work.

She'd included their employee files, asking me to treat them with discretion.

I opened Laura's first, noting she'd earned a degree in fine art before working first at a design studio then as a buyer. She'd taken some time out to retrain as a gemologist after which she'd joined the family business. She'd officially become their buyer as well as representing the firm at trade shows and exhibitions.

Alan's career was always orientated towards the business, and I wondered if that were through genuine interest or because he was not only the older sibling but the son, presumably being groomed into taking over one day. He'd studied business while working part time at the shop. After a few years in project management, he'd joined the family firm as assistant manager, taking over as manager a few years later.

Jonathan Mazzina had been with the firm for many years, joining long before Laura and Alan, and I made a note to check if there were any sour grapes about Alan's promotion over him. Laura had noted Jonathan designed his own jewelry too and included a website link. I clicked on it, impressed with the pretty, delicate pieces, the prices not so incredibly high that they were out of my orbit.

Tansy McDonald had been their shop clerk for four years. She was young, bright, and balancing business classes at night at the community college with the tasks of being the mother of a young child.

Finally, their cleaner was Monika Balint, an Eastern European woman who came in for two hours, twice a week. The morning of the theft had been her first shift of the week. She'd worked for them for several years. Her employee application listed a university in her home country and a range of cleaning jobs since her arrival in the States.

Jonathan and Tansy had both been in the shop on the day of the theft, but otherwise, Laura noted there hadn't been any incidents involving any of the employees.

I was able to run credit and social media checks for all of them, finding nothing suspicious.

When the door behind me opened, I turned my head.

"Hey, Lexi, is the boss around?" asked Lucas, our resident tech geek.

"He's on a case," I said. "Is it urgent?" As I asked, my cell phone buzzed, Solomon texting he was on his way to the jewelers'.

"Nope, just need some paperwork signed off."

"I'm on my way to meet him. I'll let him know."

"It can wait. I'll leave it on his desk," said Lucas, passing me with a few slips of paper. He deposited them on Solomon's desk. When he returned, he asked, "Are you on a case?"

"Just got assigned one last night. Heading out to check security footage now."

"Let me know when you need assistance. I've been coding some new software I want to try out."

"Will do." I grabbed my purse and followed Lucas out before we separated paths, he going upstairs while

I headed for my car, texting my dad I was on the way.

I stood facing the jewelry store a short while later, unsure if I should have been surprised to see there was no obvious evidence of a crime. Of course, I wasn't expecting shattered windows or crime scene tape fluttering in the breeze, but I also hadn't expected this air of normalcy. It was like nothing had ever happened. Just like yesterday when I'd been on the same street drinking coffee with Lily. I glanced over at the coffee shop across the street, shrugging off the odd coincidence.

Stepping forwards, I pushed the plate glass door between two large windows. It didn't budge. So I tried again, only to be met with the same resistance. I stepped back, assessing the problem. The door looked operational and there was a bald man inside behind the counter. I waved to him and in return, he pointed a finger to my right and motioned to push.

"Ahh," I muttered, spying the doorbell sunk into the frame. I pressed it and the buzzer sounded. This time, when I pushed the door it opened easily.

"Good morning," called the man jovially, offering a warm smile from behind the far end of the horseshoe-shaped counter. "The doorbell confuses everyone until you know it's there. I can just press the buzzer to let you in, of course, but it's best you know the doorbell is there too just in case you don't see anyone on the shop floor. How can I help? Is there anything you'd particularly like to see today?"

"I'm Lexi Graves-Solomon, with the Solomon Detective Agency."

"Of course. I was told to expect you. Mr. Solomon is in the back with Alan," he said, offering his hand to shake in a way that I found both gentlemanly and friendly. I wondered if he were this charming with every customer, or just the ones potentially investigating him. "I'm Jonathan Mazzina, assistant manager. Can I show you around while you wait?"

"I can't just go through?" I asked, looking around him for the employees' door that had to lead to wherever Solomon was. I spotted it at the rear, unobtrusively camouflaged in the paneling, a keypad at shoulder height.

"Store policy prevents me from allowing anyone not employed by us in the back of the shop without an escort. Someone will come to accompany you. Allow me to show you around the shop while we wait," he offered again.

I glanced around, looking for any signs of security cameras and found none. "Thanks, that would be helpful."

"As you can see, this is where we display all our goods and our customers can view or try pieces on, as well as make purchases." Jonathan skirted the counter and stepped out of a slim gap, crossing the floor to the front. "Our window displays are locked during the day, and emptied during the night to be stored in the safe. We use a keypad locking mechanism since there are a few employees and we each have our own code."

"Do you all know each other's codes?" I asked, surprised that he wasn't just showing me the jewelry but explaining the security in place too.

"We're not supposed to, but I know birthdates have been used in the past. Here, I'll show you how it works." Jonathan indicated I should join him in front of the window display. He entered his code, blocking my view with his hand and the glass partition popped open.

"There're four keypads. One for each window display," he said as he reached for a display case, "and we only ever open one at a time. That's store policy too. Open one, lock it. Put things away, lock again. Open another, lock it." He pulled out a velvet tray and placed it on the counter, indicating a sparkling array of bracelets, either made entirely of, or studded with, diamonds. "Would you like to try on anything?" he asked.

I peered at the bracelets, wanting to try on the lot until I glittered like a Christmas tree. The temptation of theft was understandable but not justifiable. No one *needed* a diamond bracelet. "They don't have price tags," I said.

"Well observed. This tray ranges from five thousand," he said, pointing to the simplest of the bracelets, then to the middle one made up entirely of diamonds "to fifteen thousand dollars."

I tried to brush that off with a nonchalant, "Do you sell many?"

"You'd be surprised. The least expensive is our entry-level diamond bracelet. Perfect for a treat or a gift," he said as though he'd said it a thousand times. Jonathan picked up the tray and entered the code, returning the tray to the window display. Then he locked it and opened the adjacent display, pulling out two small, vertical stands from which dangled gold earrings. "These are just in," he told me. "They're subtle enough for everyday wear and there are matching necklaces if you want a more glamorous look for the evening."

I lifted the gold drops with the tip of my forefinger, studying them. "They really are pretty," I said. "How much would this pair set me back?"

"Three thousand, four hundred dollars."

I winced. "Maybe later."

"Of course." Jonathan returned the stands to the display, going through the motions of entering the code and checking it was locked, ensuring I watched his every move before returning to the employee side of the counter. "You'll see in the counter displays that we have a wide array of other jewelry items and watches, for both men and women, and all kinds of occasions. Anniversaries, birthdays, weddings, *apologies,*" he added with a wink as he swept a hand over the glass counters.

"How much will an apology set me back?" I asked, tearing my eyes away from the gold, silver, and platinum underneath the glass surfaces. Every kind of gemstone appeared: rubies, sapphires, emeralds, and diamonds of all shapes and sizes.

"It depends on what you did, and how apologetic you feel," Jonathan quipped. "Shall I show you the cufflinks? Or perhaps you'd like to see the watches?"

"Okay," I agreed as we moved to the opposite counter, which housed a fine selection of watches, seeming to cater to everyone: from the rugged outdoors, to adventurous types who might need to suddenly dive 100 meters, and people who simply sought an elegant, everyday timepiece.

"If he's threatening divorce, I'd try this one," he said, pointing to an elegant silver watch. "It's not a desperate, flashy, buying of affection, but it will hit your bank balance for a more subtle shock."

"I like your sales technique," I said, trying not to smile.

"Thank you. I'm a lot more subtle usually. Would you like to see our small vintage selection? Ahh, here's your boss," he said, turning as the rear door opened and Solomon stepped through, followed by Alan Reynolds. "I'm taking Ms. Graves-Solomon through our inventory," he added.

"What do you think?" asked Alan.

"You have beautiful items," I said, "and Jonathan has been running through some of the security too."

"Glad to hear it."

"Join us in the back," said Solomon. "There's something I want you to see."

"Nice to meet you," I told Jonathan and he nodded politely, indicating with a sweep of his hand that I could step through the gap in the counter to follow Alan and Solomon through the paneled door into a narrow corridor.

"Ahead of us is the breakroom and kitchenette, the restroom, and that door leads to parking for two vehicles," said Solomon as we headed through the security door into a narrow corridor. "The middle door is for the office and this room is for the CCTV and the safe."

We stepped inside a small square room, neatly occupied by a desk, two chairs, and a large vault set into the wall with a full-sized door.

"I explained to Solomon that the vault is fully reinforced and set into the fabric of the building," said Alan. "I can show you both inside but as I already told you, I'm positive the theft happened on the shop floor and not from the vault. We accounted for the ring at the start of the day but not at the end when we were returning everything back to the vault."

"That does narrow the time window for the theft considerably," I said.

"That's what Solomon said," said Alan. "Can I get

you a coffee? Or water?"

"Nothing for me, thanks," I said. My phone buzzed with a message from my dad: *Just parked.*

"I've viewed the internal cameras from the day of theft," said Solomon, dropping into a seat, "and made a list of any person inside the store who wasn't on staff. It'll take a while to identify them all."

"It's a big list?" I asked, thinking about all the diamonds in the shop.

"Mercifully small. There were twelve customers that day."

"I was making the list already and can definitely identify three as repeat customers," said Alan. "They've been clients for so long, I hardly believe one would steal a ring now."

"It does seem unlikely to go from committed customer to thief," I agreed. "And the others?"

"I recognize two, maybe three others. I have receipts from two more. The ladies I didn't know, nor one of the men. They were new faces to me but I'll need to run their pictures past the other employees."

"We can handle that for you," said Solomon. "Lexi, I was taking an initial look at the external cameras to see if anything suspicious occurred outside."

"Like a getaway driver?" I wondered.

"More like a disturbance that could cause the shop clerk to glance over, becoming momentarily distracted, but not so obvious that they would remember it later."

"Distraction theft is common," I said, picking up his hint. "Could that be what happened here?"

"I think it's a strong possibility."

"I'm hopeful it's the *only* possibility," said Alan. "Jonathan has a great knack for sensing when someone is trying to give him the runaround."

Solomon tapped the keys and moved the mouse, scrolling back through the external footage until he stopped.

"What am I looking at?" I asked.

"Wait for it?" he said as the recording played.

"Still not seeing it," I said after a minute had passed.

"Watch again," said Solomon and rewound. This time, he pointed to the top quadrant playing. "This screen is the camera that takes a wider view of the street. The bottom screen covers the shop front, immediately outside. Tell me if you see anyone you know."

"That's Lily and me!" I said, spotting us taking a seat in the coffee shop across the street. Almost immediately, Lily put the binoculars to her eyes.

"Correct," said Solomon.

"We went for coffee," I said, quickly adding, "obviously." Then for Alan's benefit, I explained, "Lily is my best friend and sister-in-law."

"So far, you two are our only eyewitnesses for part of the time of the theft window."

"I wish I could say I saw something interesting but I didn't. We didn't even stay long," I said, feeling disappointed and wishing I could go back in time to the moment on screen so I could take a better look around. Then, when I watched Lily lower her binoculars, speak to me, then raise them again, I thought of something that had seemed tiresome and ridiculous yesterday. I almost laughed as I said, "Lily was spying on three old ladies that went... oh! I remember now. They came into the store. She was convinced they were casing the place. I thought she was just being paranoid."

"What gave her that impression?" asked Alan.

I glanced at him, then at Solomon. A puff of color reached my cheeks. "Lily saw the ladies earlier, bumbling around. Then, while we were getting coffee, she was watching them amble down the street. I think they walked past Reynolds', then turned around and walked back, and seemed to have a discussion before going inside. That's what got Lily even more interested in them. They couldn't have been in there longer than, I don't know, ten... maybe fifteen minutes? Maybe less. Then they shuffled to the coffee cart and went to the bus stop and got on. Lily left and I had to go so I forgot all about it until I was outside, just now."

Solomon paused the video and glanced at Alan. "Did you identify the elderly ladies?" he asked. "How many were there?" he asked me.

"Three, I think."

Alan shook his head. "No, I don't recognize them. I don't think they're regular customers."

Solomon leaned back in his chair. "What made Lily think they were specifically casing this shop?"

"I don't know. I just thought she was bored and hopeful they were casing somewhere." But now I wondered if there could be more to it. Lily had certainly thought so. Had her instincts been right all along? And how had I missed it?

"She didn't mention anything in particular? Had you encountered these ladies doing anything suspicious when you first spotted them?"

"No, I don't think so. I think we saw them down the street, maybe half an hour before, when we were browsing and they were looking in windows, but we didn't interact with them. When they were window shopping still, I insisted we get a coffee. Lily was particularly eager to take a window seat. She wanted to observe them."

"But you didn't see anything strange going on?" pressed Solomon.

"Define strange? Actually, it doesn't matter. No. I didn't see anything strange. Like I said, I thought Lily was just bored and hopeful, more than on to anything. I thought they were three elderly ladies doing some window shopping and maybe one of them was buying a gift or treating herself to something special. After Lily and I parted, I didn't think any more about it until I walked up to the store today."

"We'll still need to track them down."

"I think Lily might have followed them," I said, holding back a wince. "The trio got onto a bus before Lily said she had to go, and a few minutes later, I saw Lily driving in the same direction."

"What happened then?"

A creeping feeling of guilt overcame me at the weird turn of events. "I wish I could say I asked but I really forgot all about it until now." What I wanted to ask was had I done something wrong, but I was sure I hadn't. Lily's suspicions had seemed so fanciful but now we'd been thrust into the investigation, she was going to be thrilled!

CHAPTER FIVE

"Should I call Lily?" I wondered, knowing I would never, ever hear the end of it when I did.

"Not yet," said Solomon, who didn't appear at all perturbed by Lily's potential reaction. "It would be good to complete the surveillance and identify as many customers as we can. If the elderly ladies do appear suspicious, it would be wise to discuss her perspective, but we should complete other tasks first."

"We need more information about the ring too," I said. "There was only one picture in the packet you gave us." I hadn't studied it carefully but it was a pretty gold band with a large sapphire surrounded by diamonds, old-fashioned but in a desirable, vintage way.

"Laura's on her way," said Alan. "She bought the ring from one of her contacts so she's in a better position than me to give you more information. We should have given you all the information yesterday evening but we were in too much of a hurry to find help. I'm not sure if my sister even listed it on our website yet so I suppose she's pulling together all the details. Laura felt it was remiss of us and I agree."

"Don't be," I said. "We've only just begun the investigation. This is part of discovery." As I said it, I wondered how much I was reassuring Alan he hadn't done anything wrong, and how much of it was for my own benefit. I couldn't help feeling guilty I hadn't taken Lily more seriously yesterday. Could we have prevented a crime? Surely, those old ladies were witnesses, not thieves.

A buzz sounded in the small room and I turned, looking for the source of the noise.

"That's the shop floor buzzer," said Alan, opening the door. A pair of voices seeped through as another door opened: Jonathan and a woman. "Here's Laura now," he added. "Jonathan probably buzzed to let us know she was coming through."

"Does everyone come through the shop's front door?" I asked.

Alan nodded. "We prefer it that way. There's an emergency exit at the back but we decided entry from the front is better for security."

"Alan showed me before you got here," said Solomon to me. "I agree it's a sensible protocol to use one entrance and exit given the value of items in the shop."

"Hello," said Laura when she appeared in the doorway of the small room, followed by my dad right behind her, making it feel a touch claustrophobic. "You don't know how good it is to see you all at work already. I spent half the night fretting about the theft."

"Theft can be unsettling. You remember our consultant, Steve Graves?" said Solomon.

"Of course. Mr. Graves was telling me about his

detective days," Laura said, nodding.

"And that I'm very happy to assist on the case," added Dad. He wore a button-down shirt and jeans, every inch the retired detective. "I'm sure I'll get up to speed quickly."

"I'd really like to talk to you about the ring," I said to Laura. "It would be great to get a few more details about it."

"Anything to help," she said, without trying to step inside. "This room is a little too cramped for all of us. Would you like to come into the office?"

"Please," I agreed, already rising. "We won't take long."

"Take as long as you need," she said pleasantly.

The four of us followed Laura to the end of the short corridor, past the closed door to the restroom, the small breakroom—the kitchenette little more than a fridge, microwave, sink and coffee pot all squashed together in one unit—and into a room twice as large as the security room and considerably plusher than the breakroom.

The office was furnished with a large, antique desk with scrolled legs and a thick top, behind which was a modern, ergonomic desk chair, and further on, two occasional chairs opposite. The credenza displayed several antique magnifying glasses and weights, while the walls had framed posters of gems with diagrams for cuts and clarity, both artistic and practical. Filing cabinets took up another wall, a new printer on top.

"Do you have any suspects yet?" asked Laura as she sat down in the desk chair. Solomon and I took the occasional chairs, Dad propped himself against the filing cabinets, and Alan leaned against the wall between us, folding his arms and crossing one ankle over the other.

"With Alan's help, I've whittled down the customers we'll concentrate on," said Solomon. "But now, we'd like to know more about the ring that was stolen."

"Alan tells us you make the purchases," I added.

"That's right. The ring was in our vintage section. We have a small display for vintage jewelry and we're currently carrying a dozen rings of various styles, amongst other pieces, a few necklaces, and a couple of bracelets. Vintage jewelry is a passion of mine but there's only so much I can buy for myself and sometimes, I see a good piece that isn't my taste or size but I know will sell. My brother indulges my passion since it's proven profitable." She flashed a warm smile at him.

"I hardly call it indulging," said Alan. "Laura is being modest but the vintage pieces produce a good turnover. She has a great eye and many of our customers want something that has a story attached, or feel it's more ethical not to buy new."

"What can you tell us about this particular ring?" I asked.

"It came from a private seller in Europe a little over a month ago," said Laura. "Family heirloom, now unwanted. They didn't have a receipt but I wasn't concerned about that. It's often unlikely the seller has one if it's a family heirloom passed down through generations. All kinds of things happen over the years from poor record keeping to fire, water damage, and my least favorite, rats. However, they provided a picture of their mother wearing the ring back in the forties and another photo at a gala in Paris a decade later. Since it was made roughly in the 1930s, the photos were a good indication of how long it'd been in the family."

"Nothing earlier? Before the 1940s?" I asked.

"Unfortunately not, although photographs are, of course, rarer the further we go back in history and, like I said, record keeping isn't always possible. I was satisfied with the provenance, and after examining it, I was assured of the ring's value. It was a stunning, eight carat sapphire, beautifully cut and set, with round-cut diamonds. I paid forty thousand for it, and we listed it for sale at fifty thousand," said Laura.

"Wow," said Dad, the only word he'd uttered since we'd entered the room.

"A lot of people hear 'vintage' and think 'cheap' but I see marketable history. We prepared a sales pack with copies of the photos for the eventual buyer. There's an online listing too but the sellers' photos aren't available there."

"How soon did you market the ring for sale?" asked Solomon.

"Almost straightaway. It's a big investment for us. We cleaned it and put it up for sale within the week."

"Have there been any inquiries? Or anyone asking to try the ring on?" I asked.

"No to the latter, and yes to the former. A woman called last week to ask if we still had it for sale. I remember because I was pleased there was interest. I said we did, told her the same information I just gave you, although it's all on our website, and also that we would include secure shipping if she chose to pay online. She declined."

"Did she say why?"

"No, and I didn't ask. I just told her it would be available as long as the webpage was live. After that, I said it was unlikely we'd secure something similar any time soon. It really is a one-off piece. I was glad to acquire it."

"What do you remember about the caller?"

"Aside from being a female… American. Young-ish voice. At least, not elderly and not a teenager either. Why? Do you think that's significant?"

"We're covering all the angles," said Solomon. "Did she say where she was calling from?"

"No, but I remember the call came from an international number. It might still be logged. Should I take a look?"

"Please," said Solomon.

Laura reached for the desk phone and scrolled through the digital panel. "I think this is it," she said, grasping a pen and notepad. "The number starts with a 49."

"That's Germany," said Solomon.

"Is it?" said Laura.

"Let's dial it," said Solomon, holding his hand for the phone. Laura pressed the display and then put it on speakerphone. A moment later, someone answered.

"Guten tag! Hotel Ingrid. Kann ich ihnen helfen?" came a strong male voice.

Solomon deposited the handset back in the cradle without saying anything and contemplated it for a moment. "We'll make a note of that and see if we come up with a connection to Germany or Hotel Ingrid," he said.

"So it's not a dead end?" Laura brightened.

"Not entirely, no."

"Have you bought anything from the sellers before?" I asked, struck by a new line of thought while Solomon mused over the phone call.

"No, I haven't."

"Did they approach you, or you them?"

"They approached me via another contact who knows I have an interest in vintage jewelry. That's not uncommon," said Laura.

"I think we should speak to the sellers," I said. "Can we have their name and number?"

"Of course, but I'm not sure how it helps. They sold the ring fair and square and I made the bank transfer myself."

"We're just covering all the angles," I said.

"Okay, but please be discreet. I don't want them to think we're accusing them." Laura opened her phone, tapped the screen and a moment later, wrote a new number on the notepad. Tearing the sheet off, she passed it to me.

"What's the next step?" asked Alan.

"I'd like to see the display case where the ring was lifted. I assume it's just as it was yesterday," said Solomon, rising. "Understanding where the case is situated and how customers are able to view the items will help us when we review the security footage again." I got to my feet, and Dad straightened, ready to follow us.

"I'll take you through to the shop," said Alan. "Jonathan will be able to help with that."

"I'll be here for a while if you think of anything else," said Laura.

We followed Alan back along the corridor to the shop floor and waited as he disengaged the lock and opened the door. Only Jonathan was inside the shop, buffing the glass display tops with a microfiber cloth, glancing up as we trooped in.

"Jonathan, the investigators would like to talk to

you about yesterday," said Alan.

"Of course." Jonathan stowed the spray bottle and cloth under the unit that held the cash register, walked around the displays to the right side, and tapped on the glass lid. "The ring was in this case. The vintage section. I've been thinking about it and I'm sure the only people I got the case out for yesterday were the old ladies, the deli guy, and the dad. I know those descriptions aren't helpful but I'm sure I can point them out on the recordings."

"That could narrow things down significantly," I said. "We can confirm they were the only customers to see the case through the video playback."

"That's what I figured. I could be wrong, of course, but I can't see how anyone else could have gotten into the case without employee access. No matter what else I was doing, I would have noticed if someone leaned over the counter, picked the lock, and pulled out a display," said Jonathan. "It's not an easy or quick thing to do."

"I have no doubt," agreed Solomon. "So we'll work with the theory that the case was open and the jewelry was available to the thief."

"I feel awful about it," said Jonathan suddenly. "We've had attempted thefts before. Sleight of hand, distractions, but I've always spotted them. I feel terrible that I didn't this time."

"You're only human," said Dad and I nodded in agreement.

"Jonathan, we don't blame you at all," said Alan. "Laura and I talked about it. You've been here longer than us and we don't want you to feel under any suspicion."

"I appreciate your trust in me but still... this was

on my watch and such an expensive ring too!" said Jonathan as he unlocked the display and pulled out the tray to place it on top of the glass.

I stepped closer and gazed at the display of vintage rings with all kinds of stones, some engagement style, others cocktail rings, plus, several necklaces, bracelets, and two brooches. "Are they all acquired the same way? Do you ever buy from walk-ins?" I asked.

"No, we're not a pawn shop and we wouldn't want to encourage anyone to think we are," answered Alan. "Laura finds them usually. She's a big fan of antiquing and has a good eye. Exhibitions are the most expensive since those items are being sold by dealers, and they've already done their due diligence, but she also picks them up at estate sales, house clearances, or smaller shops. Sometimes on one of her trips overseas. She likes being able to examine and pick things up and she can often spot a real gem, if you'll excuse the pun, that the owners have ignored. She's even purchased some from the internet and online auction sites although that's a little riskier."

"Why's that?"

"To value a stone, it really needs to be in your hand. Anyone can put a picture of anything on the internet or give any kind of description or authentication. You don't necessarily receive what you think you've bought. But Laura has a small network of sellers whom she trusts and they have their own networks to scour."

"Reynolds' isn't a big vintage dealer so Laura only buys a few pieces a year," added Jonathan.

"What's the market like for vintage items?" I asked.

"Solid. Like Laura said before, some people like to have an item with history, or be one of a kind, rather than mass produced. The earrings, brooches, bracelets and necklaces are reasonably easy to sell. The downside with the rings is that it can be difficult to resize the bands as the stones can be so delicate, so it's usually on a wing and a prayer to know if the piece a customer falls in love with will actually fit."

"What about provenance?" I asked. "Is every piece checked?"

"Laura keeps track of where she finds things, whom she bought it from, how much she paid. Then she authenticates it, decides the retail value, based on current market trends, and gets a second opinion to confirm. Sometimes there's a maker's mark, or a style that ties it to a particular era or company like Cartier. Beyond that, it can be hard to pin down who bought the piece originally, and for whom, and how it was passed down unless it comes from a family clearance with paperwork. If there's scant or no information, like with the missing ring, Laura tries to build up a file."

"Such as using the photos of the sapphire ring?" I asked.

"That's right. Sometimes the sellers don't want people to know they're selling off family jewels, especially when the item is as distinctive as this ring but she always promises discretion."

"Why?" asked Solomon.

"We've often found sales are due to a change in fortunes. Inherited wealth can disappear with profligate lifestyles and bad investments. Selling off jewels, art, and furniture keeps some old families afloat."

"Laura said you're advertising the ring online," I said. "The sellers don't mind?"

"We try and remain discreet but they don't have much recourse regarding what we do with it after they sell it. Plus, with the difference in countries, there's plausible deniability. Maybe it was their ring, maybe not," said Alan with a shrug. "We all have access to the shop site but Laura is responsible for adding our inventory."

"What about any regrets? What happens if the seller wants to buy the piece back?" asked Dad.

Alan shifted his attention to my dad. "Like, I said, we're not a pawn shop. We've never had an issue with any of the pieces Laura buys and she always makes sure to either get a receipt or give one, just in case," said Alan. "In the instance of this ring, we haven't had any contact with the sellers since so there's nothing that indicates they regretted selling it."

Solomon nodded thoughtfully. "Had anyone made any inquiries in person about it?" he asked.

"Not to me. And I don't recall any emails or other calls about it either. Laura would have mentioned if there were anyone else. Jonathan?"

"I don't recall anyone asking," said Jonathan with a quick shake of his head, "but there've been plenty of people through the shop in the past month and I must have lifted this particular tray out multiple times."

I picked up a delicate silver necklace, the chain interspersed with tiny gemstones while Solomon reached for the matching bracelet. "It's gorgeous," I said, turning it over in my hand. "I can't imagine how you make such a piece." I set the necklace back on its velvet pillow and Jonathan adjusted the pins holding it in place. Solomon deposited the bracelet.

Jonathan hesitated, then he said, "And the ring please."

Solomon opened his palm, revealing it empty.

"Oh, c'mon," said Jonathan, patiently.

This time, Solomon grinned, flicked his fingers, and there was a ring. He handed it to Jonathan who slipped it over a pin, then locked the whole display away under the counter where light fingers couldn't make fast work.

"That was amazing," I said. "I didn't even see you lift it."

"But *he* did," said Solomon, nodding to Jonathan.

"I've seen all kinds of tricks and I have a lot of experience," said Jonathan, a trace of amusement in his eyes at catching Solomon's trick.

"Which means our thief has even more," said Solomon.

CHAPTER SIX

"What was your first indication the ring I lifted was missing?" Solomon asked.

"That's easy. There was a gap in the display," said Jonathan. "There was a little bit of confusion with you both picking up items but I noticed you did something with your thumb that gave away what you doing under your palm."

Solomon smiled. "I'm impressed. I'll need to work on my sleight of hand."

"Not around these jewels. I don't think my heart can take it!" said Alan. He clapped Jonathan on the back. "Well caught. I missed it."

"What about with the sapphire ring? How come you didn't notice?" I asked, curious. Jonathan had seen movement in Solomon's hand so subtle that I hadn't clocked it, even while standing next to him. Yet, hadn't I been distracted by the necklace in my hands? And didn't Solomon and I both return the items we examined at the same time? That was four hands in a small space. No wonder I hadn't noticed. Perhaps

Jonathan was simply observing more closely since he'd been potentially hoodwinked yesterday.

I gazed through the clear counter displaying where Jonathan had deposited the vintage tray and ran my hands around the edges, finding the glass case perfectly sealed. To unlock it from the other side, I would not only have to lean my whole body across the case, but I would also need the key that Jonathan carried on a small chain at his waist. One end was attached to his belt loop, the other was tucked into his vest pocket. There was no way a thief could dislodge the key without Jonathan noticing.

"Because there wasn't a gap," Jonathan was saying. "It wasn't until we were putting the displays in the safe at the end of the day that I realized the ring that should have been there was now a crude replica."

"If Jonathan hadn't noticed then, it could have gone undiscovered for days," said Alan.

"A replica?" I repeated.

"I have it here," said Jonathan, reaching under the counter, then dropping a ring on the glass top. It landed with a small clink, spiraled, and swiveled to a stop. I reached for it, knowing as soon as I felt it that the band was cheap, coated metal. The stone was the right size and color but set wonky and the prongs weren't quite identical to the missing sapphire ring. "It's similar from a distance and since there wasn't an empty spot and no one had asked to see the ring, it totally bypassed me," he said. "Pushed into the velvet tray, once it was under the counter, I wouldn't look at it any closer unless I had cause to. It's very embarrassing."

"Easily done," I said, covering the band with my thumb so I could just see the top of the gem. If I didn't know it was a fake, and a poor one at that, nestled in the velvet amongst other pieces, I wouldn't have noticed it was a substitute either. "I think anyone would have made the same mistake," I decided.

"I shouldn't have though," said Jonathan. "I should have noticed right away!"

"What do you think of the replica?" I asked.

"Cheap crap. Poorly constructed. I will say the blue is right for the sapphire, the crystals are the right size for the diamonds, and the band is the right color for gold, but scratch it and you'll see it's just a coating." I dropped the ring into his palm and he demonstrated, running his nail along the band. The paint immediately peeled.

"Interesting," said Solomon.

"Honestly, I would have expected something better for a dupe," said Jonathan, frowning.

I glanced at my dad, where he remained slightly behind us, watching silently. I was sure he'd ask questions if he'd had them but he was politely leaving Solomon and me to lead.

"Does any of this help?" asked Alan.

"Any information you have helps us work out what happened," I said.

"Lexi's correct. We need to review some more footage but we'd like to interview you in more depth shortly," Solomon said to Jonathan.

"Of course, I'm here all day."

"Just say when and I'll man the store," said Alan. "I'll buzz you back through."

"While we're checking the video, can you give us a list of the people you recognized when we viewed it?" asked Solomon.

"Sure can."

Ensconced in the small security room, the door firmly shut behind us, only Dad, Solomon and I remaining, I said, "I feel bad for Jonathan. He's obviously taken the theft to heart."

"I think having it happen on his watch must've wounded his pride," said Solomon. "Let's sit for a moment to review our notes before we confirm that. What do you think of Laura's comments?"

"She's helpful. She doesn't seem perturbed by anything we asked."

"Which is a good sign. Steve?"

"I agree," said Dad.

"Is the hotel call a dead end?" I asked. "Anyone could stay at a hotel or come in off the street to use their phone."

"We shouldn't write it off yet. I'm going to ask Lucas to run down the guest list for the day of the call. We might find our female American caller." He made a note, then glanced at me. "What occurred to you about the sellers?"

"That maybe they're not as honest as Laura thought they were. Perhaps they wanted the cash *and* the ring back, or maybe they wanted a quick sale to an overseas buyer for some reason."

"Interesting theories. Alan?"

"He seems sincere. He certainly trusts Laura and Jonathan."

"I agree. And Jonathan?"

"Like I said, I feel bad for him but I think his success at catching you probably pumped his ego back up a smidge."

"He's got a sharp eye. Whoever pulled the wool over his eyes was very efficient," said Dad. "I didn't see you take the ring."

Solomon grinned, apparently pleased with himself. "I think we should review the footage again and see if we spot any distractions. It's a shame there's no sound but most likely, any distraction probably came from within the store."

"What about more than one person working together?" I asked.

"That makes sense."

"Two people in on it as a team might not enter together and could have tried to appear to be strangers," said Dad.

Solomon nodded. "We'll look out for any sign of that."

"There's one more thing. I keep thinking about the replica ring. You didn't handle it but it really was poor quality. The stone is the right color and size but everything else is off. There's no way it could not be discovered quickly. So why use it?" I wondered.

"Perhaps it's what they had on hand at the time," said Dad.

"I think if someone plans to steal a ring like the sapphire, and wants to make sure no one finds out, they'd invest in something higher end. Look at our last case, the lab grown and paste jewels were utterly convincing. This dupe looks like something you'd find in a cheap accessories shop at the mall," I said.

"What's your theory?" asked Solomon.

"The Reynoldses only had the ring in their possession for little more than a month and they listed it for sale quickly. What if the thief simply didn't have enough time to get a nice fake made so they just worked with what they could get? The plan was put together quickly and they didn't have time for any finer detail. I can't decide if it's slapdash or simply audacious."

"Perhaps both."

"I'll look into where the dupe came from. Perhaps we'll get lucky," I said.

"Don't spend too much time on that avenue. We've got more time-consuming issues here. After we review the footage, we should interview Jonathan properly, without Alan observing."

"Do you think he's hiding something from his boss? If there're any sour grapes about Alan's promotion over him years ago, he hides it well."

"I agree, and I'd like him to speak freely. So far, he's only given us pointers on how the theft could have happened but he admits he's not sure exactly. The video is where the evidence lies. Actually, change of plan. Maybe we should talk to Jonathan now."

"Alan's identifying the shoppers he knows, so he's occupied," I said.

"We make a good team," said Solomon.

"Don't I know it," I said, delighted when he leaned in to plant a small kiss on my lips. "But I will need to call HR about this harassment."

"Oh?"

"Yeah, there's not nearly enough of it," I said with a laugh.

Dad coughed and looked up at the ceiling.

"Like you said, time is of the essence here," said Solomon, reaching for the CCTV controls. "The trail is around twenty-four hours cold. We might be able to narrow that time window."

Before he could do anything, a knock came at the door and Alan stuck his head around. "I got the receipts from yesterday's customers," he told us, holding up a sheet of photocopy paper. "I added the names and addresses we hold on file. The second sheet has the names and details of the three repeat customers I recognized who didn't purchase anything."

I reached out my hand and took the paper, scanning the list. All were locals. "Thanks, this is very helpful," I said and passed it over to Solomon.

"I'll be on the shop floor if you need anything else and then I need to do some admin in the office with Laura," he said.

"We'll be out shortly," said Solomon and Alan nodded and shut the door. "Change of plan again," said Solomon. "We'll start with the video."

"That's half of the customers identified," I said, pointing to the sheet. "We should check with Jonathan about the ones he recognized and those he didn't."

"Let's watch the video. I've noted the times where the customers enter and where Jonathan and Tansy are alone in the shop. We'll focus on the customers first, and get the clearest screenshots available so we can identify them."

Solomon hit *play* and we buzzed through the footage, looking closer at what they did, with Dad confirming no one was familiar to him in his detective days, even though the possibility was remote.

By the time we'd finished, I could confirm what Jonathan had told us was accurate. The only people who had perused the vintage tray outside of its glass case was the trio of old ladies, and two men that Jonathan had called "the deli guy" and "the dad" although I couldn't be sure who was whom.

However, one of the customers had looked at other items from the same display case so I didn't want to rule him out either.

"This corroborates what Jonathan said," I said.

Footsteps sounded in the hallway and Dad ducked his head around the door, mouthing, "Alan."

"Let's see what else Jonathan can tell us," said Solomon.

We pushed back our chairs and headed out of the room and onto the shop floor, buzzing our way in, the three of us making the small corridor seem crowded. The shop was empty except for Jonathan. He was standing behind the cash register organizing a box of smart shopping bags with corded handles.

"How's it going?" he asked. "I can talk until a customer comes in. How can I help?"

"Alan identified some of the patrons from the day the theft occurred. We hoped you might identify the rest," said Solomon, pulling out his phone where he'd emailed himself screenshots of the patrons. "Can you tell me if the list is correct and if you recognize anyone else?"

"I can probably remember without the prompt," said Jonathan but he took the phone anyway and swiped through the camera roll, confirming names from Alan's list. Then he returned to the remaining photos. "This man isn't a regular customer but I do know him, sort of. He works at the Little Italy deli down the street. Hence why I called him 'deli guy'," he said.

"The nice free-standing place with all the amazing cheese?" I asked, and the mere thought of the glorious deli made me drool.

"That's it. I think he owns it. Anyway, that day was the third time he'd been in here browsing. He was looking at engagement rings, including the vintage tray. I remember him saying he'd been trying to get his girlfriend to drop hints about what she likes but apparently, she doesn't have any serious expectations or dream rings, so he's second guessing himself on what to buy."

"Aww," I cooed.

"I suggested he buy something cheap to propose and come back with her to pick from a range in his budget. That threw up a whole new set of problems and now he doesn't know which cheap ring to buy." Jonathan grinned.

"What about the others?" asked Solomon.

"Let's see." Jonathan scrolled again, twisting his mouth in thought. "This woman always pays in cash," he said, pointing at the screen. "I think I've sold her four items in the past year, but didn't sell her anything that day. She likes earrings mostly. I didn't show her any rings and she's not into vintage pieces. Oh, this guy was from out of town. Dallas, I think. Wanted a gift for his wife, and another for his mistress. Left without buying anything."

"How come?"

"No two-for-one deals," quipped Jonathan. Then his mouth tugged down. "Sorry. I know it's not funny. He wasn't sure what he wanted for either woman and I didn't feel overly obliged to assist him in the mess he'd made of his life. Oh, I remember him saying he was on his way to Boston to catch a flight that afternoon."

"And the last man?" asked Solomon.

"Let's see. No, no, I don't think I've seen him before. He spoke with an accent. European. French, maybe? I'm not sure. He asked a few questions and I think he mentioned his mother so he might have been shopping for a gift. He said he'd return this week if he had time. Is any of this helpful?"

"It is," I told him.

"Can you look though this next set of photos and tell me what you remember about them?" said Solomon.

"I think Tansy served the first two. This man has been in a few times. He's the man I called "the dad". I sold a necklace to him for an eighteenth birthday present for his daughter. It was a heart-shaped locket from the vintage section and he looked at the vintage pieces yesterday too. Let's see. This woman is also a repeat customer. She bought earrings for herself. And this woman has shopped here for years. She has very specific taste, nothing wildly expensive usually, so I call her when something comes in I know she'll like. In this case, it was a necklace with a bee pendant. She's very fond of wildlife."

He scrolled on, pointing his index finger at the screen. "These three ladies came in together. I think one of them wanted to buy something for herself. She might have been celebrating something, I'm not sure, but she wasn't sure what she wanted. So this one encouraged her to try on a few different items. I got several trays out for them while Tansy was arranging some boxes, I think. One of the ladies fell over, this one I believe," he said, pointing to the woman in the middle, "and she felt sore so they decided to call off their shopping and take her home to rest. To be honest, I wasn't sure I was going to make a sale but they were a friendly, lively trio."

"This is a big help," I told him as Solomon withdrew his phone but didn't tuck it away in a pocket. "I heard you design your own jewelry?"

If Jonathan were surprised I knew that, he didn't react. "I do. Would you like to see some?" he offered.

My eyebrows arched in amazement. "You have some here?"

"Yes. Once I felt my pieces were refined enough, I showed some to Alan and Laura and they insisted they wanted to stock some items under my own name. I was flattered, I can tell you. They've been helping me with setting up the business even though I've assured them I have no intention of leaving here."

"Why not?" I wondered. "Don't you like the idea of being your own boss?"

"It's not that," he said as he beckoned for us to follow him to the end of the display case opposite the door. He unlocked the case and extracted a display with several delicate silver and gold items, placing it in front of us. "I don't think I'm cut out for the solitary workshop life. I like talking to customers, getting to know them, and learning what they like."

"Your bosses aren't worried you'll poach their customers?" asked Solomon.

Jonathan laughed. "Oh, no, not at all! If anything, they seem to think my design skills make me more of an asset; plus, I've been able to take on a few repairs for the shop's clients since I have the tools and the knowledge. What do you think?"

"They're lovely," I said, teasing the delicate silver and gold with the tip of my forefinger. "I can't imagine how you make anything so dainty."

"It took a lot of practice. My first few years were about making simple, clumsy pieces, but the more I learned and practiced, the more refined my work became. I'm currently focusing on creating a core collection, some of which you see here, and some customized items."

"I don't see any gemstones," said Solomon. "You

don't like to work with them?"

"I do, but they require considerable investment. I've just started making a simple line with small gemstones and Laura has already said she'll stock them too. It's not only a boost to my ego, but to my wallet too," he added. "The Reynoldses have been very supportive. But I know you didn't come to the shop to talk about my side hustle. What else can I help you with?" He slid the tray back into its locked case and waited.

"Of the people who looked at the vintage tray, you identified 'deli guy' as one of them. Another is the dad you mentioned, and you definitely don't recognize the elderly ladies, is that correct?" I asked.

"Yes," said Jonathan. "There's one more thing. The man with the accent. He did look at the vintage tray and he asked about the items but he didn't ask me to pull it out. Is that pertinent?"

"Definitely," said Solomon. "Thanks again for your help."

We headed into the security room, resuming our seats at the desk. "Alan noted the dad on his list and we can locate the deli guy easily."

"That leaves the old ladies, and the guy with the accent."

"We might not find everyone," said Dad. "It'll be hard to track down the man who went to the airport." His phone rang and he glanced at it. "It's your mom. Excuse me." He stepped into the hallway, pulling the door closed behind him.

"We'll see if the other employees can narrow down the list. For now, I want to show you something."

I brightened. The office was dark and secluded. We were all alone.

"No," said Solomon, a ghost of a smile on his lips.

I sighed. "What *do* you want to show me?" I asked, finishing just as Dad stepped back into the room.

"When we viewed the footage again, my focus went to the trio of old ladies. I want you both to watch closely again and give me your observations. The tape runs for around fifteen minutes at this point."

"Okay, sure," I said, and adjusted my seat so I could watch the screen. Dad stooped next to me, his hands on his knees, his neck craning but he waved me back into the seat when I started to get up and offer him mine.

Solomon cued the footage and it began to play. We watched as the old ladies were buzzed in and Jonathan greeted them, then Tansy. The ladies headed for the first case, leaning over to point at items and talk between them. Jonathan moved around the employees' side of the cases to talk with them, pointing out this and that. Tansy's head bobbed in and out of shot near the cash register where she'd busied herself stacking gift boxes.

"I'm planning to recommend they install more up-to-date tech with audio," said Solomon. "It's entirely owing to Jonathan's memory that we know about the man with an accent to add to the suspect list."

"Even though he didn't get his hands on the vintage tray?" Dad asked.

"He could have been casing the place. Keep watching."

My gaze remained glued to the screen as the three women asked to try things on, their mouths moving silently, and then one broke off to browse the other cases, the other two following their friend. Jonathan extracted a display case for them and they spent a couple minutes trying on bracelets before shaking their heads and Jonathan returned the case, locking it.

They split off again, then reformed as a trio a minute later and another display tray was produced for their perusal. This time, they tried on rings and held up earrings, checking their reflections in a small stand mirror Jonathan had produced from under the display cases. A couple of times, their hands crossed and then the display case was put away and another was produced.

Apparently in no hurry, they tried on some more items, then one of the ladies slipped and landed on her butt with a thump and another one of the ladies stooped to gather her up, fussing around her as they levered their friend to her feet. Meanwhile, Jonathan leaned over the counter, saying something I couldn't quite decipher as the third lady flapped her hands around, fussing over them some more. On the other side of the shop, Tansy started to round the counter and was waved away by one of the ladies.

The fallen lady rubbed her hip and I could imagine her insisting she was all right before wincing. She started shaking her head and the other ladies fussed some more before she linked arms with one of the other ladies while the third pulled open the door, holding it for them before following them outside, out of view. Inside the shop, Jonathan put the tray away, locked the case and walked around the counters, watching them leave as Tansy came to join him, the two of them talking briefly.

Of course I knew what happened next because I'd watched the ladies head for the bus stop only yesterday.

Solomon hit *pause* and said, "What do you think?"

"I couldn't work out who was doing the shopping.

One or all of them," I said as Dad scratched his head, frowning.

"Anything else?"

"They were definitely looking at ladies' items but they seemed indecisive. Bracelets, rings, earrings…" I trailed off, thinking. "Rings," I said again.

"Go on."

"Their hands were all over the rings."

"Tell me more."

"That was confusing, and then one of them fell over. Was that the distraction?" I frowned, wondering. It looked like a chaotic couple of minutes. "Jonathan didn't immediately put the tray away."

"That's what I think."

"Play that part again," Dad instructed. I leaned in, curious to see what I'd missed.

Solomon played it again. Then twice more, once in slow motion.

"I just don't see the theft occurring," I said. My elbow was on the desk and I leaned my chin onto my palm, confused. "I don't see a hand closing over anything. Or immediately going into a pocket or a purse."

"That's my issue too. The chaos suggests it's them but I don't have any hard evidence to conclude it is." Solomon leaned back in his seat. "So, until we can find some proof, everyone on the shop floor that day remains a suspect."

CHAPTER SEVEN

"I think it's time to call Lily."

"I agree," said Solomon.

"I thought you'd say you were afraid of that," I replied as I rummaged for my phone. I was already wondering what I'd unleashed at saying those potentially fateful words.

"I thought I'd keep that inside."

"She might have a clue," said Dad. "Because so far, we don't have a lot to go on."

I scrolled to my "favorites" list and hit Lily's name. She answered after a few rings with a cheerful "Hey, bestie!"

"Hey, you. So remember those old ladies yesterday?"

"What old ladies?" Lily asked breezily.

"The ones we were watching from the coffee shop yesterday."

"We were?"

I smelled a rat. Lily was being far too nonchalant.

"The ones you insisted were up to no good."

"Oh. Vaguely," she drawled airily.

"I need to find them."

"Why?" Lily snipped and I knew her attention was aroused.

"I think you might have been right."

"I knew it!" yelled Lily, forcing me to move the phone a couple inches from my ear. "I told you! I told you they were trouble! What did they do?"

I sighed softly. I would never hear the end of this. "Maybe a robbery."

"Yes! Lexi, I know you can't see me but I'm fist-punching the air!"

"It's nothing to be pleased about."

"It is! I called it, you *pooh-poohed* it. That's a lot to be happy about! I knew they were up to no good!"

"So do you know where they went?" I continued as Dad motioned to get on with it or something of the like. I flashed a hand at him, silently asking *what more can I do?*

"I do."

"And that would be?"

Lily paused. "I can show you," she said and I could only imagine the smile spreading across her face right now that she realized I needed her.

"She can show me," I mouthed to Solomon and he nodded.

"I'm at work now but Ruby can take over at noon. Why don't you pick me up and I can show you exactly where I tailed them?" said Lily.

"You tailed them?" Of course Lily did. I'd suspected as much yesterday when she shot out of the coffee shop only to drive past me in the direction of their bus.

"Well, duh! Where do you think I went? I followed

those no-good geriatrics all the way to… I'll tell you when you pick me up," she finished quickly.

"I'll be there at noon."

"Good. Can you bring me lunch?"

"I can. Why? Don't you have any food at the bar?"

"I do but apology lunches taste so much better. See you at noon!" Lily hung up before I could say anything else.

"I have to buy her lunch," I said and Dad laughed.

"Expense it," said Solomon. His phone buzzed and he paused to read, his face expressionless. "I need to go and I'm not sure when I'll get back. I hate to jet when we're at this early stage but it's unavoidable. Can you handle the case together for now?"

"Of course. There's nothing dangerous to get myself into and the thief doesn't know we're onto him or her yet, which could work in our favor. Plus, Dad can help me with getting the details of the other suspects while I chase down this trio."

"I'll email all the footage and the screenshots too, to all of us. I'll also alert Lucas to allow you privileges at the agency," Solomon added to my Dad. "They're at your disposal. Until then, can you find addresses and background info for the names we do have?"

"What about the unidentified?" Dad asked.

"If anyone remembers anything, note it. The European man is top of the interest list there, but mostly we should rule these people out first, as much as we can.

"Cool. On it. I'll stay here a while then see myself out," said Dad.

Solomon and I made our goodbyes to Alan and Laura, then to Jonathan, and headed for our respective vehicles where Solomon kissed me goodbye and told me to send up the bat signal if anything went badly wrong.

"So little faith," I said with a shrug.

"Faith in it going wrong," said Solomon with a wry smile. "But I live in hope."

I picked up lunch from a sandwich shop near where I'd parked my car, then I headed over to the bar to collect Lily, just a few minutes past noon.

"I knew you'd come to your senses," said Lily when she climbed into the passenger seat and peered into the paper takeout bag. "Oh, my favorite. You did good."

"Since when is that your favorite?"

"Since I asked you to bring lunch. We can eat when we get there."

"And where would that be?" I asked, curious about what Lily had gotten up to yesterday. How long had she followed these women, and how far? I didn't know the bus route, only that it didn't run towards my neighborhood, nor my parents'.

"Head for Century Street and I'll give you directions from there." Lily did a funny little seated dance in the passenger seat and clapped her hands.

"You're enjoying this, aren't you?" I asked. "You could just give me the name of wherever they went, but no, you want to hold that secret over me."

Lily pushed a straw through the lid of her soda and grinned. "Absolutely. It's like the gang is back together."

"The gang," I said, waving a hand between her and me, "never broke up."

"Yeah, but when did we last investigate anything together? It's been too long, buddy."

"It was two weeks ago," I reminded her.

"I rest my case."

Lily continued giving me directions while refusing to reveal any details, until we pulled up outside Harmony Retirement Village. Parallel to the long stone wall was a bus stop where two elderly gentlemen lingered, one resting on a rolling walker and the other shaking his cane as he spoke.

"I followed the old ladies here," she said. "They got off the bus and went inside." She pointed to the building.

"I didn't expect to see this place again. At least not quite so soon," I said. Only a couple of weeks ago, we'd just narrowly missed my nemesis, who was quizzing one of the residents for information. That we were here again seemed like a very weird coincidence but at least no elderly racers were trying to run us over with their mobility scooters this time.

"Did you happen to follow them inside?" I asked.

"Duh! Of course I did."

"And?" I asked, feeling exasperated.

"Sorry, I'm just enjoying this so much I have to milk it!" Lily reached for the bag, passing one package to me and opening the other on her lap. She pulled out a baguette and bit into it, making happy noises. Between chews, she added, "I followed them inside and they went through the lobby and into the big recreation room. They seem like popular ladies, because I heard people calling out 'Hello, Evelyn' and 'Hello, Judy' as they walked through. They didn't stop to chat to anyone, and the three went outside to the gardens and headed down the path towards the apartments. They all went inside and a minute later, the third came outside."

"What did she do?"

"She walked away from the rec room and went past

the trees. I can show you just as soon as I finish eating this. Unless time is of the essence?" Lily shot a glance at me, her mouth wrapped around the baguette and ready to bite, like she was daring me to disturb her moment.

"No, it's okay. You can finish eating." I stared at her, hoping she'd eat quickly.

"That won't work," said Lily without even glancing my way. "I'm a mom. If my toddler can't break me at meal times, neither can you."

"Okay, fine," I said as I pulled my sandwich from the bag and peeled back the paper wrapper, the delectable scent of freshly baked bread hitting me. I bit into it. Hot, oozy cheese and warm butter filled my mouth.

"How's the baby-making going?" asked Lily.

"It keeps getting interrupted by cases."

"Damn shame. I'll show you where Evelyn, Judy, and their friend went so you can wrap the case up quicker and get back to your funsies. My little girl needs a new cousin pronto." Lily crumpled up her paper sandwich bag and stuffed it into the takeout bag. I finished my sandwich and did the same, then took a long sip of my drink. The ice was already melting in the summer heat and I was sure it would have disappeared entirely by the time we returned to the hot car, leaving warm raspberry juice behind.

"Did you catch the third lady's name?" I asked as we jogged across the street.

"No, just the first two. I figured maybe the third lady was new and nobody had a chance to learn her name yet. Or maybe no one liked her? Evelyn and Judy sure seemed popular."

"Good morning, young ladies," said one of the

elderly gentlemen at the bus stop.

"Hello, handsome!" chirped Lily and the man's face lit up with delight.

"Hope you're moving in," he said, adjusting his tie and giving her a cheeky wink.

"In forty to fifty years," said Lily.

"I'll hang around!"

"You'll be dead," said his friend, leaning on a cane.

"I'll haunt the place," he said, and winked at us.

"I like it here already," said Lily, placing a hand over her heart.

"You're married," I pointed out as we carried on walking without an ache in the world.

"Yeah. And? I'm hardly going to run away with the guy. He uses a walker. Besides, Jord might be dead in forty to fifty years, and we all know women live longer than men. I'll need company."

"This guy will be dead too."

"His grandson might not be," said Lily. When I sighed, she added, "I'll check and see if he's got a brother for you. We can still be sisters-in-law."

"What if Solomon outlives me?" I wondered aloud.

Lily snorted. "Unlikely. We all know you'll be the death of him. He may maintain that cool as a cucumber façade but we all know deep inside, he's terrified of whatever you'll do next and how he'll have to rescue you."

"It's not like I do it deliberately," I said and Lily snorted again.

The driveway was curved, with one entrance and one exit. An ambulance drove up and parked at the door next to several unmanned mobility scooters. We stepped back to let a paramedic wheel out a lady clutching an oxygen mask. She tore it off to yell, "Tell

Glynis I know she pushed me over. She can have Bernie, the fickle, old coot!"

"What happened?" I asked.

"Love rivalry," said the paramedic. "Happens once or twice a month."

"Ouch," whined the lady. "I think my hip is broken. Tell the staff I'm going to need one of those mobility scooters and for Edward to give me a sponge bath every day for the next month."

"I'll relay part of that message," said the paramedic; then we were through the door, leaving them to deal with the calamity in the wheelchair.

"Who's Edward?" I wondered as we looked around the lobby. A long reception desk was more akin to a mid-priced hotel than a nursing home, and the staff wore spa-like wrapped tunics and pants in pastel shades.

"I think that's Edward," said Lily, gaping at the tall, dark-haired man with biceps bulging from under his pink tunic. "I can see why Glynis is ready to give up Bernie. Sponge baths from Edward sound like the perfect medicine."

"Concentrate," I said as we turned towards the noise coming from the rec room. "Your husband is still alive."

"Hi," said an orderly in pale green before we could take more than three steps. "Can I help you?"

"We're here to visit my... aunt," I said, a cluster of names ready to use in the ruse. "We've visited before."

"Wonderful! Is she expecting you?" The orderly beamed toothily. Her eyes were slightly unfocused and I darted a glance at the cart she pushed. It was full of little paper cups with pills of all different colors. I wondered if she'd sampled one or if she were perpetually dazed by the octogenarian fighting, flirting, and escaping.

"Uh… no. It's a surprise visit."

This time, her face creased in sweet appreciation. "That's so lovely. Our residents love surprises… ow!" She jumped as an old man jogged past her. "What have we said about pinching, Donald?" she called after him.

"Duck!" he shouted.

"No. We said *don't do it.*" She shook her head, and smiled again like a robot and I had to wonder again if she'd been freely imbibing in some resident's medication. "Donald is a live one! Please make sure to sign the visitor's book and then you're free to make your way to your aunt's apartment. Don't forget to stop by the café! It's staffed by our residents. Eduardo! Guests!"

"Guess we're signing in," I said, as Edward—or Eduardo—waved us over.

"I thought you were called Edward," said Lily as he pointed to the guestbook. The name tag on his tunic clearly said, "Eduardo."

"So half the residents seem to think. Either they're illiterate or it's benign racism," said Eduardo with a half-hearted shrug as he glanced up from the forms he filled.

"Is there such a thing?" I asked.

"I hope so. Otherwise I just work with a bunch of old racists," said Eduardo. "I don't recall seeing you before. Are you visiting a new resident?"

"No," I said, ready to claim Evelyn or Judy. Or even Bea, whom I'd visited before.

"Good. We like to encourage our residents to receive regular visitors so that their home here feels like, well, home. Who is it?"

"Who is who?" I asked, hesitating with the pen over the entry line. Did I write my name or someone else's? If only I had the benefit of hindsight to know if there would be any fallout later.

"Your relative?" prompted Eduardo.

"Oh, um. Evelyn," I said.

"Love her," said Eduardo. "Absolute peach. She's doing much better after her fall too. It's so nice of you to visit her. She doesn't get nearly enough visitors."

"How long has Evelyn been here now?" I asked.

"Seven years, I think."

"Feels like yesterday," I said, wishing I hadn't grasped at one of the only three residents' names I knew but it seemed prudent to go with that. Plus, now I could get some information from the staff. "Her friend, Judy is so nice to her," I prompted, hoping Eduardo would run with that.

"Thick as thieves," agreed Eduardo, nodding and smiling pleasantly.

"And the other lady? I forget her name?"

Eduardo frowned. "Other lady?"

"Maybe she's new. They all went out together yesterday. I think that's when Evelyn fell."

"Oh, I wasn't at work yesterday so I only heard about her fall this morning. I don't remember a third friend they regularly hang with but maybe someone tagged along on their trip. You know the way to Evelyn's apartment?"

"Of course," I said, more confident now. I pointed towards the rec room. "Through there."

"And along the path to the right," added Lily. "We should head there now. She'll be waiting."

"Enjoy your visit, ladies," said Eduardo, his attention already moving on to the next guest now queuing behind us.

"Should we get flowers or chocolates or something if we're going to pump them for information?" asked Lily.

"Not yet. We'll take a look around first, work out who's who, and see if we can identify the third woman and where she went."

"Then we'll interrogate them," said Lily determinedly.

"We'll ask a few questions," I said. "Lead the way."

Lily led me past the loud rec room, newly decorated with bright murals akin to a kindergarten and furnished with couches, coffee tables, and a number of game tables. A long table spanning one wall held tea and coffee urns, water jugs and there were a couple of cake stands, now largely littered by crumbs. Residents sat around playing cards and chess or shooting the breeze. I had to admit, it seemed nice. There was plenty of sunshine and a breeze and no one seemed to be forced into armchair yoga or left drooling alone. Most of the residents seemed spry and sociable.

Outside was a neatly manicured lawn surrounded on all sides by flower beds in full bloom. Picnic tables and umbrellas had been set out but since it was the height of the day, most of the residents seemed to be inside their apartments or the community building, availing themselves to the air conditioning. The building covered three sides, split into three blocks, then a treeline appeared with paths winding through it.

"That's the apartment they went into. I remember it because your parents' old neighbor, Bea lives in that one," said Lily softly, pointing to a closed door, before we strolled past an open door framed by large flower pots. I glanced over my shoulder, with bare seconds to ascertain two women sitting inside fanning themselves. "The third woman went this way," she said as we continued on to the treeline. The path forked quickly, one side heading into a small woodland, the other leading to a parking lot.

I hadn't been any further than the apartments before, so this was all new territory to me.

As we stood there, looking at the small array of vehicles, I asked, "Did you see the woman return?"

"No, I stood in the shade and waited but she didn't."

"So perhaps she got into a vehicle and left," I said, curious as I glanced back toward the apartments.

"What's the point of taking a bus all the way here from downtown, only to get into your car straightaway and leave?" asked Lily, echoing my own thoughts.

"Good question," I said, turning to make my way back when I spotted something odd hanging out the trashcan tucked off the path, almost obscured by the neatly clipped hedge. A strand of gray hair lay limply over the edge.

Fearing the worst, I hastily crossed the path, my heart rate quickening, and gingerly peered inside.

"What is it?" asked Lily, stepping forwards.

I reached in and pinched the hair with two fingers, lifting it. "A wig," I said.

CHAPTER EIGHT

The wig was beautifully made and far better quality than any I'd seen before. Admittedly, most of the wigs I'd handled were from Lily's collection in the days when she dressed up for her ever-evolving curious roster of jobs, but it gave me an indication of what the gray bob with feathery bangs might cost.

Even stranger was the rubbery residue around it. "What is that?" I asked, raising it to my nose to sniff before wishing that wasn't my first inclination.

"There's a nose in here," said Lily, peering into the trash can. She extended her arm, pulled a face, and leaned in.

I stilled, fearing the worst. "What?"

"Not a real one, silly. It's one of those putty, fake noses that actors wear," she said as she pulled out the pale lump with torn edges, examining it closely. "There's more of the putty and… is that a blouse?" Lily stared into the trash can.

I pulled disposable gloves from my purse and prepared to explore. Unfortunately, dumpster diving

was a sport I had some experience in—and didn't like
to relive—but at least the chances of my falling into
this trash can were non-existent... and that had to
mean our elderly target was unlikely to have suffered
such a fate. At least not in her entirety. Chopped up
was a different matter but Lily hadn't screamed when
she pulled out the fake nose so that was a good sign.

I plunged my gloved hands inside the can and
within a couple of minutes, a variety of clothing lay at
my feet. A floral blouse. A beige, sleeveless cardigan, a
pair of beige loafers that had seen better days, pale
green slacks and a cheap purse, completely empty. Not
even a tissue or a couple of bucks lay inside.

"Did she melt or something?" asked Lily, looking
around like there might be a puddle or trail of human
goo nearby.

"Or something," I said. "This was what one of the
women was wearing yesterday. I remember the floral
blouse from the video." Now that I thought about it,
the sleeveless cardigan had been too warm a garment
for such a hot day but it hadn't seemed out of place for
a very elderly lady.

"Definitely. I remember the blouse was cheery but
the rest of the outfit couldn't be more dull. Beige,
beige, beige. Her outfit was so bland, it was a crime
against fashion."

"That's exactly it. Hardly memorable but it gave full
coverage." I knelt and picked up the items, turning
them over. Inexpensive fabrics, well-used, the type of
garments and accessories you'd find in a thrift store.
The pants' pockets were just as empty as the purse.
"Lily, I think this was a costume."

"Why would anyone want to wear *that* as a
costume? There's way cuter stuff out there. Only last

week I bought a French..."

"Don't tell me," I said.

"But it came with lacy..."

"No."

"And a feather..."

"Lily!"

Lily rolled her eyes and shrugged. "Jord liked it."

"I'm happy for you both. I meant, this outfit was a disguise."

"Oooh," cooed Lily. "Undercover Granny!" She pulled out her phone. "I have to tell your mom."

"Don't tell my mom," I said, waving for her to put her phone away but instead, she snapped photos. I pulled out my phone and did the same, like it had been my idea all along. "If she even was a granny," I said, examining the fake nose now. It was remarkably good. Wide across the bridge with a thickened tip and hollowed out nostrils, yet the skin color and texture were astonishingly real. If I hadn't turned it over to see the inside, I would have thought a terrible dismemberment had happened here.

"There're more bits," said Lily, peering into the trash can again.

I joined her and reached in, pulling out what looked like strips of skin. Yet, even through my gloves, they had a slightly rubbery texture.

I turned back to the residents' communal areas, then to the trash can, and then the parking lot, thinking. When I gathered my thoughts, I said, "I doubt whoever wore this was a resident here. She just wanted everyone to think she was. She parked in this lot, wearing a disguise, and walked through the retirement community. Maybe she stuck around for a bit to see whom she could attach herself to, and got on the bus downtown with a couple of other residents, making everyone think she was an elderly resident too. If no one recognized her, well, she must have been unknown to the community. I'm not sure now she actually even knew the other ladies, no matter how friendly they seemed yesterday."

"They were walking with linked arms."

"Sure, but she could have made friendly with them here and then roped them into whatever she was doing as part of her disguise. All she had to do was go downtown with them, use them to cover what she was really doing, return on the bus with them, and say her goodbyes. She ditched her disguise in the trash, got into her car, and poof! Gone! Like she never existed, which she didn't," I added, holding up the fake nose in one hand and the wig in the other.

"I hate to say it, because I absolutely love it, but this is mostly conjecture," said Lily. "Maybe she wore a wig because she's losing her hair, and the nose could be because she has a facial deformity."

"Explain the clothes," I challenged.

"Okay, you got me. I can't. They're *sooo* beige. Even the flowers on the blouse are on a beige background. I can't imagine no one told her it's not a good look."

"It *is* conjecture, but I think it's a solid guess, given the evidence she dumped," I agreed as I peered into the trash can, hoping for something that could give me a valid clue as to the perp's real identity. Unfortunately, all I could see now were candy wrappers, empty chip bags and other useless detritus. Pulling a face, I reached further inside, gingerly moving trash out of the way in case there was something sharp, or a candy-stuffed chipmunk lurking at the bottom, waiting to spring out at me. Fortunately for me, there really was only trash.

Unfortunately, none of it was useful. No wallet, no ID cards, and no hope. "Do you have a bag I can put this stuff in?" I asked.

"Jord makes us carry reusable shopping bags," said Lily, producing a blue pouch from her purse. "He's on a recycling kick. We're saving the planet one plastic bag at a time." She unfolded the pouch into a large shopping bag and held it open while I scooped up the disguise and tossed it in. Then I peeled off my gloves and threw them in the trash.

"Let's go talk to Evelyn and Judy," I said. "Perhaps they can shed some light on the situation."

"Good cop, bad cop?" asked Lily. "Wanna toss for it?"

"How about we just ask them gentle, probing questions, and try not to scare them," I suggested.

"It would be easy to rough them up a little. Just one prod and those old ladies would go down like a pile of bricks."

"We're not roughing anyone up. We're gathering intel."

"You sound like a spy. Which you sort of are. A really cute spy. Where are your pants from? I like that shade of pink."

"Thanks! I got them at the mall last week. Do you think I look like a walking sausage?"

"Nope. But if you'd gone a shade lighter, I might think you were semi-naked. You made a good call on the darker pink. I can definitely tell you're dressed and no one will think you're gathering intel. Someone should tell the FBI to update their standard outfits to something jollier. Maybe they'd get more information out of people if they didn't freak them out on sight with those dull, official suits."

"The FBI don't freak me out on sight."

"Because you know what one of them looks like naked," pointed out Lily, and winked.

"Maddox is going to Germany on assignment. Why don't I get assignments like that?" I asked, contemplating it. "I'd like to go to Europe again."

"Have you asked Solomon? I don't think you'd even need to take a job. He'd take you just because you want to go there."

"In that case, I'd rather go to France. Or Italy."

Lily cut me a side look. "They're in Europe," she said.

"I know that! I meant I'd rather go to France or Italy than Germany. France and Italy are pretty dresses, berets, croissants, pasta, and courtyards with lots of sunshine."

"Germans have pastries, rivers, and a lot of beer."

I pondered that. "I like pastries."

"Aim high. Ask for all three. But if you go to Paris, I want to come too."

"I don't think Solomon would see it as a romantic getaway if you came too."

"That's what he thinks. We both know different. I would romance the heck out of a trip like that. I'll get you a padlock for that famous bridge in Paris that the couples attach their locks to as a declaration of their love, and I'll take the best pictures of you looking wistful on Italian balconies. I'll take you on picnics and tours of all the sites and I won't even complain when you want to spend a day shopping because that's what I'll want to do too!"

"That does sound nice," I admitted.

"Exactly. Who needs men when you have a bestie to nail the assignment with?"

"Feminist," I said, nodding.

"Practical," said Lily.

We stopped outside the apartment Lily had pointed out when we walked past only a few minutes ago. The door was still open and the ceiling fan was making a squeaking noise. One of the ladies sat on the couch while the other moved around the adjacent kitchen at the rear of the small apartment. Two internal doors were closed and I guessed they were probably the bedroom and bathroom. The apartment was cozy and cluttered, but well-appointed. It looked like a regular starter apartment except for the long panic rail that wrapped around the walls. I knocked and waved through the open door.

"I can hardly see who you are with the sun behind you," called the lady on the couch, shielding her eyes. She was the rounder, shorter of the trio and I recalled she'd been wearing light slacks and sleeveless blouse. Now she wore a batik midi skirt and a matching t-shirt, the bright colors very becoming on her. "Come in so I can get a better look at you. Ah, there you are. Who might you be?"

"I'm Lexi, and this is my friend, Lily," I said as we stepped in. "I hoped you could help me with something."

"Unlikely with my hip. You're too young to be in here. Are you looking for someone?" she asked, shifting to see us better. "Are you lost? It's easy to get around once you realize the numbering system makes no sense. Do the opposite of whatever seems natural and you've cracked it."

I laughed at that and nodded. "I'm looking for my grandma," I lied smoothly, almost surprised at how easily it slipped out. "One of the employees said she saw her with you yesterday when you came back from your shopping trip and we can't seem to find her."

"Your grandma, huh? Judy, have you seen any missing grandmas?" called couch lady, or Evelyn, as I now assumed.

"Nope, I just see a bunch of grandmas stuck in this joint," called back Judy, barely turning around. She was tall and lean with wild, curly, gray hair pushed back with a headband. She wore pale blue slacks and a shapeless floral blouse, not too dissimilar from the one we'd found tossed in the trash. Judy continued, "Although there was Sylvia, who went missing for three days in the spring but turned out she was just in bed with Roger and they both did something to their hips and got stuck. Do you remember the firetrucks coming out, Evelyn?"

"Epic," said Evelyn. She turned to us. "That's what my grandkids say. *Epic*. I think I got the context right."

"I think so too," I said, unsure whether I should ask more about Sylvia and Roger or just leave it to my horrified imagination.

"Three days, huh?" said Lily, nudging me out the way.

Evelyn shifted uncomfortably and Judy passed her a cold pack, which Evelyn pressed to her hip. "That's not how I got this," she said.

"Evelyn fell over like an old lady," said Judy, returning to the kitchen to collect a tray that she deposited with a jug of iced water, two glasses and a bowl of chips on the coffee table before flopping in the armchair and fanning herself. She leaned in to fill Evelyn's glass and pass it to her.

"I didn't fall. I was pushed!" said Evelyn indignantly.

"She fell," insisted Judy. "So Angela is your grandma? We didn't socialize with anyone else yesterday."

"Where're your manners, Judy? Get these young ladies some glasses. This heat is something else today," said Evelyn. She pinched the material at her cleavage and wafted it while she pressed the glass between her collarbones, then on her forehead.

Judy rolled her eyes at the order but got up and returned with two fresh glasses, passing them to us before pouring from the jug.

"Angela? Yes, that's right," I said. "She mentioned going shopping. Have you known her long?"

"No, we only got acquainted yesterday. I never saw her before then and I think she said she just moved in. I'm not even sure which apartment is hers. Do you know, Evelyn?"

"I figured she got Ruthie's. Ruthie died two weeks ago," Evelyn added for our benefit, then, "Terrible to die in the summer and not be found quickly. They spent a week fumigating the apartment; then they had to repaint and get rid of the bedroom furniture."

"No, there's a man in there," said Judy. "I saw him getting the welcome tour with his kids."

"How old?" asked Evelyn promptly. "Teeth? Hair?"

"He said he's eighty-nine but he looks eighty. Hollywood teeth and a smattering of hair, mostly in his ears."

"But single?" Evelyn persisted.

"Widowed," said Judy and the pair grinned like teenagers faced with their heartthrob.

I needed to get them back on topic before they decided to go in search of the new man. "So you only met Angela yesterday?" I prompted.

"That's right. We got to chatting and she seemed like a fun gal. She should liven up the place a bit. We were sitting out in the garden, enjoying the sun and thinking about how to pass the time when Angela strolled up and introduced herself. First thing she did was suggest we break out and head downtown. She said it would be fun!" Evelyn winced and pressed the pack on her hip. "Plus, the bus has air conditioning so that convinced us."

"She saw the necklace I was wearing and said I had great taste and she needed help buying a gift for her granddaughter. Guess that's you," said Judy.

"Uh, yeah," I said. "It's my birthday soon."

"So we probably shouldn't tell you anymore," said Judy. She mimed zipping her lips and throwing away the key.

"We're actually worried Granny usually spends too much," said Lily, jumping in. "She's a little reckless with her money. We don't want her to spend a fortune on a birthday gift."

Evelyn and Judy exchanged glances.

"Oh, no," I said, putting my hand to my mouth. "Did she go to a jewelry store? I told her not to be so extravagant! We want her to spend her money on herself, especially after that credit card incident." I flashed a look at Lily and she nodded, her face full of concern.

"Terrible impulse control," added Lily.

"Maybe we should tell them?" said Judy to Evelyn. "She didn't buy anything anyway."

"I suppose it won't matter if we do since that's true and we're not spoiling any surprise. Angela really was insistent we went to Reynolds'. That's a nice jewelry store downtown. She said we should try some things on, really have some fun for the day, do things that we wouldn't normally do. I suppose I'm a creature of habit. Anyway, we wanted to go to a dress shop but Angela insisted she needed to buy a present. She was quite forceful about it and we had plenty of time so we went to both stores and more," said Evelyn.

"We figured why not?" said Judy. "Your grandma seems like a fun sort and we need more of that type around here. Some of the new residents just seem to give up and we like to live a little. Plus, who doesn't like a little shopping trip? There wasn't anything we liked in terms of clothing but Angela said we should try on a few rings and other things while she tried to pick something; then, in the middle of all of that, Evelyn fell."

"I didn't fall!" huffed Evelyn. She pulled a face as she shifted, adjusting the cold pack on her hip, clearly uncomfortable.

"Then how were you upright one moment and on the floor the next?" asked Judy.

"I told you already, Angela pu—" Evelyn trailed off, looking first at me, then the floor, clearly uncomfortable with the accusation she'd been ready to divulge.

"Did Angela, uh, Granny, push you?" I asked, confused. I hadn't seen that in the video tape. "I'm so sorry! She can be very clumsy."

Evelyn shook her head. "Not pushed exactly. My leg collapsed from under me and I toppled over. I think she hooked her foot around my ankle and gave it a yank!"

"That's a mean thing to do!" said Lily looking stern as she shook her head. "Shame on Granny!"

"We'll have words with her," I said. "She needs to be more careful!"

"Well, I didn't much want to go shopping anymore after that, what with my hip hurting and all, and Judy wanted an iced coffee but the coffee cart didn't have any. Then I was feeling so sore that we all rode the bus home. Judy and Angela helped me to my apartment and Angela said she had to go check on something and I haven't seen her since," finished Evelyn. "I hope you find her. She did liven up the day and she seems like a fun gal but not if she's going to go around and do things like that. I'm tempted to have words with her!"

"You've no idea where she might be?"

"None," said Judy. "I tried asking her about moving in but now that I think about it, she didn't really say much. She was just so keen to get to the shops and buy a gift. Your birthday must be soon."

"It is," I said. "Do you recall anything else she might have said?"

"Just a few things about downsizing and liking the area and seeking a like-minded community," said Evelyn.

"Did she say she was planning on meeting anyone? Or going anywhere soon?"

"Not that she mentioned. Judy?"

Judy shook her head. "She's a spry thing so I figure she likes keeping active. I told her we have badminton, croquet, and an aerobics class on Mondays and Thursdays and there's a bus that takes us to the public swimming pool. Such a young voice too. If I hadn't seen her with my own eyes, I'd think she was decades younger. She sounded like you girls."

"Your eyes are terrible and you should wear your spectacles all the time," said Evelyn. "She's right though. Your granny does have a youthful streak."

Since it didn't seem like either women knew anything pertinent, I thanked them, and then thanked them some more for their birthday wishes, and told them we'd look out for them next time we were visiting.

Back in the main building, we headed for the reception desk. Eduardo had been replaced by a young woman examining her nails. "We're looking for Angela," I said, "Can you direct us to her apartment?"

"Angela? I don't think we have an Angela," she said, glancing up at us with little interest.

"I think she's new," I said.

"You're not relatives?"

Continuing the grandma ruse might result in questions I couldn't answer. "Neighbors checking in on her," I said swiftly just as Lily said, "We're physiotherapists."

The young woman narrowed her eyes. "Which is it?"

"Physiotherapist neighbors," I said.

"Pro bono," added Lily.

"Is that a thing?" asked the young woman, frowning. She tapped on her keyboard and waited, then she shook her head. "We don't have any residents called Angela."

"Are you sure?"

"Are *you* sure?" Lily repeated, raising an eyebrow, her face mildly threatening as she leaned in.

I took a deep breath. "She might have moved in only yesterday," I said. "Perhaps she isn't in the system yet."

"The paperwork would be done before then. No, we don't have any Angela listed and we haven't had any new residents this week. Are you sure she moved here?" she asked,

I shook my head. "Must be our mistake," I told her and thanked her for her time.

"That's disappointing," said Lily as we crossed the road back to my car. "I thought we'd glean more information but now we don't even know what this Angela looks like. I really thought I did a good thing trailing them here."

"You did," I assured her, "your instincts were correct that something was suspicious, and without you we wouldn't have this." I held up the bag with the prosthetics and clothing.

"Fat lot of good that'll do. You can't even wear those clothes. Next time we follow someone, let's make sure she's wearing designer labels in *our* size." Lily glanced back at the retirement home as we walked down the driveway. "Should we stake out the place in case Angela comes back?"

"I don't think Angela *is* coming back," I said. We walked across the road and climbed into the car. I immediately regretted it with the stifling heat, rolled down the windows and stepped out, leaving the door open in the hope of cooling the car's interior.

"Not that we'd recognize her if she did," sighed Lily, speaking across the car roof. "What kind of person dresses up like a senior, sneaks into a senior community home, and encourages old ladies to go on a robbery expedition with her? Apart from an absolute badass! You have to find her, Lexi. She sounds awesome. I want to be her friend." Lily clapped her hands gleefully.

"She's a criminal!"

"And? Evelyn and Judy are right. Fake Angela

definitely livens up the place."

"Because she made them accomplices to her crime!"

"I wonder what she'll do next." Lily took on a faraway look, clearly dreaming about grand larceny.

"Go to prison," I said.

"Really? That's disappointing."

"Maybe," I conceded. "All I have to do first is find her."

"At least we know she's called Angela," said Lily.

I looked at her and shook my head. "I think the name is as fake as everything else about her."

"What are the odds?" said Lily and sighed.

CHAPTER NINE

The discoveries we'd made about "Angela" were so suspicious, I was ready to write off all the other potential suspects. Yet I felt I couldn't return to the office without doing a little more due diligence in my investigating, especially since my dad had texted me the names of the other two men who'd perused the vintage jewelry tray. It was partly wanting to make sure we were on the right track and partly due to knowing how long it took my dad to type a text message.

"Want to check out some other suspects?" I asked Lily. We'd just gotten back in the car and although it wasn't much cooler, I could now touch the steering wheel without feeling like steam might billow from my palms.

"Sure. I love a criminal shakedown."

"It's only to absolutely rule them out," I said. "Although there's a small chance these guys could have cased the place in advance. Both men on my list went into Reynolds' in the morning and our missing woman Angela was there mid-afternoon."

"She's bold. Imagine committing a crime like that mid-afternoon! I'd wait until the dead of night," said

Lily.

"Then you would have to contend with breaking in from the outside, bypassing the security alarms, and making a clean getaway before the police rolled up."

"Yeah, I suppose being handed the goods is easier."

"And with her disguise, no one even caught her on camera." We were driving back downtown and I was thinking hard about the costume. The wig and prosthetics were both high-end, not the sort of thing she could pick up from a costume shop. The clothes could have been easily scraped up for cash from anywhere in the country. "We've got one top suspect with no face and no name."

"Maybe it was one of the guys from that morning?"

"They were a few inches taller, and Evelyn and Judy didn't have any suspicion Angela wasn't a woman. I think she was, just heavily disguised and probably not as old as she appeared," I decided, remembering the description of Angela's youthful voice and spry movements.

"Perhaps they were stooping?"

"We'd see that on camera."

"*I* haven't seen the camera footage," Lily reminded me.

"Okay, well, the men were both taller and broader."

"Could they have shorter, less broad, wives or girlfriends?"

"That's a possibility," I said, thinking. If they were in cahoots with a partner, that would make sense. Now, thanks to Lily, I didn't feel like I was sucking up crucial time with a wild goose chase.

"The dad is in West Montgomery so we'll go there first, then to the deli guy since he's downtown."

"Now do we get to good cop, bad cop someone?" Lily asked, her voice so full of hope I hated to disappoint her.

"No. We'll just tell them there was a theft and we're asking anyone who might have witnessed it what they saw."

"Won't that tip them off if they were behind it?"

"Yes, but it won't make them think we suspect them."

"You're so good at this! You're a great PI!"

I beamed. "Thanks for the hype!"

The dad shopper's real name was Miles Wilson and he lived only a few streets from my parents' house. As we walked towards the front door, I saw him in the living room, typing on a laptop on a desk facing the front yard. He glanced up as we approached, adjusted his black-framed glasses, and then got up, walking towards the door.

"Hello?" he said, opening the door a fraction.

"Hi, Miles Wilson?"

"That's me."

I produced my license and passed it to him. "I'm Lexi Graves, a private investigator. I'm looking into a theft that occurred yesterday at Reynolds' Fine Jewelry downtown."

"Gosh. I was there yesterday." He stroked his clean-shaven jaw, frowning. "I can't say I saw anything suspicious though. I think I was the only one in the shop at the time."

"Can you tell us what you did while you were there?"

"Sure. My daughter's birthday is coming up and I bought a locket from there last year for her eighteenth. I thought I'd get her earrings this year so I looked at a few pieces but I didn't see anything I liked."

"Did you take a look at the vintage section?"

"Yes. I think the locket I bought was vintage, but, like I said, there weren't any earrings I liked."

"Did you notice anyone near the store?"

"Can't say I did. I was in and out pretty quickly as I had a meeting downtown, then I wanted to get home to take client calls. I'm in tech support."

I gave him my card and asked him to call me if he thought of anything else. He said he would and closed the door, leaving us to walk away.

"He doesn't look like I imagine a jewel thief would look like. He's kinda nerdy," said Lily. "You know what a jewel thief does look like?"

"If you say Ben Rafferty, I'll scream," I said, thinking of the handsome rogue who'd become my nemesis.

"Tempting but I won't say it even though that's exactly who I meant."

We got back in the car and I gave one last glance to the house. Miles Wilson was head down, busy at his desk.

"Could *You Know Who* be back?" Lily asked.

I shuddered. "I don't think he'll come anywhere near Montgomery in the foreseeable future. His face is too well known. Let's head to the deli and see if that guy can replace Angela on the top of the suspect list."

The Little Italy deli had a small parking lot at the back of the building and Dad had added a note saying we should look for him here and not at his home. We parked and went inside. Lily immediately grabbed a wooden basket. "Have you seen the cheese counter?" she asked when she saw me looking.

"Yes, but we're not here to buy cheese." The scent

of it hit me and I breathed in, contemplating the meaning of life.

"Then what is the purpose of life?"

"Fair point." The deli wasn't somewhere I shopped regularly, given that its goods were priced twice as high as the nearest big supermarkets, and although it seemed to have a lot of things that I knew were ingredients, I had no idea how to use them. How did one chop *pak choi?* What did a person do with a dragon fruit? And just what, exactly, was the point of sugar-free, gluten-free, and dairy-free cake?

"Do you see him?" asked Lily as we paused by a rustic-edged, oak table piled high with boxes stuffed with every flavor of cookie I could think of.

I'd been looking for the man from the security video as soon as we stepped inside. There were employees dressed in Little Italy t-shirts and striped, linen aprons stationed at the deli counter, the cheese counter, and the wine section, but none of them were my guy. Then I saw him, coming through a set of slatted saloon doors, carrying a crate of produce. He said something to the cheese counter girl as he passed and she laughed; then he walked over to the open fresh produce refrigerators, setting the crate on the floor and began to restock the wooden crates.

"There he is," I said, nodding in his direction.

"Let's box him in. I'll advance from the rear by the apples. You round the table and approach him from the other side. He won't be able to get away."

I let out a long sigh, then thought better of arguing. "Fine, but we don't need to stop him from getting away. We're only asking a few, simple questions." But it was pointless; Lily was already gone. By the time I reached the produce, Lily had sidled up next to him and was intently examining the apples.

"Noah Levin?" I asked.

He looked up and gave me a half smile, polite but disinterested. "That's me," he said. "Can I help you with anything?"

"I'm investigating a theft down the street yesterday and I'm looking for potential witnesses," I said, producing my license and introducing myself. "I hoped you could help."

"Oh, no. Which shop?" he asked as a tall, red-headed woman in a striped staff apron strolled past with a stack of cakes in waxy paper. He followed her movements, his attention entirely on her as she paused by a table a few yards away to unstack her cake portions.

"Reynolds' Fine Jewel—"

"Let's talk outside," he said, his attention snapping back as he swiftly cut me off. He dropped the leeks he held into the display crate and motioned to the front doors.

"Okay," I said, frowning, and followed him, Lily on our heels. We passed through the automatic doors and the alarm started to beep.

"Whoops. That's me," said Lily, stepping back inside.

"She's with me," I explained.

"The baskets have a security tag on the base, otherwise, people can walk out with them," explained Noah. "That's what you get for going chic instead of using the standard metal baskets but we wouldn't be us if we didn't do that little bit extra. You said there was a theft at Reynolds'? When?"

"Yesterday, possibly in the afternoon. We're asking anyone who was in there yesterday if they saw anything."

"I went there in the morning so I can't see how that's any help to you, sorry. If it does matter though, it was Jonathan who assisted me. I think he's the manager or the assistant manager."

"Did you see anyone suspicious lurking around?"

"Inside? No. There was only me and Jonathan. I think his assistant might have walked in but I don't think we spoke. I'm afraid I didn't really notice anyone outside. I was in a hurry to get back to the deli. I might be the owner but I don't want my staff to think I'm taking liberties. We're an everyone-pitch-in kind of place."

"Was there a reason you wanted to talk outside?" I asked, curious about the flash of panic I'd seen crossing his face as soon as I mentioned the shop.

"My girlfriend works here part-time and I didn't want her to know I've been… I'm assuming Jonathan told you I was looking at engagement rings? I want it to be a surprise." Noah scratched his head, his eyes darting nervously.

"The red-haired woman who walked past us?" I guessed.

His face lit up. "Yes, that's Livvy."

"Do you remember what you looked at?" I asked.

"Uh… lots of different rings but I wasn't sold on any of them. Some new stuff, the vintage tray because I thought maybe that would suit Livvy better, and then I wasn't sure. Anyway, Jonathan locked everything in the case when I finished looking at them. There was a lot of choices and I guess I got a little bamboozled by all the options. I figured I'd go back later in the week and try again. I don't suppose that's any help to you though?"

"It's plenty," I said, "Thanks for your time."

"Anytime. Hey, what was stolen anyway?"

"Some jewelry."

He cracked a smile now. "I figured that. I guess we should all be on the lookout for thefts. I can let you know if I hear anything, although I think it's unlikely a jewelry thief would be bragging about it in the deli."

I gave him my card and he walked past Lily into the store. "I'll be right back," said Lily who was waiting near the doors with her basket. She darted into the shop and a few minutes later, returned to where I waited by the AC vent, carrying her items in a cotton tote bag bearing the deli's name and an artist's drawing of the shop.

"It's reusable and it only cost fifteen dollars. Saving the ocean, however, is priceless," she said when I raised an eyebrow at the bag. "Plus, I got cake. What now?"

"To the car," I said, pointing to the rear doors.

"Prolonged AC, hurray!" said Lily as we headed through the shop to the rear doors. Just as we reached the car, I heard a woman's voice calling, "Excuse me? Hey? Hello?"

I stopped, turning around, and found myself facing the tall, red-haired woman Noah Levin planned to propose to. "Did I hear you say you're from Reynolds' Fine Jewelry?" she asked.

"Not quite. We're investigating a robbery on their behalf. We're canvassing the local area. If you saw anything happen there yesterday, we'd appreciate you telling us," I said.

Instead, her shoulders slumped. "No, sorry, I didn't. I was working in the deli, covering for one of the other workers who had to pick her little girl up from school. All kind of last minute but I did see Noah

121

coming out of there when I drove past."

"We spoke to him already."

"I know. I saw. I just..." Livvy stopped and laughed. "Sorry, it's silly. I just had a hunch that he'd gone there to buy me a ring."

"Oh?" I tried to keep my face impassive.

She laughed. "I feel silly now. I was going to tell you that if you were from there and you wanted to talk to him about rings, I would love it if you dropped the hint that I inherited my grandmother's diamond ring. My grandfather bought it for her engagement ring and that's what I want more than anything for *my* engagement ring. It just needs resetting. I know he's been hinting. He's not exactly subtle."

"I couldn't say what he was doing in there," I said, "but if it comes up in conversation with my clients, for some reason, I suppose I could mention it." I tried, and failed, to hold back a smile.

Amusement crossed her face, like she wasn't quite sure if I were confirming her suspicions or simply being helpful. "I'm sorry I wasted your time. I think I was just overeager. He might not be planning that at all." She started to stop back, uncertain and apologetic.

"No problem," I said. "I'll keep my fingers crossed for you."

"That's sweet of you," she said, darting a glance toward the store. "I'd better get back inside."

"Aww," said Lily. "She's going to be thrilled when he does propose. Can we cross him off the list?"

"Yeah," I said, "And her too. She's too tall to be the woman in disguise. They're definitely not our thieves." I tapped out a message to my dad, asking him to relay Livvy's request to Jonathan Mazzina, so he could be ready next time Noah went to Reynolds'. As

I hit *send*, my phone buzzed with a text. "Let's go to the agency," I said after reading it.

Lily and I walked into the agency office twenty minutes later. Delgado was seated at his desk on a call, which he wrapped up quickly.

"Note how I never bring any family members to the office," he said, looking from me to Lily as he swiveled in his chair and leaned back, relaxing for a moment.

"I'm here and I'm your sister-in-law too so technically, you have," said Lily and stuck out her tongue.

"*I* didn't bring you," said Delgado.

"I'm still your family member. Lexi is merely the method of delivery."

"Please never bring my sister," I said, contemplating what I would do to keep my workplace a Serena-free zone. I wasn't sure I had limits to safeguard that boundary.

"No problem," said Delgado. "I like to keep my personal life and career entirely separate."

"Explains why you married into my family," I said.

"And became in-laws with your boss," added Lily.

"Forget I said anything," said Delgado with a small eye roll. "Make yourself at home."

Before we could do anything of the sort, the door opened and Solomon strode in, heading for the boardroom, beckoning us to follow. I hurried after him, Lily on my heels and Delgado joined us with a, "What's up, boss?"

"Our case is getting complicated. We'll need to head back out there soon," said Solomon to Delgado. "How did it go with you two? Did your dad get you what you need?"

Lily practically squeaked with excitement, "We found the thief!"

"You did? Well done! Why didn't you call it in?" The last part was addressed to me.

"We didn't find her exactly," I said as I tipped the contents of Lily's reusable shopping bag on the table. The rubber prosthetics, wig, clothing and shoes tumbled out in a heap. "We found what was left of her."

"She's dead?" Solomon frowned as he reached for the blouse.

"No! She was in disguise. We found all this stuffed inside a trash can at the retirement village where Lily tracked the old ladies to," I said, before explaining our conversation with Evelyn and Judy.

"Weird," said Delgado, reaching for the prosthetics. "That's a lot of trouble to go to in order to steal a ring. I don't think I've seen anything like it. This is remarkably like skin." He passed the nose to Solomon who turned it over in his hands.

"This is definitely professional quality," he said.

"That's what we thought," I agreed. "Our thief clearly had an airtight plan, including dropping Evelyn to the floor as a distraction. I'm positive now that's when she swiped the ring and they left within minutes while it was still chaotic. I think Jonathan was distracted by everything as he put the case away. Meanwhile, 'Angela' was in the wind within an hour of leaving the jewelry store. I think she had a car stashed at the retirement home, ready for when she ditched her disguise."

"This kicks the case up a notch," said Solomon as Delgado passed him the strips of skin. "We're dealing with a professional who has access to the kind of resources that would buy them an expensive disguise like this. Not just financial resources, but someone with the knowhow to make or commission prosthetics and a thief who can convincingly act the part."

"Everything except the voice," I said, thinking. "The ladies said their fake friend sounded decades younger."

"They said she was spry too so maybe she wasn't all that good an actress," added Lily. "She should have gotten a cane to appear like she was slower."

"I wish we had more to tell you other than we're looking for a much younger woman. If it weren't for Lily being able to identify where they went, we wouldn't even have that."

"That's right!" said Lily, beaming and standing a little straighter. "You're welcome!"

My dad walked through the door a moment later, a lanyard swinging around his neck identifying him as a contractor for the agency. "This seems to be a family affair," he said, smiling, the sparkle in his eye telling me he was trying his best not to show how absolutely thrilled he was to be here, and part of the investigation.

"Hi, Dad," I said, as he tucked an arm around me and pulled me in for a side hug.

"Steve is going undercover," said Solomon, without preamble.

"Where?" I asked.

"At Reynolds' Fine Jewelers. This new development clinches it. He's going to be a shop clerk for the next week in case our thief returns for another attempt. This single theft could be the precursor for something much bigger."

I was momentarily stunned, having assumed it would be me to go undercover but it made sense. Dad would be able to observe the comings and goings of the shop, leaving me free to follow the leads as we'd done today. It was a perfect allocation of the resources available.

"Steve has also been able to give us some background information on comparable robberies over the last decade although there's been nothing similar reported. Steve?" Solomon nodded to my dad.

"That's right. I checked in with my contacts still on the force…"

"Jord?" asked Lily.

"Garrett?" I asked.

"No and no."

"Uncle…" I started.

"Tara?" asked Lily.

"I do know more people beyond our family," said Dad. "Okay, I might have mentioned it to them. Yes, all right, *all of them*, but I asked around too."

"Please continue," said Solomon, waving him on.

"Thanks. So, I spoke to my contacts and there have been seven reported burglaries or attempted burglaries at jewelers in town. Three unsuccessful attempts at a chain store, different crew each time, each of them caught and convicted. Two more robberies at pawnbrokers, and the attempted thieves were the sellers who thought they'd just help themselves to the goods. The other two were a smash-and-grab, and a distraction attempt. The last one caught my eye."

"Go on," prompted Solomon.

"Obviously, it's long odds that our distraction thief was also this distraction thief but it's the only similar crime," said Dad, as he pulled out a notepad and flipped the cover. "I noted it happened more than a decade ago. One of my retired buddies caught the case and said the thief made off with ten thousand dollars' worth of earrings and rings. Not exactly big fry for a jewel thief but the thief was also a woman. She came in like she was some kind of big shot, asking to see this and that and the vendor got all muddled with the display cases and didn't realize the items were missing for more than an hour. By then, she was long gone."

"Could she be the same woman?" I asked.

"It's possible. Maybe this is how she started out. Small thefts, perfecting her craft, then she moved up to the big stuff."

I thought about it. "What's the likelihood of this woman committing that theft, sticking around town and not targeting a single other jeweler until more than ten years later?"

"Seems low," said Dad. "Most thieves I caught didn't just stop cold turkey. Of course, that's not to say that thief didn't steal other stuff or commit other crimes. I have a note here that says the jeweler filed an insurance claim and beefed up their security. They went out of business a few years ago when the owner passed away but there was some question that not all of their goods were on the up and up."

"What do you mean?" I asked.

"Like, they weren't too scrupulous about whom they bought their merchandise from," said Dad. "I can ask around more."

"Did anyone mention the woman wearing a disguise?" I asked.

"Nope, unless you count the smart outfit. Just that she was young and pretty."

"It's too tenuous a link," I decided. "But I can put a call in to Maddox and see if he knows anything about similar crimes state-wide or in neighboring states,

127

anything that might have got on the federal radar."

"Do it now," agreed Solomon.

I stepped outside to leave them to talk and placed the call. Maddox answered quickly with a cheerful, "Hello to my favorite nuisance. To what do I owe this pleasure?"

"Hello to you too. I've got a case that I wanted to run past you."

"Fire away. I've got time."

"Have you come across any cases of jewelry thefts, possibly involving a distraction, and maybe even a disguise?"

"Like your dead body cold case?"

"Similar but more alive, more recent, and more local," I said.

"A disguise? Can you narrow it down?"

"A woman using high-end prosthetics to change her face and a very good quality wig."

"There was a distraction theft at a jewelers' in town years ago. That was a woman. I didn't work on the case but I remember it. She scored a few thousand dollars' worth of jewelry."

"Dad mentioned the case. He said the shop closed down a few years ago and there were rumors about their purchasing scruples. I got the impression the thief wasn't caught."

"No, she was. I remember it because I was good buddies with a detective from the burglary squad and he was all abuzz about it, although it wasn't his case. She hit up a couple of places in Boston and she was caught. If I remember correctly, she got fifteen years."

"So, she's still inside?"

"I would think so. How high-end are these prosthetics you're talking about?"

"Good enough to make a younger woman appear like a senior citizen. Face, nose, gray wig."

There was a long pause and then Maddox said, "And this woman committed a jewel theft in town? You're sure?"

"Given the disguise, yes."

"Huh."

"Huh, what?"

"What did she steal?"

"A vintage ring worth a small fortune."

"Hmm."

"What occurred to you?" I asked, sensing Maddox clamming up.

"Nothing. Thanks for calling. Catch you later!" And with that, Maddox was gone.

I stared at the phone, puzzled by his weird behavior, then I reminded myself I should be used to it by now.

CHAPTER TEN

"What did I miss?" I asked as I stepped through the doorway.

"Not much," said Lily. "You'd think investigating a jewel robbery would be more dynamic and glamorous than being stuck in a sweaty boardroom with all my in-laws."

"This isn't the movies," replied Solomon.

"Don't I know it," said Lily. "If it were, I'd be a foot taller, ten pounds skinnier, and my character would be married to a guy forty years older than me, and no one would bat an eyelid."

"The robbery was dynamic," I said, wondering about the voraciousness of Lily's segues. "And so far, she's outsmarting everyone."

"I kinda like her," said Lily, "She's ballsy. Hey, what's the feminine equivalent for ballsy? Ovary-y?"

"Does it matter?" asked Dad.

"I want to raise my daughter as a feminist. We can't always use masculine words."

"Can you do it later?" asked Dad. "We need to

catch the bad guys first."

"What's the female equivalent for 'guys'?" asked Lily.

"'Guys' is unisex," said Dad.

"Yeah? How many guys have you kissed?" asked Lily, raising her eyebrows while I stifled a laugh. "You want new vocabulary now, huh?"

Solomon clapped his hands. "Back to work," he said, barely able to conceal his exasperation. I had to wonder if he regretted hiring my dad, allowing Lily into the investigation, or marrying me? Probably all of the above but he was definitely stuck with one of us. Hopefully, me, but it really depended on how well my dad performed in his undercover role.

"Lexi?"

"Hmm?" I blinked, realizing Solomon had said something.

"What are your next steps?"

"I'm sure the deli guy and the dad aren't our perp. I want to concentrate on the mystery woman, Angela. I need to find out if there are any security cameras near the retirement home that might have picked up our thief's vehicle," I started.

"Get Lucas on it," said Solomon.

"Will do. While we figure out who our thief is and where she went, I think we should also approach this case from the other side. I want to double check on the ring's provenance to be sure it's on the up-and-up," I said.

"Is there any possibility the Reynoldses lied?" asked Dad.

I shook my head slowly, contemplating the question I'd already asked myself. "I don't think so. Laura and Alan both appeared sincere but that doesn't mean they weren't lied *to*. I'd like to take a look at the list of hotel guests Lucas is generating, which could possibly include our caller from Germany. Maybe there's something we can cross-reference."

"Good call."

"I think we should talk to the Reynoldses about the next steps too. If they want to file a claim with their insurance, the police need to be called in. If they're not planning to claim it, why not? The ring is worth a small fortune. It looks like the business is doing well but I doubt they can just write that kind of loss off."

"That's a good point," said Dad. "And, why employ private investigators at all? I can poke around, ask a few subtle questions."

"Good idea. They did make a point about wanting to keep the theft quiet so it didn't attract more thieves to the shop," I said, thinking. "I didn't get the impression there was any subterfuge going on and none from Jonathan either. We still have the assistant and cleaner to interview. My gut says it's not an inside job but perhaps they'll have a different take."

"We should interview them before the day is out," said Dad. "I took a look at their files so I know we have their addresses already. I'm not sure if they're aware of the theft but if not, it would be good to catch them both off guard before we decide to rule them out."

"That makes sense," I agreed. "We can go together now."

"It sounds like we have a plan," said Solomon. "You both check out the last of the employees today. Then, Steve, you go undercover starting tomorrow and keep us posted. Lexi, you're in charge of tracking down the thief. Make sure you check in with Lucas on following up the Germany lead. It's tenuous, but I don't think we should ignore it."

Solomon and Delgado's phones both buzzed. They checked the screens and did some sort of imperceptible silent bro-mmunication. "We have to go," said Solomon, then to me, he added, "I might not be home until late but call if you find anything serious."

"What about me?" asked Lily.

"Thanks for your assistance," said Solomon. "We couldn't have gotten this far without you."

Lily beamed at the praise. "You're welcome," she said. "Guess I'll go then. Bye!" She gave a cheery wave, turned on her heel, and headed out, but not before my suspicions were piqued. First, because Maddox was way too cheerful on the phone, and now, Lily didn't even attempt to muscle in on the action? I hurried after her, catching her at the door to the office before she could make her incredulously fast exit.

"What gives?" I asked.

"Don't know what you mean!" She grabbed the door handle. "Bye!"

"You're giving up too easy. Why?" I narrowed my eyes.

Lily shrugged and her face made a too exaggerated show of not understanding. "You all seem to have it under control. Your dad's going undercover, you've got all the leads, and I've done my bit. So… bye!" She slipped through the door before I could stop her, leaving me to grab it before it closed, and hurry after her.

"Hold on," I said as Lily pressed the down button for the elevator. "What are you really up to?"

Lily sighed. "Fine. I thought I might head back to the retirement village and see if there's anything we missed. There has to be a reason the thief picked that place above all others. It can't be because the bus route is good."

I thought about it for a moment. It was strange that only a couple weeks ago, one thief had been there and now another. What was so appealing about Harmony Retirement Village? "It *could* be because the bus route is good. It goes directly from the retirement home to Reynolds' street," I said. I thought about it for a moment. Could it really be that simple? Were ease and location the real reasons the thief had picked that facility to start her plan? To put her plan in motion so quickly after the Reynoldses acquired the ring and listed it for sale, she had to already be in possession of her elderly-appearing prosthetics. More and more, this looked like a well-targeted theft from a criminal who had a lot of experience in pulling off something so tricky.

However, maybe Lily was also right? What if there were another reason that we hadn't thought of yet?

"That's a good idea," I decided. "Maybe she knows one of the residents or she's been there before and knew it would be a safe bet for her plan. Perhaps she's worked there, although it seems like an odd career choice for someone with a sideline in grand larceny."

"But you never know," said Lily. "Of all the disguises she could have picked, why that one? Why pick Evelyn and Judy? I figured I can snoop around a little more and see if anything turns up."

"Okay," I agreed. I felt like stamping my foot. I should have thought of that! I should have insisted on following the lead too but my dad was waiting inside the PI's office. It felt like I was being pulled in two directions. "But be careful. Call me and Dad and I'll come straightaway, and if anything feels off, leave."

"They'll never know I was there," said Lily, clearly excited about staying on the team even if she hadn't planned on telling anyone she was still on it. What harm could it do? It felt unlikely the thief would return to the retirement home but Lily might still pick up a clue just by hanging around.

"You could have said that's what you wanted to do," I said, a brief moment of worry that Lily had attempted to hide her plans, just like she did yesterday. "Your instincts are what gave us this break."

"I know. I'm awesome." Lily bounced into the elevator car, saluted me, grinned, and disappeared behind the closing doors.

As I headed back to the office, I placed a call to Lucas asking him to find any cameras on the day of the theft and the time window in which I wanted him to pinpoint any vehicles leaving Harmony. I hadn't noticed any obvious security at the building but that didn't mean they didn't have any. We'd driven past a lot of residential housing on our way there but I hoped there might be businesses at the other end of the street that had security cameras facing the road. The bus networks wouldn't be much use since the thief was already equipped with her disguise for both journeys. I decided hacking into those would be a waste of Lucas's technical skills.

"Did you get anything for the call from the German hotel?" I asked after I'd laid down my parameters.

"Not yet but I'm working on it," said Lucas.

"Sorry to add more to your list."

"Not a problem. It's what I'm here for. I'll call you when I have something."

Solomon and Delgado had their heads together, discussing plans in the boardroom but my dad was ready and waiting for me by the time I reached him. I grabbed my purse and we went out to my car.

"The file said the assistant, Tansy, doesn't work today so I hope we'll catch her at home," I told him.

"The Reynoldses mentioned she's part time although she often works extra hours when they need it. Laura mentioned Tansy is a single mom," said Dad. "School's probably letting out around now."

The address the Reynoldses had given us was not far from my old high school. I drove there, filling Dad in on the conversations with Noah Levin and Miles Wilson while Dad ran through the notes he'd made from watching the camera footage one more time, culminating in our agreement that, in his opinion, the old ladies were definitely the most interesting suspects.

Tansy McDonald's home was a small duplex, perfectly twinning its neighbor with matching doors, paint colors, and even identical window boxes with the same pretty pink and purple flowers. A small hatchback was parked in the driveway on Tansy's side.

We took the path and I knocked on the door, hearing the sound of a TV inside. A woman answered the door, a tea towel in her hand. "I'm sorry," she said, giving us an apologetic smile, "I don't buy anything at the door. I don't even keep cash in the house."

"We're not selling anything," I said, producing my license. "We've been retained by your employers, Alan and Laura Reynolds, to look into a theft on the premises. They told us you have a keen eye for details and could help us with a few questions."

"Oh, well, yes, of course. Will you excuse me for a moment to call and check with them? I don't like to let people I don't know inside the house."

"Of course," I agreed. "We'll wait."

She shut the door.

"That was a good move to appeal to her willingness to help," said Dad.

"I figured she'd have more to say that way than if she feared she were a suspect," I said.

Tansy returned, and beckoned us inside. "Come into the kitchen," she said. "My son just got home from school and he's supposed to be doing homework in the living room, not watching TV." She shot her son a look and he gave her a lopsided smile from where he sat on the floor, his legs curled under him, homework sheets and colored pencils spread out on the coffee table. "I'm sorry to keep you waiting outside but I figure you can't be too careful when someone you don't know appears at the door. Laura said she'd appreciate any help I might be able to offer you."

"It was sensible of you to make the call, ma'am," said Dad. "Anyone legitimate would want you to feel comfortable."

"I hope you don't mind if I bake while we talk," she said, moving around the small island in the bright kitchen where a large mixing bowl stood amidst open packages of flour, sugar, and eggs, like she'd just been getting everything ready when we knocked. "There's a cookie bake sale after school tomorrow to raise funds for the new library and I promised two dozen chocolate chip cookies."

"Not at all. We're just glad you can help," I said.

"Laura said it was the vintage sapphire ring that was stolen but I didn't even touch it yesterday so I'm not sure I can offer anything of interest. I don't think I saw a thing."

"You'll be surprised what people don't realize they know," said Dad.

"Well, go ahead with your questions. I'll tell you whatever I can." Tansy sifted the flour into the bowl.

"We'd like to know a little more about the day of the theft. You were working yesterday?"

"That's right. I work flexible hours. I don't have much of a choice while Olly is still in elementary school. I started at nine-thirty and worked until two-thirty. Jonathan was there too and he works longer hours than me so the only time I was alone was when he took a lunch break. I took a coffee break at twelve for twenty minutes but I don't get lunch until I finish for the day," she explained. "I think Alan was with Jonathan while I was getting coffee. I went outside to breathe some fresh air since it was such a warm day."

"Where did you get your coffee from?" I asked.

"There's a coffee place across the road. I treated myself to an iced coffee and did a little window shopping since it was so hot and I didn't want to walk too far.

"I like that coffee shop," I told her. Lily and I had been there only a couple hours later than Tansy.

"Me too. I usually make coffee at home to save money but it's nice to have a treat every once in a while."

"Treats make life worthwhile," I agreed.

"Did anything stand out to you as unusual that day?" asked Dad.

Tansy shook her head. "No, I can't think of anything right now but I don't know if that's due to the surprise of hearing there was a theft. It felt like a normal day. Are you sure it isn't a big mistake?"

"Do you think it could be?" I asked.

"Well, I guess there's never been a theft before so I suppose it's possible! But no, I guess it must be true.

It's just... the security is really good! There's a buzzer entry system so people can't just waltz in, and all the jewelry is kept in lockable cabinets or inside the safe. It's almost impossible for anyone to steal anything. I can't think of any way it could have happened!" Tansy shook her head and dipped a measuring cup into the sugar bag, pouring the sparkling granules into the bowl before reaching for the eggs.

"What can you tell us about the customers?"

She pulled a face, giving a quick shake of her head that loosened strands of hair from her ponytail, which she pushed back. "I'm not sure I totally remember. There were a few customers that day. Men and women, and a gaggle of old ladies who arrived just before I left. The guy that works in the deli down the road, and a man who wanted to buy something for his daughter, I think, and another man who wanted to... oh!" She pulled a face. "Yeah, I remember him. He wanted to buy something for his wife and mistress. Jonathan was not impressed with that."

"You have a good memory," I said. "Go on."

"Some women bought things. I rang up a necklace, I think. The old ladies were looking for a gift, I believe, until one of them slipped on the floor and hurt herself so they decided to go home. Jonathan helped them. I was unpacking an order of gift boxes and bags, putting them under the counter near the cash register and trying to stack them into a nice display."

"What do you recall about the old ladies?" I asked.

Tansy reached for a wooden spoon and began to stir her mixture. "Nothing much," she said. "Chatty and cooing over everything, and then the one that fell down was upset about how much the other two were fussing over her. It was quite sweet really. They looked like they'd been friends forever."

"What about Jonathan?" I asked.

"Oh, he was worried about them, asking if they were okay and did they want to call a taxi. But one of them said it wasn't so bad and they'd catch the bus. When they left, I think he said he was sure they'd be back, or something like that."

"I meant, do you two get on well?"

"Oh! Yes, I think so! He's technically my boss but he doesn't throw his weight around. Did he show you the jewelry he designs? He's very talented."

"He did," I said. "I liked his pieces a lot."

"Me too. I hope he doesn't leave us to work on it full time but he says he's not planning to. He's nice to work with and that counts for a lot in retail jobs."

"I wonder what kind of income a side hustle in jewelry-making earns," I said to my dad, not because I expected an answer from him. Instead, I watched Tansy from the corner of my eye.

"I haven't asked him," said Tansy, "but I think he makes a little bit of extra money. Not enough to afford anything flashy. I think he's been driving the same car for at least ten years."

"He should take a vacation sometime," I said. "The side business must take up a lot of his time on top of having full-day working hours."

"That's what I said to him and he did say he's saving up for a trip to Europe. I think he wants to see Paris. Can you imagine? I bet it's even more beautiful than it looks on TV."

"You haven't been there?"

"No. Between bringing up Olly solo, working part time, and going to school, Europe is totally out of my budget. A girl can dream though." She smiled warmly before she glanced at her recipe, running her finger down the ingredients list.

"And what about the Reynoldses? What's your relationship like with them?"

"Good, I think. They've been very fair to me. They're happy for me to work around Olly and if he's ever sick or anything like that, and I've needed to stay home, they've never complained. They know I can't work weekends but they're okay with that too. My last boss was nothing like them. I think they trust me and I wouldn't want to ever let them down." She looked up and smiled, then her smile faltered. "Do you know how the ring was stolen? I've been so worried that they'd think it was me and I couldn't prove it wasn't but they haven't said anything like that at all. Actually, they haven't said anything except to answer your questions," she added, worry flitting into her eyes.

"We think it was a distraction theft. At the time we think it happened, you weren't anywhere near the jewelry case," I told her.

She heaved out a sigh. "I know it probably sounds awful, and like I'm only interested in myself, but I'm *so* happy to hear that. I hope you catch whoever did it. The Reynoldses don't deserve having something stolen from them. They're nice people."

"What do you know about the ring?" I asked.

"Nothing at all. Except that it's vintage and Laura brought it from a family seller, I think. It's sapphire and diamond. Very pretty. That's it. There's probably more information on the website but I don't own a computer and I'm not very tech-savvy with my phone either."

"Do you remember if there were any inquiries about it? Maybe someone came in and wanted to see it or know more about it?" I asked.

Tansy wrinkled her nose. "I think I tried showing it to someone last week but he wasn't interested. He wanted a new sapphire ring for his girlfriend, nothing vintage, and I sold him one. Otherwise, no. At least, I didn't handle anything. Jonathan could have, but I suppose he would have told you already," she said. "We didn't have it long. I remember Laura showing it to me with a couple of other things she bought."

"Oh? What other items?"

"Another ring, I think. And two necklaces."

"Do you know if they came from the same seller?"

She shook her head. "I don't think so but if Laura said otherwise, I don't remember."

"You've been very helpful," I said, reaching for a card in my purse. I handed it to her but she wiggled her flour-tipped fingers so I placed it on the counter, away from the mixing bowl. "If you remember anything else, could you please give us a call?"

"Sure," she said, reaching for a towel to wipe her hands, then escorting us to the door. "You know there was one thing that puzzled me." She stopped, pressing her lips together.

"What's that?"

"It's just that we hadn't even had that ring for very long and it really was a unique piece. I know it was expensive but a lot of other pieces in the store are too. Why steal that? Why not steal something else that would be far easier to resell than something so unique?" she asked.

I contemplated that. "Good questions," I said. "That's what we intend to find out."

CHAPTER ELEVEN

We climbed into the car. Before driving away, I glanced at Tansy's house but if she were watching us, I couldn't tell. It was more likely that she'd returned to her baking, thoughtful about the investigation but not filled with worry. She didn't appear to think she was under any suspicion and hadn't acted defensively, both of which I felt were good signs.

"What do you think?" asked Dad. "I liked her. She was pleasant and open."

"Is that your professional detective opinion?"

"Sure is."

"Then I second it. I don't think Tansy had anything to do with the theft and she did raise an interesting point. Why that ring out of all the other rings in there?" I waited for a car to pass us, then pulled out after it.

"And why didn't Laura mention she bought other items?" asked Dad. "If they were from the same seller, she should have said something."

"Perhaps they're not and she didn't think it was relevant. All the same, we should find out."

"I like the 'we'. It's nice to feel part of a team again."

"I thought you were enjoying retired life." I glanced at Dad before returning my attention to the road. I never got the impression he was anything but happy with life, which was exactly how he appeared now.

"I am, and I do, but there's a certain thrill of the chase that golf doesn't elicit, unless you count that time your mother and I went to Florida and I whacked the ball into a lake before an alligator climbed out."

I gaped at him. "Why have you never told me that story before?"

"We didn't want you kids to worry."

I hardly dared ask but I did. "What did Mom do?"

"She got on top of the golf cart and refused to get down."

"That seems sensible." I didn't add, *for Mom*. It was more likely Mom would have given the alligator a piece of her mind until it regurgitated the golf ball and apologized. That she'd decided to steer clear of the reptile was nothing short of a miracle. Which just goes to show miracles do happen when you least expect them to.

"I drove us out of there with her on the roof. It was like that eighties werewolf film, with Michael J. Fox surfing on the van roof, except when I said that, she took offense at the comparison so I should probably be grateful I'm still married."

"Dad," was all I could say.

"I know," he chuckled. "I'm actually lucky I'm alive." He reached for his phone, pulling up the information we'd been sent about the cleaner. "We need to go to Bartholomew Drive. I'm not sure if that's the home or the business."

"That's a nice street. It's just around the corner from where I used to live."

"Bonneville? Where you had that pretty bungalow?"

"That's exactly the one."

"How's the tenant?"

"Great! I keep expecting her to give notice any day that she's moving out to get married but so far, no. If she does, the neighbor has someone who's interested in renting it though."

"That's good news. You've made a lot of smart decisions in your life. I'm really proud of you, Lexi."

Warmth filled me. "Thanks, Dad!"

"When you were a teenager, we feared you might end up in a juvenile facility so it's nice to be proven wrong."

I frowned. "You're welcome?"

"This profile says Monika Balint has worked for the Reynoldses for almost ten years and she's a trusted employee. I can't see someone working around jewelry like theirs for ten years and only now deciding to steal something," said Dad, moving on obliviously.

"Perhaps she ran into financial trouble and figured one ring wouldn't hurt. Or that she was owed it."

"That's some financial trouble."

"She might not have known exactly how much it was worth. The sales tags are tiny. Plus, its value isn't in the price tag, it's in how much someone can sell it for."

Dad spared me a glance. "That's wisdom," he said. "You must get it from me. She probably knows all about the Reynolds' security. I imagine cleaning involves polishing fingerprints off the glass and the locks. I wonder if she could figure out keypad combinations?"

"I'd guess that they've probably gotten used to her presence over the years and been lax on occasions with their pin codes. I doubt they'll admit that but I'd put money on it. Not that it matters since the ring's case is unlocked with a key, not a number code."

"Tansy does have her own pin code and she's a trusted employee too. She can easily make copies of keys. On paper, the possibility of her being the thief seems higher than their cleaner."

"Except neither of us think it's her," I reminded him. "She wasn't anywhere near the case when it was open and she's not showing any obvious signs of new wealth. She doesn't seem on edge or scared of being found out either."

"Back to the cleaner," said Dad. "Take a left down here. It's quicker."

"Are you sure?"

"Yeah. I investigated a double homicide down here once and found a great shortcut through."

"I'm so pleased you found a benefit."

"Always have to look on the bright side," said Dad. "Or I'd never have coped with that kind of work. We didn't have therapy back then. We just turned to drink."

"Did you turn to drink?" I asked, worried now.

"No. I turned to your mother."

I smiled. "I'm glad she was there for you."

"She always is. Her to-do list always kept me too busy to go entirely mad. Take this right, go to the end, and that's Bartholomew Drive." Dad pointed the way, which was useful in case I'd forgotten how to follow his simple instructions.

"What number?" I asked as we turned onto

Bartholomew Drive.

"1339. I think it's the next block. Keep going. Mind that cat," he yelled as a black cat hurtled from between two parked cars and ran across the street.

I slowed down with a hundred yards to spare. "I wasn't going to run it over!"

"Glad to hear it. There it is, just over there. Pull over here. No, not here. Here." Dad jabbed his finger towards a red sedan parked on the side.

"Dad!" I squeaked in exasperation.

"What?"

I pulled around the sedan and parked. The house to our left had iron numbers over the door so I rolled the car forward until we reached the right house. Number 1339 was a broad ranch style with a long veranda just wide enough for a swing chair, and a gabled roof. A curved stone path meandered through the lawn. A small hatchback and a new SUV were parked on the driveway in front of a double garage.

"How much do cleaners earn?" I asked.

"Must be profitable," said Dad, peering at the house. "Or maybe her husband earns more."

"I don't think she's married."

"Boyfriend then," said Dad.

"Maybe," I said. "Let's find out."

As we reached the door, it opened and a small woman with short, black hair stepped out, carrying a Dior purse in one hand and a bucket full of cleaning products in the other. She stopped when she saw us approach and asked, "Are you lost?"

"I don't think so," I said, producing my license and introducing us, adding, "Monika Balint? We've been hired by Laura and Alan Reynolds."

"That's me. What for?" she snipped, her accent

evident.

"There's been a theft," I said.

"And they think I did it! Ugh!" she squeaked, her face instantly turning to annoyance.

"No, not at all," I said quickly. "We're just talking to all the employees to find out if anyone saw anything. They told us you weren't scheduled to work today."

"That's right. I clean for them two times a week."

"This is a lovely house," said Dad, looking over it admiringly.

"Thank you," she said, clearly suspicious. "It's mine. I don't clean it. I pay someone else to do that. Why would I want to clean all day, then clean my house too? What was stolen? Why didn't they call the police?" Her questions came quickly.

"A small piece of jewelry and…"

"All jewelry pieces are small," she snorted. "What was it?"

"A vintage sapphire and diamond ring."

"Oh. Yes, there are some nice, old things in that tray. Not my style, but different." She held up her wrist where a delicate silver chain was wrapped. A thick silver ring embedded with a piece of jet was on her middle finger, modern and stylish. "Why haven't the police been called?"

"The Reynoldses wanted to handle the theft discreetly."

"Pfft", Monika snorted. "They should call the real police, not the pretend police." She waggled her forefinger at us.

"I used to be a detective with the Montgomery Police Department," said Dad.

"Used to be," repeated Monika. "What's a PI? A mall cop without a mall." She snorted again.

"Anyway," I said, before my dad began to bristle, "the Reynoldses would appreciate it if you could answer our questions."

"Why didn't they ask me?" she asked. "Why they ask you to ask me?"

"They're very busy reviewing their security procedures."

"Oh." Monika set down the bucket and crossed her arms. "What do you want to know?"

"Have you seen anyone hanging around the shop or taking extra interest in the jewelry?" I asked.

"No, but I only go in before or after the shop closes. Alan or Jonathan lets me in usually. I clean for one or two hours. Shop, bathroom, kitchenette. Vacuum floors, clean surfaces, take out trash, make it nice. I leave. That it!"

"So you don't spend any time with the customers?"

"No. I'm not a shop lady. I clean. I leave. I never in shop alone. Alan or Jonathan always there, maybe Tansy." She glanced at her bucket. "What else you want to know?"

"Do you work for many other clients?" I asked.

Monika laughed. "I see now! You look at my house, my car, my purse and you think 'how she get money for this? She just cleaner!' That what you think, yes?"

"Not ex…"

"I *own* cleaning business," she said, pushing her shoulders back and lifting her chin. "I work hard. I learn English and Spanish! I take on more jobs. I take on staff. I clean for two old client: Reynolds' and another shop to keep me humblepie! But I have my staff for other jobs. I have assistant. I have accountant. I have good revenue! I buy nice house, nice car and keep little car for cleaning job because no client like to see cleaner in fancier car than theirs. That enough?" Her jaw wobbled and I wondered how many times she had explained herself, and how many times she'd fought off stereotypes to succeed.

"I don't mean to imply anything else. I'm really impressed," I said, feeling terrible for the miscommunication. "You must have worked incredibly hard to build such a successful business."

Monika softened, her shoulders relaxing a little. "Yes, I have. So you see, I don't need to steal. I have everything I want."

"It really is impressive," said Dad. "I wish I could learn languages too."

"Just try," she said. "Not easy, but try works. No try, no works."

Dad nodded and glanced to me.

"There's just one more thing. Have you ever noticed the employees taking out the jewelry from the cases?" I asked.

"Yes, always at end of day. They put in safe."

"But never to try anything on? Or to look at anything?"

"No, not that I see. They take cases from window and from cabinet and put in safe. No playing with sparkly things. Jonathan very nice. Tansy very nice. Alan and Laura very nice. Someone steal something, it is not them. Nice people. Like me," she added, pointing to herself with a decisive nod.

We thanked her and headed back to the car. As I buckled my seatbelt, I watched Monika cross to the hatchback, open the trunk, and put her bucket inside. Then she shut it and walked over to the SUV, climbed into the driver's seat and dropped her purse on the passenger seat.

"She's impressive," said Dad. "She saw an opportunity and worked her way up. Three languages, at least! And look what she's made for herself. Great house, great neighborhood, her own business."

"Do you feel bad about thinking she had a husband bankrolling her now?"

"I feel sexist. I think the kids call it unconscious bias. I have things to relearn."

"This is new, Dad. I like it."

"Thanks. I read that in a book at Serena's house. She said I could take it with me but I forgot so I don't know what the rest of it says but I'm sure she'll tell me."

I nodded. Serena would probably buy him his own copy and highlight all the passages she found relevant, then spring a pop quiz on him later when he was most likely to have forgotten just so she could lecture him.

Monika's SUV pulled out of the driveway and headed down the street, away from us. "We should get going too," I said. "I don't think she did it. She doesn't seem to have anything to gain financially and she wasn't in the shop when it looks like the ring was stolen."

"I agree. Can you drop me back at Reynolds'? Alan said to meet him there and go over the schedules before I go undercover. I haven't been undercover in years," said Dad, his excitement hanging in the air, which probably just went to show exactly how long it had been. Undercover work wasn't usually any more exciting than sitting in a car for hours on end, conducting surveillance, and wishing for a restroom break.

"Are you excited?"

"Sort of. The idea of it is always more exciting than

the actual job. I pretty much stopped when we started having you kids. I didn't want to be away from you all."

"Awww."

"I was scared of the chaos that would greet me on my return. It was better to stay put and get eased into the chaos day-by-day until it became my normalized existence."

"Dad."

Dad glanced at me. "What?"

"Never mind," I sighed and turned on the engine.

I dropped Dad outside Reynolds' and headed for the agency. As soon as I parked in the underground lot, my phone rang.

"Hi, Maddox," I said, surprised to hear from him again so soon.

"Sorry for disappearing last time. Work's so busy. You know how it is. I've been thinking about your case," he started, his voice too smooth to be casual, "and I'd love to know more. It sounds super interesting. Do you need any help? I've got time."

I pulled a face at the phone, both confused and suspicious. This was so unlike Maddox that I immediately sniffed a rat. "Aren't you on your way to Germany?" I asked.

"Oh, sure. Soon. Can't wait. So where did you find these prosthetics?" he asked, suspiciously jovial and like he was asking for nothing more interesting than the weather report. Definitely shady.

"In a trash can," I replied as unhelpfully as I could.

"Uh huh. And that would be *where*?"

I could imagine him waiting, a pen poised above his notepad. "Near a parking lot," I said, purposefully vague.

"What did she steal? Big ticket item, was it?"

"Just a vintage ring," I said. "I told you that already."

"Right, right. And were there any inquiries about it before the theft?"

I paused, choosing my next words carefully. I had a puzzle piece that didn't fit and the connection seemed to be on the other end of my line. Regardless of what information Maddox was trying to ascertain, perhaps I could fact-find too. "Funnily enough, the only inquiry came from a German hotel phone," I said. "And you're the only person I know with a recent connection to Germany."

A pause then, "Where in Germany?"

"Berlin. Hotel Ingrid."

"Huh. Fascinating. What a great case. Did you track down the caller?"

"Not yet. Lucas is working on it."

"Terrific. Great. Yeah, sorry can't help you there. So a vintage ring? Where did it come from?"

"France. I'm working on that too, but it looks like my client did their due diligence before the purchase."

"France? Well, isn't that interesting? And it was just the one ring?" Maddox continued.

"Why are you being so nosy?" I asked, narrowing my eyes even though he couldn't see me. "Why the twenty questions?"

"Professional curiosity from one law-abiding professional to another," he said, far too upbeat.

"That's not what you usually call me."

Maddox ignored that. "I thought you might appreciate some help? Do you have any names you want me to run? Any photos? Possibly a vehicle?"

"Why are you so keen to help me?"

"I thought you'd appreciate the resources at my

disposal that I am literally offering to you on a plate. On. A. Plate, Lexi."

"I have to go," I said. If he wasn't going to tell me, I wasn't playing the game. "Have a nice time overseas! *Auf Wiedersehen!*" I disconnected before he had a chance to ask anything else or find out that I only knew three words in German, two of which I'd just used. I couldn't quite work out his interest. Was he actively trying to be helpful? Or was he trying to ferret information out of me? Either way, I felt bamboozled.

I jogged up to the office, glad I'd chosen my rainbow-striped sneakers for all this running around, and relieved to flop down at my desk. Solomon was on the phone in his office, Delgado was long gone, and someone had brought in a free-standing fan, sending a deliciously cool breeze across the room.

I opened my laptop and made a start on my searches. The dupe ring was easy: it was widely sold through a women's accessories chain store. In other words, a dead end. Laura Reynolds had forwarded the link for the real ring's page and I clicked on it, skimming through the photos. It really was a lovely ring; beautifully designed and still highly wearable. Laura had included the contact information for the seller, adding that Madame Michel spoke perfect English and that she hadn't been informed of the theft. Laura also inserted a note that she would prefer it if our investigations were as discreet as could be as she was unsure whether it might affect future deals if word of the theft got out. I was pretty sure few sellers would care once they got their payment, but I appreciated her concern for business matters.

I shot her a message asking if she'd brought any other items from the same seller and almost immediately a reply appeared: no, she'd only purchased the ring.

Next, I checked online for the time in France and now, convinced I wouldn't be waking anyone in the middle of the night, I placed the call.

"*Bonjour!*" chirped a female voice.

"*Bonjour... er, je cherche...* Do you speak English? I'm looking for Madame Daphne Michel."

"Yes, I do. I am Madame Michel. What is the call concerning please?"

I introduced myself, adding, "I'm an associate with Reynolds' Fine Jewelry and I'm calling to ask some questions regarding a ring you sold to Laura Reynolds."

"Oh? I 'ave sold several pieces zis year. I'm not sure I recall which ring I sold to Madame Reynolds."

"It's a sapphire and diamond cluster on a gold band."

"Ah, *oui,*" she said, drawing out the little word in her charming accent. "I remember. It was a family heirloom but I did not like it so much. Best to sell it and let someone else enjoy it, *non?* Much prettier on a finger than collecting dust in a box."

"I agree."

"I do not 'ave any more pieces like it, if zat is why you are calling. It is a... let me find the words... a one zing. No! A one-off! Yes, zat is it!"

"We have a potential purchaser who is interested in a more complete history," I lied. "She would like to know if the jeweler who made the ring is known, or if there is a sales receipt?"

"Ah, *non,* I am sorry to say there is not. I gave everything I 'ad to Madame Reynolds. Just pictures. My father bought the ring for my mother during ze war, you understand? Many papers were lost during zis time.

I am thankful to 'ave the photographs. My mother was very fashionable. A great example of the era, despite ze 'ard times in Paris."

"Did your father ever mention who he bought it from?"

"*Non*, but he 'ad magnificent taste. He liked to buy *Maman* many items on his travels."

"His travels? Did he buy it in France or elsewhere?"

There was a long pause, then her voice came a little cooler. "I don't know. He was a businessman. He went 'ere, he went zere. I was a *bebe*. I would not know zese zings! I am afraid I cannot 'elp you anymore."

"Our client loves that your mother was so fashionable," I said, seizing on something I thought Madame Michel would be interested in talking about as soon as it seemed like she wanted to end the call. "Is there any possibility she wore it anywhere where there might have been celebrities? Our client loves glamorous histories."

"I don't know. Maybe. Zey entertained many people. Minor royalty, the popular people… what do you call zem, ah! I remember. Socialites! Even film stars but I could only find two photos with *Maman* wearing ze ring and I gave zem to Madame Reynolds. I can give you some names, per'aps? But I don't know if an American would know zese people."

"That would be wonderful. What was your mother's name?"

"*Maman*? 'Er name was Cosette Durand. Maybe if you find old magazines, *Vogue France* or *Paris Match* maybe, although zat magazine was much later, you will see 'er photographed. She was very pretty. Everyone said so. A society beauty and intelligent too. She spoke English and German as well as French. Per'aps zat is enough for your client? 'E or she likes the chic connection to the French *aussi*?"

"Very much," I lied. "Was there a lot of interest in the sale?"

"Of ze ring? I zink zere would be if I sent it to auction at Sotherby's or Christie's but it is a…. 'Ow do you say? A bother? Madame Reynolds 'as a good reputation and she is discreet. She offered me a good price. I could not say *non*."

I made a note, another question occurring to me. "So no one else knew about the sale?" I asked. "The ring wasn't advertised anywhere?"

"Just my friend who suggested Madame Reynolds. She needed a new roof for 'er *chateau* a few years ago and Madame Reynolds' purchase enabled it wizout gossip."

"I see," I said.

"I am sure you do not! We are not poor! We 'ave too much and do not need zese trinkets. I must go. I am dressing for lunch and I do not like to keep my 'usband waiting."

"Of course," I said. "Thank you for your—"

"*Au revoir*!" She cut me off and hung up.

Wincing at the abruptness, I scribbled my notes in the file, disappointed with the lack of information, although I thought I'd gleaned something. Madame Michel wasn't as well off as I imagined she might have presented herself to Laura Reynolds. Like her chateau-owning friend, she seemed to want to keep up appearances, and selling jewelry quietly to an overseas buyer was a way of guaranteeing discretion.

I plugged Cosette Durand into a search engine and found several women of the same name but all too recent to be Madame Michel's mother. It took several more pages of scrolling to stumble upon an article that seemed to present the correct woman and a dapper older man. She wore a beautiful formal dress with cap sleeves, a gathered bodice, and frothy skirt. One hand in front of her skirt displayed a ring, her other hand on the arm of the man flashed an engagement ring. I looked closer. Was that the ring I searched for now? They stood with two other stunningly dressed young women on a beautifully curved staircase, smiling and looking like they were having a wonderful time. It was written in French beyond my comprehension but I had the page translate, reading aloud, "Mademoiselle Cosette Durand at a winter ball with her fiancé, Jean Dupuis, and friends, Mademoiselle Sidonie Martin and Frau Ilse Bauer, 1942."

"Holy crap," I said, sitting back, the backdrop of the staircase now grabbing my attention as a cold shiver ran down my spine. There was only one explanation for the images on the flags. Cosette Durand was at a Nazi ball!

CHAPTER TWELVE

After printing the picture, and adding it to my file, I took a long moment to think about what I'd discovered. No wonder Madame Michel was so tight-lipped and eager to end the call at my pressing. Who'd want to admit that their socialite mom partied with some of the most evil people in history? And what did that make her mom?

As much as I searched, I couldn't find anything else to support the opposing theory that Cosette Durand was a secret French resistance fighter. Yet I also couldn't find any further evidence of her shocking associations. There wasn't even anything to uncover on her friends; it was like they'd faded from memory, decades ago.

That didn't mean there wasn't any evidence either way.

It just meant a lot of time had passed and I couldn't find the evidence now.

I couldn't even be sure Madame Michel knew about her mother's past.

Yet I could be almost positive that Cosette Durand was wearing the ring in the 1940s. Madame Michel had said so.

When Solomon emerged from his office, I'd exhausted my options.

"Why the face?" asked Solomon. He leaned against the door to his office and folded his arms, waiting.

I passed him the printout and he stepped forward to take it, studying it thoughtfully. "This is the former owner of the ring," I said. "I think she's wearing it in this photo. This photo wasn't supplied to the Reynoldses."

Solomon raised his eyebrows. "Is that what I think it is? In the background?" he asked.

"Yep."

"I didn't have Nazis on my bingo card for today."

"Me neither but it is making me wonder about the Michels."

"Plenty of Europeans were collaborators whether they agreed with Nazi ideology or just figured compliance made their lives easier during occupation. Although there were others who used their connections to pass intelligence along to the Allied forces."

"I'm not finding any evidence of resistance but I'm not sure I'm looking in the right places. I'm not even sure where the right places are," I admitted. For the first time in a long time, I felt beyond my depth. I'd come across terrible people in our line of work but this magnitude was something else entirely.

"Even if there is, it might not have been digitized. Plus, a lot of activity from that era is still officially secret."

"I like your optimism." I leaned back in my chair,

contemplating resting my ankles on the desk, as I thought. "The Reynoldses didn't mention this. I wonder if they knew."

"If they did, I can see why they didn't say anything. These types of connections are bad for business, and should be."

"They'd have to know the Nazi connection could come out. They had to know we'd look into the ring's provenance beyond just calling the former owners. It didn't take me long to find that photo."

"I would think most people would want to get ahead of something like that," said Solomon. "Especially if they were innocent at the time of the sale."

"Do you mean, if they didn't know then but found out later?"

"Yes."

"It's possible. I didn't get any sense the Reynoldses were Nazi sympathizers. There was nothing in the office or shop to indicate that and I'm sure I would have noticed." Solomon placed the photo on the file and I couldn't help glance at it. Jean Dupuis and the trio of women wore big smiles, clearly having a good time. I couldn't imagine the kind of human misery their fancy ball was built on.

"Agreed. So work on the assumption for now that they didn't know, but keep digging."

"Okay," I decided. "And I'm going to let Dad know so he can keep his eyes and ears open for that while he's undercover." I drafted a message as we spoke and sent it to my dad.

"Good thinking."

"What if it's not just the Michels and Durands that have Nazi connections? What if the ring does too?

161

Could that be a reason for stealing it?"

"It could provide a motivation. Is there any evidence it was a gift from a particular figure?"

"No, but the Reynoldses already said there's no real provenance at all. No receipt. No identifiable maker. They said it was made in the thirties so it was already at least ten or twenty years old during the forties and fifties when the photos the seller provided were taken." I sighed. "I'm not sure what to do next."

"What does your gut say?"

"Find out more information."

"Sounds like a plan."

Thankfully, Solomon didn't ask me what my plan was for that because the desk phone rang. I picked it up, pleased to hear Lucas on the line. "I've got some information for you regarding a possible vehicle," he said. "Come up when you're ready."

"We'll come now," I said as Solomon nodded in agreement.

Lucas was waiting for us when we entered, partially hidden behind several monitors that took up a large portion of his long desk, his messy blond hair peeking over the top. The rest of the office staff were working quietly and intently at their stations, a radio playing in the background, stopping the atmosphere from feeling entirely sterile.

"The retirement village's security is reasonable," said Lucas as he scooted his chair over to make space for us. He pointed to the middle screen. "They have a camera overlooking the parking lot but unfortunately, there's a tree close by and the branches are partially obscuring the view."

My heart sank. "I hoped the news would be more positive."

"Oh, it is. One of the cameras at the front picks up vehicles entering and exiting the rear parking lot. Parking is supposed to be for residents only but there doesn't appear to be anyone checking so it's easy for anyone to come and go. I started at the time of the robbery, cross-referenced it with the bus times arriving at the retirement home and then focused on any vehicles leaving the lot in the next two hours. There're only four vehicles. I'm sending you screenshots and videos of each, but they're not great quality. I need you to narrow down who I'm looking for to track them further."

I checked my phone and scrolled through the screenshots. The first picture was a man alone, the second was a senior couple together. The third and fourth pictures were both women. "Not the man or the couple," I said, "We should focus on the women but I'm not sure which."

"One of the couple is a woman," pointed out Lucas.

"The prosthetics were ditched before she left so we're not looking for a woman of the couple's age. It has to be one of the younger women."

"I concur," said Solomon. "Cue the videos for both women."

"You got it," said Lucas. The monitor closest to me came alive with a video feed. A woman in a white shirt, big, black sunglasses and a neat ponytail glided out in a silver hatchback. The small car turned right and disappeared from view.

"And the second," I prompted.

The video was replaced by another. This time, a black minivan exited the lot, pausing at the junction with the main road. The driver checked her phone and then tossed it on the passenger seat. She wore a cross-over tunic with a name badge attached but it was too far away to possibly read the name.

"This woman looks like she might work there. The orderlies wear that kind of tunic," I said. "Both women could be in their thirties, but I wouldn't put money on it. I couldn't say it was one over the other."

"I ran the plates of all the cars," said Lucas. "The first two belong to men registered as living at the village. The silver hatchback is registered to a rental agency. The minivan belongs to a woman who lives here in town."

"Can you find out the name on the rental?" I asked. "The other three have ties to town but the rental is the outlier."

"Give me a few minutes," said Lucas. He scooted his chair closer to the desk and tapped at the keyboard.

While he worked, I asked, "What are the odds that this woman has even stuck around? We're twenty-four hours late."

"She might have if she were stealing to order and the handoff is here," said Solomon.

"Is that what you would do?"

"I'd want to get rid of hot goods as fast as I could, then I'd put a helluva lot of distance between me and the crime," said Solomon.

"Maybe it's got nothing to do with the Nazis," I said, frowning.

Lucas stopped typing and glanced up. "Nazis?"

"I'll fill you in later."

"Okay. Got it," said Lucas after returning to his search. The videos disappeared and a driving license appeared on screen. "Sally Smith, age thirty-six, Boston resident, rented the car in Boston from their airport office around a week ago for the period of ten days. It's due to be returned in four days," he said.

"Sally Smith?" I repeated as I looked at the photo of the unsmiling woman. Long bangs swept down to her eyes, a choppy, shoulder-length cut, artfully styled. Tan, minimal makeup. Or at least it had appeared to be. I leaned in. No, she was wearing a lot of makeup in the effort to look makeup-free. Round, thin, gold-framed glasses. Sweetheart-shaped face. Pussy-neck bow blouse in an unflattering print. "What are the odds that is really her name?" I asked, already skeptical. "And why rent a car from the airport of the city where you're a resident?"

"See what you can find on her," said Solomon.

"On it," said Lucas and we waited impatiently as his fingers flew across the keys. "So the address on the license is for an apartment block but there's no Sally Smith listed as an owner or renter. Plus, the block is marked for renovation and appears to be empty. I can't find any social media that matches both her name and face. There's a Social Security ID but the owner is listed as deceased."

"So we have a fake identity in Sally Smith and a missing ring," I said. "What are the odds these two crimes aren't connected?"

"Low," said Solomon.

"This woman has access to fake IDs and elaborate disguises," I said, musing out loud.

"That's not wholly true," said Solomon. "We now know what she looks like. Lucas, put the driver's ID and the camera footage next to each other."

Lucas tapped his keyboard and motioned to the screen where the two images were now displayed.

"They match," I said, nodding. "But I doubt even

165

this is what she really looks like. Her makeup is expertly applied and that hair… it's too perfect. I'll bet it's a wig too. She took off the gray wig and ditched it, then put on this one. She probably doesn't need glasses either, but the big sunglasses shield her face. We need to know more before we can think anything definitive about this woman."

"Let's find out where she goes next," said Solomon.

"That might take a while," said Lucas. "I'll send the DMV picture to the printer and call you when I have anything concrete."

"Make it a priority," said Solomon.

Solomon and I headed back to our own office, my mind whirring. "This woman can't have appeared here out of the blue," I said as I grabbed the printed sheet with Sally Smith's license on the way to my desk. "She had to have traveled here, and I don't just mean hiring a car. She might have flown in, probably to Boston, where she rented the car using her fake ID. She has to be staying somewhere since she picked up the car. She had to have scouted out Harmony Village and picked out her targets for the ruse. She had to have bought the prosthetics from somewhere, and the clothing disguise too. The clothes would be easy but the facial prosthetics? Would she need to purchase them specifically? Could she have done all that in between picking up the car and the theft?"

"It's possible," said Solomon. He rested against my desk, not quite sitting or standing, his arms folded, biceps bursting from his t-shirt's short sleeves, his legs stretched out. "The prosthetics would have to be created in advance. She could have had them made for another job prior to this, and like you said, the clothing is easy enough to pick up anytime. She could have created her plan and then staked out a few retirement homes over the course of a few days. What stumps me is her doing all that *and* scoping out Reynolds'. It strikes me that she might have split the tasks in two. Stakeout Reynolds' first to know what she's dealing with and how she's going to do it, and the ruse second since it's easier to put together."

"So we can track her?"

"We could be sifting through hours if not days of footage and there's no guarantee Sally Smith didn't use a disguise for the reconnaissance too. She's definitely a pro. She would be careful about leaving any evidence tying her to the crime."

"Yet she probably also assumes the theft hasn't been discovered yet. So far, she thinks she got away with it. She doesn't know we're onto her. That should work in our favor."

"That might be her big mistake," said Solomon. "She's cocky."

"What are the chances that she's been caught before? I don't mean recently. I mean a long time ago? She can't have had a perfect career. It must take time to perfect the kind of skills she's got and that means making mistakes that might have led to her being caught."

"It's possible."

"She made the mistake of allowing the car to appear on camera. She didn't figure on Lily following her to the retirement home after the theft either."

"There's no accounting for a wild variable like Lily," said Solomon, smiling.

"I'm going to check in with Lily. She should see the photo too," I said.

"Ask Maddox too."

"He's been asking weird questions. Until he tells me why, I'd rather not hand him any particulars of the case."

Solomon's cell phone rang and he put it to his ear, listening, then hung up. "I have to go soon," he said. "The Reynoldses decided they definitely want the security of their shops overhauled and they're a little edgy about it. Plus, there was a question about providing security for an inventory collection. We can catch up over dinner but call me before that if there any important developments."

"I will," I agreed. "Hey, the car was hired for ten days, right? Where does it get returned to?"

"I would assume at the same rental office where Sally Smith rented it."

"Then we know where she's going to be in approximately four days' time," I said, smiling now. "Even if we can't find her, we can get ahead of her."

"Assuming she doesn't plan on ditching it."

"Wouldn't that burn her ID?" I asked. "Or at the very least, draw attention to it and to her photo? Even if she didn't plan on using that ID again, she wouldn't want the rental company to hand her fake driving license with her face on it to the police for auto theft."

"I agree," said Solomon. "That would be a bad move. We'd need to potentially run a twenty-four-hour surveillance on the rental agency to cover the return window but it's doable. Fletcher and Flaherty might be free by then. However, I don't think we should rely on that. The chances of her dumping the car are high and if we waste time over the next few days and she doesn't turn up at the rental agency, then she's in the wind. Finding her is the priority above all else and I can't think she'll stay in town long, now that the job is completed." He straightened, then leaned down to kiss me. "I have every confidence you'll find her," he said, his lips inches from mine.

"Thanks," I said, wishing I felt more reassured. I might have had a lot of experience in tracking people down, but something told me this woman had even more experience evading capture. Not only that, but she had a plan, time, and significant resources on her side. I could only assume she had as solid a plan for getting out of town as she had for entering it.

As soon as Solomon headed to his office, I called Lily and updated her on what we'd found out.

"Now I feel like I wasted my time here," she said. "I haven't gotten one bit of information and I've been talking to a lot of the seniors. No one remembers an Angela at all. Barely anyone even remembers seeing Evelyn and Judy with another senior and those that do, all have something different to say."

"That's not a waste of time. You've confirmed this Angela is the fake we're looking for."

"The only interesting thing was when Maddox showed up."

My interest piqued. "Maddox showed up?"

"Yeah! He was really pleased to see me too! He came over and chatted about the case a bit."

"He did?" I frowned. There was that rat stench again. First, the overly cheerful call to me, then the readiness to chat with Lily about the case. The man was sniffing around and he was barely trying to hide it. That had to mean something. My guess was he wanted information fast. But what did he think we knew?

"Yeah, he said it was all fascinating," continued Lily. "I showed him the photos of the prosthetics and he was really impressed and even more impressed when I told him how the thief got Evelyn and Judy involved. He said it was very clever to do something like that and how cool it was that I'd tracked the thief here and was investigating."

"That so?" The rat was getting stinkier by the minute. There was no way Maddox just happened to think Lily was cool. She *was* cool, but that was beside the point. Maddox wouldn't be praising her for involvement for no reason. What was he up to?

"Yes! He asked if the disguise had been turned over to the police and I said no, because the Reynoldses didn't want them involved. I said maybe he should take a look at everything as a favor and he said that was a good idea. That we might get fingerprints or DNA off something."

"That *is* a good idea," I said. "I have everything here and the agency has access to a lab but we'd need something to cross-reference it too and right now, there's nothing." I held back on telling Lily about Sally Smith, even though I'd planned to, cautious that Maddox would pry the information from her before I was ready. What I couldn't fathom was why he didn't just come out and state the reason he was so interested in my case. Instead, he was trying to wheedle information out of the one weak link in our investigation: Lily. No, that wasn't right. There were my parents too! If Lily were a weak link, my parents were chocolate under his flame.

"Should I hang around Harmony some more?" asked Lily. "I have the rest of the day off and Jord is taking Poppy to the park."

"No, I think that avenue is exhausted. We have a lead thanks to you, and Lucas is tracking down the woman's movements so we can take it from here. We uncovered another false identity."

"So exciting! I love this!" she squeaked.

"Why don't we get together tomorrow and I'll fill you in. I might have some more to tell you by then," I suggested.

"Okay!" Lily said perkily. "What's next?"

"Can you do me a favor?"

"Sure! Anything!"

"Call me if Maddox comes around asking any more questions."

"Of course. Is there something wrong?" She paused. "Shouldn't I have said anything? He was so interested. I figured it was... professional courtesy, or something. I... did I do something wrong?" she asked, her voice slipping away into worry.

"You didn't do anything wrong. Maddox is just asking a lot of questions and I want to know why. He called me too."

"Have you asked him?"

"He's being evasive."

"Have you asked Sadiq?"

I pondered that. Maddox's FBI partner would know what he was up to. The question was whether or not he would tell me. "I might just do that. I'll call you soon."

"Make sure of it," said Lily.

I kicked back, despondent at where my leads had ended up. Sally Smith was a fake name but how was I supposed to find out her true identity? And for that matter, what was I supposed to say to the Reynoldses?

The Reynoldses could be put aside for now. There was nothing concrete I could give them and the Michels' dubious connections might yet materialize into nothing to do with the case. Plus, there was the small matter of where was the ring? Something that size would be easy to dispose of. It could be FedExed anywhere in the country, maybe even the world, leaving no need for a physical exchange. Or it could be worn on a finger as a person boarded a train or plane and no one would even look twice. It could easily be concealed in anything from a sock to face cream. Solomon was wrong. The job wasn't finished until the ring was in someone else's hands.

I turned to my laptop, knowing it was futile to type Sally Smith into the search bar, yet doing it anyway. There were plenty of search results but after skimming them, my thoughts were justified. No results that pointed to a thief.

Lucas had emailed the list of guests from the Berlin hotel and I opened it, cross- referencing the names to the fake identity but there were no matches and no name that begged attention otherwise. It was probably a ludicrous leap that this Sally Smith had made an inquiry from Germany and then flown here to snatch it, yet... I couldn't shake the idea that things were connected in ways I didn't yet understand.

France, Germany, and the United States. What was going on?

There were too many names to search all of them, and nothing that could help me narrow down the parameters. I couldn't even be certain of the names' nationalities and in some names, not even the owners' sex. Even if I did spend all night trying to track these people down, there was no guarantee the call was anything more than from a curious online browser who liked pretty, sparkly things.

"You should head home," said Solomon, stepping

out of his office and closing the door behind him. "Let Lucas work his magic and we'll pick it up in the morning."

"And give the thief another half day to get away? I don't think so."

"I like your commitment but there's nothing more you can do until there's a viable lead."

My shoulders slumped. "I guess."

"There's no urgency for Sally Smith to leave town yet and if it's a case of our best option being to wait her out until she returns the car, we'll do that."

That cheered me up, then another thought occurred to me. "There has to be a reason she wanted the car for extra time."

"It could be that she wanted to give herself a buffer and didn't expect the theft to go so well."

"Maybe."

"She could be combining this trip with something else."

"Another theft?"

Solomon shook his head. "I was thinking maybe she has someone in town. That could be a plausible cover story if she were ever questioned about her reason for being here. It would also explain how she knew to target the retirement village for unwitting accomplices in this distraction ploy. Anyway, we'll know more when Lucas gives us more to work with. Until then, I'll pay a call to the Reynoldses, then home, dinner, sleep. Power down and we'll head out."

"I need to do a few things first," I said. "Go ahead without me." I closed my laptop, a thought occurring to me. In Solomon's hand, the phone rang and he waved goodbye, turning his back to me, answering as he left the office.

I pulled the picture of Sally Smith closer and then reached for my phone. Maddox had recently sent me some photos of a woman who was a master of disguise. A woman so clever he couldn't catch her.

I'd met her only a couple of weeks ago.

I put my phone next to the DMV photo and stared at the two women side-by-side.

Oh, boy.

CHAPTER THIRTEEN

A month ago, I'd been blissfully unaware of Cass Temple's existence.

Two weeks ago, she'd outsmarted me and stolen millions of dollars in jewels.

Today, she was in a photo on my desk.

Of course she was disguised in the photos but now I'd printed the one on my phone, and added Lucas' surveillance shot, side-by-side, there was no mistaking the sweetheart face.

What the hell was going on?

I was pretty sure there was one person in Montgomery who could join the dots together and unfortunately, his name rhymed with Schadam Schaddocks.

Even more unfortunately, his nosiness suggested he might already have suspicions of his own about the case. So why hadn't he shared his suspicions? Why was he sniffing around, pretending to simply be curious?

He'd asked me to share any news of Cass Temple. Yet, he hadn't done the same.

Now I wondered how long he'd been sitting on the information that she's returned to town…. and was he thinking the same thing about me?

Except I'd tipped him off about Hotel Ingrid in Germany… the country Maddox was supposed to be visiting in pursuit of a criminal. What were the odds we now searched for the same person? "High," I muttered to myself. "Damn high."

That left me with two choices: ask Maddox what he knew and then request his help. Or mess with him.

It was hard to say which one I found most appealing.

Practicality, however, would need to win out. If I stood a chance to find Cass Temple in the next few days, assuming she was even in town, assuming it really was her, I needed help. Lucas might be tracking her vehicle but there were countless places she could hide it. She could even abandon it or switch the plates, replacing them with the originals only minutes before the drop off. Although the likelihood of her going to all that effort just to avoid losing the deposit made in a fake name seemed ludicrous. Something told me Maddox could fill in the gaps.

As I was contemplating my next move, the phone rang.

"Hi, Dad."

"I'm at Reynolds'," he said. "I have a shiny badge with my name on it but they're not sure about giving me a code to the jewelry cases."

"Do you need it?" I asked.

"Not really. Either Jonathan, Alan, or Tansy will be with me the whole time. I'm just the muscle."

"Aww." My dad probably had been the muscle once. Now he was the muscle memory.

"You doubt that but I box at my golf club. I can still pack a punch."

"Of course you can," I said.

"You sound like your mother," Dad grumbled.

I held back a laugh. "What's up?" I asked.

"I saw Maddox just now."

"He came to Reynolds'?"

"Not exactly. He was walking past, stopped to look at something in the window, saw me and waved. I was going to go out and say hello when he came in."

"Huh." It sounded exactly like he was walking past on purpose.

"He asked if I was taking on some post-retirement work. I told him, as one professional to another, I was doing some consultant work for you. He was impressed."

I narrowed my eyes. Maddox knew my case revolved around a stolen ring. "I'll bet he was."

"He was curious about how a jewelry store was involved and guessed I was undercover. He said he'd catch up with you about it sometime and told me to thank your mom for the lasagna she dropped off."

I shook my head, not quite in disbelief, but more at Maddox's blatant attempts to wheedle information from my dad. Then I recalled what Dad had just relayed. "Mom made him... oh, never mind. Of course she did!" I huffed. I'd pay good money in a bet that Maddox had used the opportunity to extract all the information my mom had.

"Her lasagna is very good. You know that. Anyway, I smelled a rat. What's Maddox up to?" Dad asked, surprising me with his shrewdness.

"That's a very good question. What made you smell a rat?"

"He was too nonchalant. Acting like he didn't really care meant he absolutely cared. I've known him long enough to recognize his behavior."

"Yeah, I think he's up to something too."

"Is he helping or hindering?"

"I don't know."

"Do you want me to throw him off the scent? I can make up some crap if you want me to."

"No, that's okay. Let me find out what he's after first. He might be willing to help." I glanced at the photos. If Maddox knew Cass Temple was in town, then surely he knew what she was doing... but if he knew that, why was he sniffing around my case like a dog at a particularly stinky tree? In an instant, it came clear. He knew she was here but he didn't know why. At least, he wasn't one hundred percent sure. Perhaps he suspected she was involved in my case but couldn't confirm it. Yet he was trying. "I've got a good idea but I need to verify it," I decided.

"Let me know if you want backup."

"That's kind of you. I'm sure I'll be just fine without you."

"I was thinking of sending your mom. She loves Maddox but she loves you more. If you want him interrogated, she's your woman. At worst, she'll simply withhold food."

I laughed. "Anything to report from Reynolds'?"

"Absolutely nothing. Let's hope it stays that way."

"There's nothing to indicate it won't."

"One-off thefts can often turn out to be trial runs for something bigger and the Reynolds' store front can easily be rammed and raided," said Dad.

"Seems an excessive step-up for a sleight of hand theft."

"It's a good thing I'm here. Saves agency manpower getting too stretched. I'll hang out until closing time, then head home."

"Thanks, Dad."

"One more thing before you go!"

"Yes?"

"The guy with the accent came back. Jonathan recognized him. I subtly questioned him and checked out his alibi. I sent everything to your email but I'm certain he had nothing to do with anything."

"Good work, Dad!"

We disconnected and I took a deep breath before calling Maddox.

"Hey!" he said, answering quickly. "I just bumped into your dad."

"You did? No way!" I feigned ignorance. If Maddox could do it, so could I.

"It's great he's consulting for you. The man is a class act."

"Isn't he?" I agreed. "I'm so pleased he's come out of retirement to help us out on this case."

"I think he's pleased too. We really undervalue the older generation." There was a pause where Maddox took a sip of something, then he asked, "So what can I do for you? Everything okay?"

"I wondered if you were free? I was thinking about what you said and I'd really appreciate some insight on my case."

"Oh? How so? I'm sure I can make time." There was that breezy nonchalance Dad had mentioned. He was too compliant, too charming.

"It's thrown up a couple of things I didn't expect and since you work with major crimes, I thought you'd know more."

"This is the ring theft? With your dad undercover, I figured it was stolen from Reynolds'. How's it going otherwise?"

"I think I'm closing in," I said. "I'll tell you more when we meet. Where's good?"

"I'm at the coffee shop at the end of the block from Reynolds'. The one on the same side, near the deli. Not the one opposite. I'm in no hurry to go back to the office and my partner has the afternoon off for a dental appointment. Why don't you meet me here?"

"I'll be there in thirty minutes." I disconnected, pleased with how effortlessly that had gone. Maddox hadn't offered any information but he hadn't pressed either. He was far too cool for that. I knew that would be a different matter once I met him face-to-face although I still wasn't sure how to play it: feign ignorance to his machinations, drop clues until he broke, or play with him.

I drove downtown rather than braving the unabating, stifling heat and pulled up a block away, walking back to the coffee shop. By the time I pushed the door open, standing back to let two women walk out through the doorway, a trickle of perspiration was making its way down my back and I had the horrible feeling my face was a lot redder than I wanted it to be.

Maddox was at the corner table, his back against the wall, reading on his phone, a half-drunk tall glass in front of him. He looked up and waved, smiling.

"You look… pink," he finished as I approached.

"It's hot!"

"I know. That's why I'm sitting in a building with AC and drinking an iced coffee."

I looked at the drink. Even my gaze seemed to be melting the ice cubes. "I'll be right back," I said, and headed to the counter.

Five minutes later, I pulled out the chair opposite Maddox with one iced caramel latte for "Recksi" in my hand.

"How's it going?" asked Maddox. He slipped his phone into his pocket, giving me his full attention. "Any strong leads?"

"We know we're looking for a woman."

"Oh, very good. That narrows it down to… would you say half of Montgomery's adult population?"

"Less than half," I snipped lightly, knowing he was teasing from the glint in his eye. "But since she was in disguise, it's hard to tell who she might have been. Where does a person get a disguise anyway? Prosthetics? Wigs?" I watched him closely.

"What kind of quality are we talking? High end, you said?" Maddox watched me equally closely.

"The best you can get. The type a person could wear and their companions wouldn't even begin to think it wasn't their own face."

"Special effects prosthetics like that can run thousands of dollars."

"Is there anyone here who could make something like that?"

Maddox sat back in his plastic chair and sipped his iced latte. "No. There isn't much call for that kind of stuff here. Plenty of freelancers elsewhere. Movie and theater industry types, either in the business, freelancing, or doing that kind of thing as a business can be easily commissioned."

"That's disappointing."

"It's good money."

"No, I meant, it's disappointing there's no one here like that," I said. That would have made my case a lot easier but instead, Cass Temple—if it really was her—must have brought the disguise with her. She could have bought it weeks or months, even years, in advance, knowing one day it would come in useful. Just like I did with shoes.

"I didn't say there wasn't. Just that I don't know of anyone."

"How long would it take to make something like that?"

"An entirely custom job? A few weeks."

I shook my head. "She couldn't have planned it so far in advance. The Reynoldses didn't take possession of the ring until five weeks ago."

"A pro could have had something like that commissioned in the past, waiting for the right moment," said Maddox.

"That's what I figured. So, my thief gets the job and she already has the right disguise ready and waiting? All she needs to do is pack and catch a flight. The rest of the details can be worked out when she's in the vicinity."

"Catch a flight?" Maddox asked, latching onto that.

"Our suspect hired a car at Boston airport. I figured she flew in." As I sipped my drink, I watched him from under my lashes. His face was impassive, but his eyes told me he was deep in thought. "She's scheduled to return it," I added. "The car, I mean."

Maddox looked up. "When?"

"A few days from now."

"That's great!"

"I have a photo of her without the disguise."

Another flicker of interest, quickly subdued. "You do? Do you want me to run it for you?" he offered.

"Why don't you take a look at it and tell me?" I

produced the printouts and placed them on the table in front of him, neatly dodging a small puddle of liquid formed by the condensation slipping down our glasses.

Maddox picked up the photos, studying them, his face carefully not showing a thing.

When he didn't say anything, I pounced. "You *knew* she was in town," I said.

"Who?"

I tapped the top of a photo. "Cass Temple."

He hesitated and when he did, I knew I had him. He didn't want to lie, but he didn't want to admit to it either. And the evidence was in his hands: the DMV's Sally Smith and the driver leaving Harmony Village.

"Why didn't you tell me?" I asked, unsure if I was annoyed, irritated, or curious. Maybe all three. Although, this was certainly easier than interrogating Special Agent Sadiq Farid.

"You didn't need to know!"

"She's the chief suspect in my last case!"

"And that case is closed!"

"And in my current case!"

"Clearly."

"Does she still have the Queen's Ruby?" I asked, leaning in, keeping my voice low enough that the neighboring table of a laptop-working couple couldn't hear.

"No."

"How do you know?"

"She's not stupid enough to hang onto a piece as hot as that."

"But she's stupid enough to stick around town?"

"I don't think it's that…"

"Oh!" Realization dawned on me. "She wasn't here for the Queen's Ruby in the first place. She was here for something else, perhaps doing the reconnaissance before her heist. She was here for this! The Queen's Ruby was what... a convenient side quest?"

"Side quest," snorted Maddox.

"Cass Temple was already here and she heard about the ruby because some jerk leaked it to the newspaper and she figured 'Why not steal that too?' and make a deal."

"I think she would call it repatriating."

"Whatever," I said, drumming my fingers on the table as the puzzle pieces clicked into place. "But she'd already arranged to steal the ring so she left, making us think she was long gone, only to turn around and come back. Now that she's got the ring, she's going to run." That was it. This was my last shot, our last shot. Cass Temple had taken a huge risk in returning; I doubted she'd be back once the handover was complete.

"Okay, let's say that's what I think happened too. What's so important about the ring?" asked Maddox, leaning in, his forearms resting on the table.

"What about Ben Rafferty? Is he here too?" I asked, ignoring his question as I tensed, bracing for the answer.

Maddox gave a quick shake of his head. "No, he's long gone, along with his real identity."

"How can you be so sure?"

"We have surveillance of him getting on a flight at JFK bound for Paris. He tried the usual ballcap and beard disguise but, lucky for us, his cap was knocked off just at the moment he turned to face a camera. The shot is clear."

"Really?" I couldn't help but be skeptical.

"We're giving it ninety-five percent it's him. Interpol have been notified."

"And in Paris? Are there photos of him arriving?"

"There's a man in the same clothing but we don't have a clear shot of his face. We did get a copy of the passport he's using. It's in the name Benjamin Thomas."

"That's similar to some of his other identities," I said, relaxing now.

"Yeah, we picked up on that too."

"How long ago was this?"

"Three days after his father's funeral."

"Do you know where he's been since? Or what he's done?"

"No clue. We lost sight of him once he left the airport so I figure he's gone to ground. He'll lie low for a while, then he'll probably resume his usual activities."

"Romancing women out of their money," I filled in.

"Yeah, but with an added *ooh la la*." Maddox winked.

"Assuming he stays there. He could already be back in the country."

"It's possible but we know he has prior connections to Paris and he's fluent in French. I think he'll wait out any heat before he makes a return. Even then, I doubt he'll come to Montgomery. He got what he came for here."

"Yeah," I agreed. "That is, he found out what happened to his father, but he didn't get the jewels."

"Side quest fail," said Maddox, smiling again. "Don't leave me hanging. I've told you what I know and what I suspect. Now you tell me what's so important about the ring. We can work together on this."

"I'm not sure you've told me anything," I said. "I

think I figured everything out for myself. How about you tell me something and I'll tell you something. Then we can see about working together."

Maddox contemplated that. "Okay. What do you want to know?" he asked.

I wanted to know everything. The problem was where to start.

"When did you know Cass Temple was back in town?" I asked.

Maddox's guilty look told me everything before he said, "Almost straightaway."

"How did you know?"

"I had an idea where she might have a safe house. I've kept an eye on the place until I caught a glimpse of her a few days ago. I wasn't sure at first so I've been making spot checks. I'm reasonably sure it's her."

"Did she see you?"

"I don't think so but I can't be sure. As much as I hate to admit it, she's usually two steps ahead."

"And the safe house? Did you go inside?"

"Not yet. I didn't want to get too close in case she spooked. I've been figuring out how to get in there and take a look around while I tried to figure out why she was back."

"What…"

"My turn," he said. "You're sure it's her?"

"You saw the photos. Hair's different, and her clothing, and the big sunglasses only cover so much. Her face shape is the same. The eyes are the same if you ignore the glasses in the DMV photo." I'd seen her up close. I was sure of the resemblance. Plus, Maddox wasn't arguing. He was adding more missing pieces to my puzzle. He'd seen Cass Temple and so had I.

"Anything else to tie her to your theft?" he asked.

"Unfortunately, no."

"And she only stole one item?"

"Yes. Dad's undercover in case she comes back. As you know," I said, subtly pointing out I was aware of the real reason for his visit to Reynolds'.

"She won't come back."

"How can you be so sure?"

"She won't return to the same scene now the job's done."

"How do you know that?"

"Because she's never done it before. Whatever she stole, that was her target. Reconnaissance, in and out. What about…"

"My turn!" I interrupted. "How long have you been tracking her?"

"A long time."

"How does she know you?"

"What makes you think she does?"

"Oh, c'mon! I saw how she looked at you after she clunked Ben Rafferty over the head with a retractable baton. She knows you. You know her."

"Fine. Okay. Yes, she knows I'm onto her. We've had several run-ins."

"Why haven't you arrested her?"

"Amongst other things, not enough evidence. Everything I have on her is circumstantial. I can't arrest her until I catch her red-handed. Her saving you from Black was the closest I got to catching her with the goods on her."

"Why did she risk that? Why did she risk saving me when she knew you could have caught her?" That was the one thing I couldn't figure out. How had she known me? Aside from working the same cases, albeit from opposite ends, our only connection was Maddox.

That told me, Maddox's run-ins with her were… what? What wasn't he saying?

"I think it's my turn," said Maddox. "What about the item she stole? You said it was a ring?"

"It's a beautiful, and very expensive, vintage sapphire and diamond ring. Sounds just up her alley."

"She rarely steals for herself. What's so special about that ring?"

"Our clients bought the ring from a family with dubious connections. I'm not sure if the Reynoldses knew and the family definitely wasn't forthcoming about it when I contacted them. I found some old photos online that proves it."

"What did the Reynoldses say? Did it sound like they did their due diligence?"

"Yes, I think they thought they had. I had to dig to find the evidence I found. They could have found it too, but I don't think they went looking."

"Did they purchase anything else with the ring?"

"No, just the ring. The Reynoldses could show us photos, including some family photos the sellers gave them, but the family claimed not to have any receipts. They said the same thing to me when I spoke to them. I have concerns now that the sellers were trying to conceal the ring's origins."

Maddox gave me a long, curious look. "Tell me more."

I took a deep breath. "The sellers had World War II Nazi connections. There's a picture of the seller's mom wearing what looks like the ring at an enemy ball during the occupation. I'm wondering if they wanted to sell the ring overseas to get the cash and distance themselves from it." I paused, collecting my thoughts as I sipped the latte. The ice was almost melted and the caramel deliciously sugary. "You said that's the sort of thing that appeals to Cass Temple," I said, remembering. What had he called her? Someone who repatriated stolen goods.

A thief with a conscience.

"It could be *exactly* the sort of thing that appeals to her." Maddox drummed his fingers on the table, lost in thought as he gazed out the window. When he returned his attention to me, he said, "The question is still what's so interesting about this ring?"

"How well do you know her?" I asked, returning to the question he hadn't quite answered.

"Who's turn is it?" asked Maddox. "I thought it was mine."

"It's definitely mine. Answer the question."

"I… we…" He hesitated again and that's when I knew. It wasn't just professional. It couldn't have been the way Cass looked at him, or the look that crossed his face now. "You get to know someone well when you're tailing them," he finished lamely.

"Professionally?"

"I suppose you could say that."

"How did she know who I am?"

"She did her research into me."

"You didn't tell her?"

"Why would I do that?" he asked, stern now as his eyebrows knitted together.

"I have no idea! Why would she research you and then me?"

"To find out who I know."

I pounced on that. "Not to find out who you are?"

Again, the hesitation, then, "She knows I'm FBI. She knows it's my job to track her down and bring her in. Know thine enemy." He shrugged.

"That's what she is to you? Your enemy?"

"We're hardly on the same side. She steals stuff. I don't want her to steal stuff."

"Even though you called her something akin to a repatriation agent?"

"I think you've hit the most important nail on the head."

It was my turn to frown. "What do you mean?"

"If she's repatriating that ring… to whom is she repatriating it? And why? There's another player here and you don't know who it is."

That stopped me. He had a point and it was more important than ascertaining whether Maddox and Cass Temple were making googly eyes at each other or not.

"Damn it. I figured she might have stolen it to order but I don't know who told her to."

"Want to find out?" asked Maddox.

I narrowed my eyes. Now he was being helpful? "How?"

"Now we've teamed up, it's time we paid a visit to her safe house."

CHAPTER FOURTEEN

I insisted on following Maddox in my car. Partly because I wanted my own vehicle if I needed to hightail it out of there; and partly because I wanted to make some calls. Yet Maddox stuck to his word and made sure I could follow him easily across town, not once speeding his way through a red light to ditch me or leave me behind.

I had to admit I was pleased with this sudden progress. We were two professionals, working together on a case... and only one of us had the hots for the suspect. Not that Maddox was going to admit that, but I had a sneaking suspicion his case wasn't quite as professional as he made out. Something else was going on but he wasn't saying anything and refused to be subtly drawn into any admission.

Of course, it could be that Maddox was merely being cautious. Perhaps Cass Temple was even an occasional informant with whom he'd developed a casually friendly handler-snitch relationship.

She was pretty, intelligent, street-smart, and a

devastating challenge to the law.

Nope. It was most likely Maddox had the hots for her.

And Cass Temple?

Yes, she definitely looked at him with the eyes of someone who fought complicated feelings.

I knew how that felt... and wished I didn't.

Maddox and I were in the past and although I thought part of me would always love him, our relationship had come to a horrible, screeching end.

We'd both moved forwards.

Never though, did it feel like we'd left each other entirely behind.

Life was complicated like that.

But I wasn't jealous.

I had a terrific husband and I wanted Maddox to be my friend, with happiness of his own.

I wanted Maddox to be just as happy.

Just *not* with the criminal suspect at the center of my case.

For the first time since that fateful day when I'd taken the temping job at Green Hand Insurance, I wondered if it was a forever friendship. Solomon and Maddox got on, sometimes grudgingly, their relationship long pre-dating me knowing either of them, and my family adored him, but would Maddox's future romantic partner want me around? Would he, one day, want me to step away? Would he fade out of our lives to become a happy memory?

I didn't like to think about it.

The idea of feeling his loss was too sad.

"How's the search going?" I asked Lucas, pleased for the mental distraction of a work call while I kept an eye on Maddox's FBI-issued SUV as it hung a right.

"I got a couple of hits. The same day as the theft, the rental car stopped at Dempster Street and the occupant got out for five minutes."

"Do you know where she went?"

"No, she disappeared off camera. There're a few businesses on that block and I lost her heading south past the laundromat. Ten minutes later, the vehicle was captured turning left and heading north."

"Where did she go from there?"

"I'm still looking. I'll call you when I get an answer. I've got a program scouring for the license plate and the car but nothing yet."

"Could she have ditched the car?"

"If that were the case, I think my program would have picked it up. There haven't been any reports of any kind involving a car with that description logged with the police either."

"Does the rental company have a tracker in the car?" I asked.

"I checked and they don't in that model."

"Figures," I said. "So nothing since we lost it after it left Harmony?"

"Not yet. She may have left it in a parking garage, a private garage, or tucked it out of the way somewhere. It'll reappear eventually."

"What about changing the license plate?"

"Also a possibility, which is why my program is scouring for both the car and the plate. There've been a few false hits. I'll call you when I have something concrete but there's still the possibility she could have ditched the car entirely and switched to something else."

"Yeah, I thought of that too," I said, feeling despondent. I thanked Lucas and disconnected, calling

Solomon next.

"What's happening?" he asked.

"I've teamed up with Maddox. He thinks our thief might have a safe house here in town."

"Why the hell would he think that?"

"He's been on the lookout for Cass Temple and there's evidence to suggest she's our thief. He thinks the safe house is legit. We're on the way over there now."

"Do you need backup?"

"I don't think so. I think we'll assess the situation, poke around, and get out of there."

"Get confirmation she's definitely using the safe house and I'll send a team to watch it around the clock."

"Will do," I said, and hung up.

Maddox slowed and his blinker flickered on. He pulled over to the curb on a street of identikit glass and steel apartment buildings not far from the office-laden area bordering downtown and I followed suit. He turned and waved, indicating I should join him in his vehicle. I stuffed my purse under the seat, out of the way, grabbed thin plastic gloves to shove into my pocket and jogged over. When I settled in the passenger seat, he pointed across the street. "Temple has an apartment in that building," he said.

"How, what, where, why?"

Maddox blinked. "Narrow those questions down for me?"

"How do you know this is her safe house?"

"I told you. I've been staking it out and I saw her."

"Yes, but *how*. How did you know to stake out here?"

"I followed her and narrowed it down. Do you

really want all the boring details? It involved a lot of sitting in my car and listening to a thriller audiobook. I already downloaded the next in the series."

I looked around the SUV. There wasn't a scrap of litter to be seen and the car smelled really nice. "Your car looks remarkably tidy post-stakeout."

"I clean it."

"Oh."

"You should try it."

"I clean my car!"

Maddox frowned. "When?"

"Let's move to what," I decided, refusing to be drawn into that very judgmental question. Just because there were a few empty packets and soda cups in my car didn't make it filthy. "What made her pick this place?" I wondered, peering up at the buildings.

"The building is owned by some shell corporation. It's mostly vacation rentals and short-term leases so no permanent residents aside from a superintendent who has a first-floor apartment and small salary in exchange for maintenance and monitoring. My guess is that all makes it easy for her to hide her comings and goings."

"How long has she rented it?"

"That's two hows and a what."

I shrugged and made a motion for him to move it along.

"No idea. Her apartment is the only one with a long lease."

"Isn't that strange?"

"Very."

As we were talking, I texted the address to Lucas, asking him to find out whatever he could.

"Where..." I stopped, thinking how to rephrase the question so it made sense. "*Why* would she maintain a safe house here?"

"I suspect she has them all over the place."

"All over the country?"

"The world," he clarified.

"Sounds expensive and paranoid." As well as glamorous and exciting, but I decided not to say that in case Maddox thought I was interested in being lured to the dark side.

"Also smart. With safe houses in key hubs, Temple can travel very lightly and not worry about lugging her stuff around or losing anything. She always has a place to stay, protecting her in case of any eventualities."

I had to admit that did sound smart. "What kind of eventualities?"

"We're back to the what. Well, let's see, not everyone she steals from is as calm or non-confrontational as your clients."

"She steals from dangerous people?"

Maddox held back a laugh. "She steals from anyone."

"But how dangerous are the people we're talking about?" I pressed.

"There was a drug lord in Columbia," Maddox started. As I opened my mouth to ask for more information, he continued, "Then there was the crime boss in Italy."

My eyebrows rose as Maddox began to count on his fingers. "There was the psycho in New York, and the old lord with the sawed-off shotgun in England. I'm pretty sure she started a gang war in Mexico and I try not to think about the Russian oligarch with the desperate henchmen armed to the teeth."

"Wow."

"Do *not* be impressed by Cass Temple. She is a law

unto herself."

"No, I was thinking about her air miles. With that kind of travel, she must get upgraded every time!"

"She doesn't travel under her own identity."

"How do you know Cass Temple is even her real identity?"

"I know." Maddox was definitively confident.

"And how do you know she committed all those crimes? How can you be sure?"

"I know," he said again.

"Yes, but how…"

"I. Know."

"Great! Good information sharing!" I gave Maddox a thumbs up. I thought about it for a moment. "Since she stole from those kinds of people, stealing from a jewelry store must have been a walk in the park. And also, she can't have charged nearly as much for her services. What *does* she charge for her services?"

"Your guess is as good as mine."

"Where's her lair?"

Maddox's eyebrows popped up as he gave me a sideways look. "Where's her what?" he asked.

"Her lair. You know, the place she holes up when she wants to take a break. Thieves do take a break, right? All that excitement would make me lie low for at least a month each time."

"You've come up against all kinds of crazy and never lain low for a month."

"Which has always been a mistake. So, where is her lair?"

"Stop calling it a lair."

"You don't know, do you?"

Maddox shrugged. "I don't, but I suspect she has several *lairs* as you like to call it. One of which is over there." Maddox pointed to the apartment building he'd indicated a few minutes ago.

"Weird place to have a lair."

"Stop calling it... oh, never mind. Where would you have a lair?"

"Somewhere remote. Or glamorous. Somewhere I could get away from everyone but also see anyone coming. A tropical island with a boat gassed up and ready to go in case I needed to make a fast escape. And I'd have an amazing wardrobe."

"Why?"

"No point being a glamorous thief on a tropical island if I can't dress the part. I'm thinking bikinis in every color, linen dresses, and sexy caftans."

"There's nothing sexy about a caftan."

"You've never seen me in one. I'd put the sex back in caftan."

"You could probably have sex *in* a caftan. Those things are like wearing a tent with enough room for two."

"Multi-functional," I agreed. "Although I'm not sure how you know what it's like to wear one."

"If I want to wear a caftan, I will."

"Please don't. Should I carry a lace parasol?"

"Why?"

"Sun protection on my tropical island," I said, "but I'd get one with a sword in the handle, just in case."

"Do you know how to wield a sword?"

"No, but I don't think I should let that stop me. I don't know how to do a lot of stuff but I can figure it out."

"Much to the fear of everyone around you." Maddox checked his watch. "There's been no movement since we got here, and no recent alerts from my surveillance setup. Let's go and check it out. Maybe then we'll find out why Temple chose this apartment as her la… I am *not* going to call it that."

"Have you been inside before?" I asked, just as my phone pinged.

"No. Put your phone on *silent*."

"I will right after I read this text from Lucas. Ah! He confirms you're correct about a shell corporation owning the building. He says the shell is owned by another firm that's owned by another shell."

"That much I know."

"It was bought for cash. He also confirms an apartment is rented on a long-term basis to another shell corp." I lowered my phone. "It all seems very complicated."

"Not if you want to make sure your name stays off any record and no one can find out where you reside."

I studied the text again, reading out, "The vacation rentals are managed by a firm here in town and all the funds go through the second shell corp and the super, taxes, and utilities are paid out of that too. The firm doesn't do any other business otherwise, and once a year, a dividend is paid out to a bank account in Switzerland."

"That confirms what I already know."

"You could have said so!"

"It would be great if Lucas could keep digging since he's on the right track. Our guys hit a brick wall at that point."

I fired off a text to Lucas asking him to do that and he replied: *Done!*

"Let's pay a visit to that apartment."

We hopped out of the SUV and strolled over to the building, as casual as if we were out for a walk. The building was a neat six-story, two apartments to every floor except the penthouse. It was one of the older buildings on the block but considerable funds had been poured into its renovation. The glass-paneled doors had keypads rather than key locks and the neat strip of garden separating the building from the street was beautifully maintained with real grass, and stone pavers that led to, then around, a slim, stone bird fountain and on to a bench tucked into the hedge at the far end. It was neat, chic, and well-maintained.

"How are we going to get in?" I asked, cupping my hand over my forehead so I could peer into the lobby. Not that I could see much through the wavy glass. I stepped back and glanced up, noticing a small camera blinking in the corner.

"Easy. I rented an apartment for the night," said Maddox as he pressed four digits into the keypad. The lock clicked and he pushed the door.

"Ooh. Which one?"

"The one below the penthouse. It came with access to the elevator, stairs, and apartment."

"Way to announce you're coming," I said.

"That's why I got your mom to rent it for me. No link to me at all."

"Why did you rope my mom into this?"

"She offered! And I gave her the cash plus twenty percent."

"I never knew my mom was so entrepreneurial."

"I said she could have it for the night after we were finished. I think she and your dad are planning a romantic evening."

"I didn't need to know that. Don't tell Mom you told me in case she decides she wants to share more."

"Prude."

"I like to think of it as blissful ignorance. Do you want to know about your parents' sex life?"

"Pretty sure they don't have one. They casually greet each other once a week and return to their respective sides of the house. That's enough for both of them."

"Why don't they just divorce?"

"Why would they do that?" asked Maddox, frowning.

We headed for the elevators, finding the car waiting and rode it to the fifth floor. Hopping out, I turned to the apartments and Maddox turned to the stairs. When he didn't wait, I spun around and hurried after him. "Stairs aren't locked on this side," he said, tugging the door open, then jogging up one flight.

"But they are here," I said, my shoulders dropping at the sight of another keypad on the door. Maddox stooped to inspect it, then pulled out a small device from his pocket. He wedged it into the lock and pressed a button. The lock fizzled and began to smoke as it released. "What was that?" I asked.

"I gave it an electrical pulse that fried the circuit."

"You could have done that downstairs and saved yourself the apartment rental fee plus twenty percent."

"And alert everyone in the building that the lock was tampered with? Plus, why deprive your parents of a sexy night? Nope."

"Stop saying that," I said and shuddered.

We stepped into a broad corridor with large windows at either end, flooding the floor with light. The elevator doors were on the same wall we'd stepped through from the stairs' door but the door to the apartment was at the far end of the hall. In front of us was a tall mirror with a slim console and an arrangement of dried flowers in a large vase. I paused, reapplied a slick of lipstick, and adjusted my ponytail.

"If you're done…" prompted Maddox.

"Catching criminals is no excuse for sloppiness," I snipped as I followed him.

Another console with a similar arrangement was in front of the elevator doors. Framed pictures of generic landscapes tried to liven up the beige walls but failed.

"Is the plan to knock on the door and arrest her?" I asked.

"I feel like I should have explained the plan to you in more depth. We don't want to run into her. We want her out of the building already. Before you ask, I'm reasonably sure she is. We're going to enter…"

"Break in?" I asked.

"Enter," Maddox said slowly.

"By non-legal means?"

"The less you know, the better."

"I'm literally next to you."

"Close your eyes."

"I don't think I should."

"Why not?"

"You might tickle me."

Maddox rolled his eyes. "We're going to enter the apartment, poke around a little, and see if we can figure out what's going on. Find out who her client is, what identities she's using, and where she plans to be next."

"What are the odds she has all that written in a handy, little notebook?"

"Low. But we have to work with what we've got." Maddox inspected the keypad on the door. "Close your eyes."

"So I can't see you break in? I just saw you break in over there." I pointed to the stairs. "And, just so you know, I'm impressed that you're breaking in. Usually, that's me."

"Just close your eyes." Maddox sighed.

I closed my eyes and Maddox booped me on the nose and laughed. I shook my head, sighed, and opened my eyes in time to watch him stick his electrical pulse thingy into the keypad. The lock popped and Maddox pushed the door. He listened for a moment, then stepped inside.

"You're getting fired for this," I decided as I pulled on my gloves.

"Let's hope not."

We stepped into a small, partially open-plan lobby that was closed in on the left side with a coat closet behind sliding doors that I slid open to reveal absolutely nothing. Not a single coat. Not even a forgotten hat or a pair of slippers. The other two sides opened into an airy kitchen. White units spanned one wall with smart, integrated appliances. The counters were devoid of the usual kitchen detritus. There wasn't even a coffee pot in sight. I walked over to the refrigerator and opened it. Several bottles of water and two fresh deli lunch boxes. "The fridge is pretty empty," I said, "but the food cartons are recent." I looked around for the trash, opening doors to reveal generic pans, plates, and counter appliances. "There isn't a trash can."

Maddox paused at a doorway. "She probably disposes as she goes. Let's split up. I'll take the bedroom. You take the living space. Look under things, behind things, vent covers. Anywhere she could stash something."

"You got it."

As Maddox headed into the bedroom, I rounded

the kitchen island, running my fingers under the counter edges, then stooping to check. Of course, there wasn't anything to find. No one would hide their nefarious notebook of illegal activities under a breakfast counter. Much less, a vintage ring.

The kitchen opened directly onto a living room furnished with a long couch upholstered in gray linen and two easy chairs around a marble coffee table. A pale wood cabinet had a TV mounted on the wall above it. A bookcase occupied the corner, which was decorated with objects I could find at any chain store in the country: glossy coffee table books for luxury locations, a large seashell, and several other trinkets. The wrap-around windows showed a nice view of the city with barely any overlooking windows. As far as privacy went, any occupant would find it here.

I started with the cabinet since it was the only enclosed furnishing. The sole thing inside it was a TV remote. I pressed and prodded at the insides, disappointed not to find any false walls.

Moving over to the couch, I was preparing to pull out the cushions when I saw it.

A mug of half-drunk tea on a side table, only visible now that I was in front of the couch.

I pressed the back of my hand to the mug.

"Maddox!"

"Did you find something?" he called back.

"Yeah." I said, straightening to turn slowly, every bit of me on alert. "Someone's here."

Maddox burst out of the bedroom, his gun drawn. "Where?"

I pointed to the mug. "This tea is still warm." I looked around. "There's nowhere to hide in here and I already checked all the kitchen cabinets. How could she get out without us seeing her?" I asked. "We came through the only doors."

"There must be a concealed exit. Head out into the hallway and see if you can spot anything."

"Okay," I said, feeling skeptical. Safe houses, secret doors... usually, this kind of fantasy was my job to think up. It felt weird that Maddox was rolling with it.

"I'm going to try and figure it out from this side."

"What if she's still here?"

"She probably bailed before we even got up here. We might have tipped our hands."

"There was a camera over the entry," I said. "She probably got an alert and saw us and took off. She was ready to go." I was already walking across the room, aiming for the main door, wondering if there was anywhere to hide in the corridor.

"Figures," said Maddox, his voice almost lost as I hurried out the front door. There wasn't anything to hide behind or under out here and I tapped all the way along the dividing wall. The mirror was firmly fixed to the wall. I pulled out the console tables and checked behind the picture frames even though the idea of her wiggling out from a hole behind them was ludicrous. Then I turned, noticing something from the corner of my eye. There was a panel in the wall between the elevator doors and the stairs, around waist height. I pressed it and it popped open, so I peered into the darkness. I flicked on the flashlight in my phone and inched forwards, then a little further, uncertain what I was looking at, my head and shoulders now inside.

Just as the chute became clear, my legs lifted abruptly, my head dropped with the sudden inversion of my body, and I was forcibly thrust by a firm shove.

All I could do was scream.

CHAPTER FIFTEEN

"Why do you have two marshmallows shoved up your nose?"

"Out of all the questions you could ask, that's what you chose to go with?" I stifled the urge to yell or sigh, mostly because I wasn't sure I could do either with my packed nose. A few minutes ago, I found myself upside-down on the corridor floor, my face wet, and a trilling near my left ear. It had taken only seconds to right myself, realize my nose was bleeding profusely, and that the trilling came from my phone, which had preceded me down the chute.

"Why does one of them have a string attached?"

"My nose was bleeding. I had to stop it," I said, my voice weirdly nasal.

"Is that a—" Maddox stopped and looked like he was going to choke "—a tampon?"

"They're very absorbent, okay?! I didn't have anything else I could use to stop the bleeding!"

We were standing in the doorway to the stairwell at the end of the corridor and even though I'd staggered to the door with relative ease, I thought I was in mild shock. When Maddox pulled out his phone and snapped a photo I didn't have the will to insist he delete it.

"Someone shoved me down the laundry chute!"

"I don't think it's a laundry chute," said Maddox, bypassing me and peering into the hatch that had opened in the wall. It took every ounce of me not to send him hurtling down headfirst like I had. "Look here. It's an escape route," he said.

I followed him, noting a smear of blood on the hatch and the slide when he pointed his phone flashlight in and up. "I think this is Temple's fast way out."

"It was certainly fast," I said, shaking off the terror I'd felt at falling and banging my face while sliding into the unknown. "Where are we?"

"Second floor. I heard you scream from inside the apartment just as I figured out Temple's escape route. You disappeared!"

"It must have been her who shoved me inside!" My jaw wobbled and I touched my nose gingerly, worried I was about to cry. My nose hurt and my cheek throbbed. But worst of all, Cass Temple had gotten away! If it was even her but who else would do such a thing to me?

"I got a glimpse of her dashing into the elevator as I was figuring how to get out. That tall mirror and console opposite the stairwell concealed a secret entrance. On the apartment side, it was hidden by the bookcase in the living area. I found a switch that opened it and there's just enough space for a person to step inside and conceal themself. I think she stepped in there as soon as we triggered her alarm."

"So she was already inside the bookcase as you busted the stairwell lock?"

"That's my guess."

"Then she waited until we were inside the apartment and the coast was clear on the corridor to make her escape. Why didn't she take the chute?"

"It's probably just a backup option in case the elevator and stairwell didn't pan out. My guess is she stayed put to listen in and find out what we knew, and then when you went into the corridor, she saw an opportunity to get you out of the way and distract me and took it, making a clean escape."

"That's smart," I decided.

"Don't go getting all impressed by her!"

"I'm not!" Well, maybe just a bit, but Maddox didn't need to know that.

Maddox peered at me. "Are you okay?" he asked, raising a gentle hand to my cheek. I winced at the brush of his fingertips against my cheekbone. "Do you need to go to the ER?"

"I'm fine. I'm... wait... why didn't you go after her?"

"I thought about it for a split second but I was more worried about you."

"You passed up catching Cass Temple to help me?" My chin trembled and now I really thought I was going to cry.

"Yeah." He paused, lifting one shoulder in a casual shrug like it were nothing to let a jewel thief go. "Also, there was no way I was catching her. Let's head back up and see if there's anything we missed. She was sloppy in forgetting the mug. She might have left something else."

"Fingerprints?"

"Certainly but we already have those anyway, not that she ever leaves them at a crime scene." Maddox inclined his head, indicating I should follow him into the stairwell and up the stairs. As we stepped out onto the penthouse floor, I stopped dead. The mirror and console table were both two feet to the right, leaving a large gap in the wall through which I could see the apartment's living room.

"This is so clever," I said, pulling the mirror, finding it slid easily on heavy duty tracks. I stepped into the small enclosure and Maddox followed, pulling the sliding mirror door partially closed behind him, not quite enough room for both of us. In the dim light, he pointed to the latch that had held the mirror securely closed. I looked up, surprised that I could see through the mirror to the hallway.

"Two-way mirror," he said.

"I reapplied my lipstick in that mirror!" I pulled a face at the idea of Cass Temple just inches away on the other side of the mirror. Had she held back laughter? Had she gazed quizzically at me as I adjusted my hair? Or was she too busy planning the rest of her escape?

"There's a latch in the back of the bookcase," he continued, "it's covered by a sliding panel that matches the rest of the wood." We slid through the small opening into the apartment, the bookcase opening just wide enough for us to shimmy through. Maddox closed it, then demonstrated sliding the thumb-sized panel back and depressing the latch so the bookcase opened. "See how the shelves aren't as deep as the bookcase? Anyone would think it had been built to cover pipes, not so a person could hide inside it."

I stared at the setup for a minute. "This is so cool! It's like a childhood dream to have secret panels, and bookcases that lead into secret rooms and secret doors!"

"I wish I could take a shot every time you said 'secret'," grumbled Maddox.

"I love this!" I said, clapping my hands. "Does she have secret doors in all her lairs?"

"I wish I knew but probably, and this setup is pretty simple."

"It's great!" There was one secret panel in my house, concealed in a closet where Solomon kept a stash of weapons, but now I had the urge to suggest we add more. Although the lack of handles and knobs in the kitchen pretty much made all our cabinets secret doors, and it had taken me several weeks to memorize what each one held. I still occasionally lost the refrigerator.

Before Maddox told me to stop fangirling our chief suspect, I stepped into the small enclosure again, running a gloved finger in the light coating of dust. "This hasn't been used in a long time," I said, showing him my dusty finger. "But there's a large dust-free patch on the floor."

"That must be where she kept her go-bag. Makes sense to keep it out of the way in case the apartment is used or infiltrated in her absence. It's likely she already has a new identity set up and cash and clothes to keep her going until she leaves town. Damn!"

"She's very resourceful," I said. Not only that, but she had access to a lot of resources. Fake identity documents that passed close inspection cost a pretty sum, leaving a stack of cash in a rarely-used apartment meant she had access to other funds and could afford to leave it until needed. Plus, there were the funds to purchase buildings like this.

It left me with one clear conclusion.

I was in the wrong business!

"How does one get into a life of crime?" I asked.

"No," said Maddox.

"What?"

"I'm not helping you!"

"I didn't ask!"

"We both know that's what you meant and it's only by sheer luck that your temp agency placed you at the insurance firm I was working undercover and brought you into fighting crime before you turned to it."

"You say that like I was teetering between the two."

Maddox raised his eyebrows and gave me a knowing stare. "Weren't you?"

"No!" Well, not entirely.

"You were technically charging the temp agency for all the time you spent playing on the computer, shopping online, and sneaking off to get fancy coffees. You were one bored step from embezzling!"

I gasped and put a hand to my heart.

Maddox's lip wobbled and then he burst out laughing. "I couldn't keep a straight face," he said between guffaws as he held his sides.

I smacked his shoulder. "I could never become a criminal! Not with my family!"

"I know. You'd bring everyone down with you. You'd turn them from a well-known police family into a network of dirty cops in your bid to create a crime empire."

"Aww, you think I'd have an empire!" Take that, one-woman show, Cass Temple!

Maddox's laughter subsided and he shook his head. "Only you would consider that a compliment."

My phone pinged, a message appearing from

Lucas.

"Lucas says the vehicle hired by Cass's alias is on the move," I said while touching my nose gingerly. It didn't feel any worse but I still didn't want to pull out my makeshift plug.

"She must have not set up access to another vehicle," said Maddox. "Did Lucas say where she was headed."

"No, only that the camera that picked her up is two blocks from here, heading north."

"Can he track her while we finish up here?"

I was already tapping a message into my phone. Another one returned almost immediately. "He will," I said. "Wanna tear this place apart?"

"I doubt the ring is here," he said. "She won't leave that behind."

"I figured but maybe there's something else."

We pulled out the couch cushions and checked inside pillows. Maddox swung the TV on its big arm out from the wall and pulled out the unit, checking behind them both. He took pictures off walls and I opened every kitchen cabinet, checking more thoroughly this time. When he took the bedroom, I headed into the bathroom.

Seeing my reflection halted any further movement. My cheek was starting to smudge purple and green, and dried blood covered my nose and chin, also spotting at my neckline. I looked like a cannibal who didn't like the smell. Easing the snapped tampon from my nostrils, relieved that the blood had stopped, I wrapped the evidence in my gloves then tissue. I washed my face with my hands and a glob of hand soap. Searching the wall-mirrored cabinet, I was disappointed to find Cass didn't have the good grace to leave moisturizer. I was clean-faced but my skin was dehydrated. Running my finger carefully down the bridge of my nose, I couldn't find any sign of a break and the pain was almost gone.

The bathroom was as devoid of secret compartments and stashes as the rest of the apartment, minus the false bookcase exit.

When Maddox and I stepped out at the same time, I knew from his face that he'd come up just as empty.

"Nothing?" I asked.

"Nothing," he confirmed. "Not even discarded clothes. She was very careful. And you look better. You looked like a maniac."

"Thanks for letting me walk around like that. Are you sure it was her you saw? Really sure?"

Maddox shook his head. "I only caught a glimpse of a flash of clothes as she got into the elevator. I think it was her but I'm not sure I would swear it was in court. Lucas's camera capture of the vehicle is the clincher for me. That had to be her."

"Where would she go from here?" I asked. "What's her usual modus operandi?"

"Backup safe house," he said without thinking about it. "Possibly a backup vehicle or a go-bag stashed somewhere else that she needs to get to. We can guess she already has her go-bag and since she's using the same vehicle, I assume she already has somewhere to relocate to. She might ditch the car on the way. She'll know it's impractical to keep a hold of it now."

"You tracked her this far? Did you see her go anywhere else?"

"No." Maddox ran a hand over his hair, ruffling it in opposing directions. "Much as I hate to admit it, even finding this safe house was one in a million luck. Are you really okay? You do look a lot better. You were white as a sheet in the stairwell except for the... you know." He waved a hand across my chin.

"It's the lack of blood smeared across my face," I said. "It's done wonders for my healthy appearance."

"And the lack of a tampon up your nose."

"One day you'll be glad to know that trick."

"Unfortunately, that'll be the same day I remember I don't carry tampons."

"I have no idea where to go from here," I said.

"Don't suggest sanitary pads. I'm not carrying them either. I'll leave some in the bathroom for lady friends but I draw the line at carrying them."

"No, I meant I don't know where to go from here in finding Cass," I said, wondering which lady friends he referred to. "We've scoured her apartment and found nothing. We know she's on the move but there's nothing we can do until Lucas calls in another sighting."

"One thing we should do is get out of here," said Maddox. "And maybe let your parents know their sexy night away should be postponed."

"You can deal with that," I decided since I never wanted to hear about it again. "You're not wearing gloves and I had to take mine off so I hope you have an explanation for our fingerprints too. I'm going to Lily's. I need a drink and snack to raise my blood sugar levels."

"You didn't lose that much blood."

"I could have died!"

"On a slide? You've dealt with worse than that." Maddox wrapped an arm around my shoulders and gave me a squeeze. "It's a miracle you've survived thus far. Today is just a mere blip in your chaotic life. After you." Maddox waved towards the door. I headed out and Maddox didn't bother pulling the door shut behind us. We rode the elevator down—Maddox pressing and knocking on every panel in the car just in case—and walked out of the building like nothing had ever happened. Yet as the door swung shut behind us, I noticed the camera panning to catch our departure.

Someone was watching us.

"Solomon can get a team to watch over this building," I told him.

"No need. She won't come back now. I'm going to head back to the office and work on those shell corporations," said Maddox. "Perhaps we'll get some new information."

"Will you share when you find out?"

"Of course. Happy to keep collaborating."

We said our goodbyes and I drove to Lily's bar. I parked out front and went inside. She took one look at me and told me there was a fresh t-shirt in her office.

"What's wrong with this one?" I asked.

"It has blood droplets on it. I hope they're not yours!"

"They're mine."

"You look far too pleased about that. Is that a bruise on your cheek?"

"Let me freshen up and I'll fill you in."

Lily tossed me the office key and I walked into the back, letting myself in. There was a stack of new Lily's Bar t-shirts on a shelf so I grabbed one, pulled off my t-shirt, and slipped the fresh one over my head, careful not to knock my nose or cheek. I reapplied lipstick, added a sweep of mascara, adjusted my ponytail again, and stuffed the dirty t-shirt into my purse as I returned to the bar and took a seat.

"Tell me everything," said Lily, so I did, and by the

215

time I reached the end, she was wide-eyed.

"She is so cool," said Lily. "The disguises, the hideouts, the secret doors, the go-bags! Her ethics! I'm rooting for her!"

"Right?" I agreed, delighted someone shared my enthusiasm. "The only thing making me not entirely like her is I haven't caught her…"

"Yet," interjected Lily. She paused to take an order and once she'd placed two glasses of wine on the bar and taken payment, she waved for me to continue.

"Yet," I agreed, "and she also stole something that didn't belong to her. And Maddox still hasn't come clean with what else he knows about her. I know there's more to the story but he's keeping silent even though we're working together."

Lily asked, "Which bothers you more?"

"I'm not sure. Not catching her. No. Maddox withholding something. No. Definitely not catching her."

Lily folded her arms. "There's only one way around that."

"What's that?"

"You have to catch her and get her to tell you everything. Remind her of girl code."

"I already figured out that the ring she stole might have Nazi connections, but I won't know for certain until she confesses, which seems unlikely now, after she shoved me down an escape chute."

"I like her less for doing that. *That* was *not* girl code. She can consider her invitation to join our gang rescinded. But I meant she should tell you everything about her and Maddox. Do you think they're lovers?" she asked, leaning in, her face full of conspiracy.

"I don't know. Maybe." I let out a huff and my

shoulders groaned. "I'm not sure how though when he seems so intent on arresting her. Ending the night in handcuffs is not conducive to a hot date."

"Speak for yourself," said Lily with a raise of her eyebrows and shake of her head. "So what now? Are you going to sit at my bar drinking soda and eating chips for the rest of the case?"

"No. I'm pondering my next steps." I paused as Ruby walked through to the bar, tying her bar apron strings behind her.

"Hey there," she said, beaming when she saw me, which was the kind of reception I hoped to get from everyone. Then she winced. "What happened to your face?"

Never mind.

"You should have seen her when she walked in," said Lily. She waved a hand over my upper body. "This is an improvement."

"Thanks," I muttered.

"Did you get into a fight?" asked Ruby.

"No. I'll let Lily fill you in later. I don't want to talk about it." Mostly because it was too embarrassing.

"I can't wait. Until then, let me get you a wine," she said, already reaching for a glass.

"Perfect. I am officially off duty," I decided as my nose twinged once more.

CHAPTER SIXTEEN

In the morning, I felt rejuvenated. My nose was fine, my cheek shades of blue and green, but not nearly as bad as I'd anticipated. The only signs Solomon had been home was that his side of the bed was warm when I awoke, the shower still damp, and a note on the mirror reading *Good morning, sleepyhead.* Smiling, I stuffed it into my nightstand drawer.

My phone was blank without any notices. Taking that as a bad omen, I headed into the office, eating toast in the car on the way, brushing crumbs from my thin denim jeans. On the passenger seat next to me lay my purse, my small gun inside. After yesterday, I was taking no chances.

For two hours, I puttered around the office, reading and rereading my case notes, texting Maddox for an update, making additional searches and doodling possibilities. Finally, Lucas shooed me out of his office, saying he would call when he had something to tell me.

Without any other clues to investigate, I called Lily and suggested brunch. When she proposed I join her and Ruby at the bar at opening time, I headed over there.

"You look sore," said Lily, waving me in.

"I feel okay."

"You also look fed up."

"Not a single hit on Cass Temple." I slid onto the stool and drummed my fingers on the bar. "Lucas and Maddox are both looking for her."

"They'll find her," said Lily decisively as Ruby appeared at the bar, carrying three dishes on a tray.

She set it down, scents of hot tomatoes and enticing spices wafting up, saying, "Our new cook is testing out shakshuka so when Lily said you were coming over, I had her make some. We can eat and rant at the same time."

"That's the best idea I've heard all day," I said.

"The day is still young," remarked Lily and Ruby laughed.

"If I don't find the thief and figure out what's going on, I may never find that ring," I said, "and time is ticking."

"You had a rough break yesterday, but you did make a breakthrough," Ruby reminded me. "You know who the thief is. That's amazing."

"Is it?" I wondered, "because all it seems to have resulted in are more questions."

"Eat," said Lily.

When I pushed my dish away, the taste on my tongue a glorious reminder of how nice the food at Lily's Bar was, I was ready to give my compliments to the cook; but as I opened my mouth, my phone rang. "It's Lucas," I said, pressing the phone to my ear and crossing my fingers for good news. "Hey," I said.

"I've followed the silver hatchback as far as I can,"

he said, "and I have a rough location for you."

I sat up straighter. "Shoot."

"I lost it last night so I figured it didn't leave the last known area. After a few false leads didn't pan out, I've pinpointed where all the traffic cameras and local businesses' cameras are, and I think you should search between the 800 and 1600 blocks on Century Street. I wish I could be more precise, but that's what the data suggests and I couldn't find any trace of the vehicle leaving Century after it was captured by the 800-block camera. Your thief's vehicle is somewhere there."

"How long ago was that?"

"Last night and it hasn't been captured on any cameras since. When I realized the vehicle hadn't gone through any of the major junctions, I felt sure it had stopped somewhere but it's a fairly popular car so I figured maybe she switched plates and that threw up a bunch of false hits. I'm still monitoring the area although the lead might have gone dead already. She could have ditched it in a high traffic area, knowing if we figured out her vehicle, we'd waste time hunting for it while she switched vehicles or made off on foot. I'm sorry, it's the best I can do."

"You're amazing," I told him. "I'm heading there now."

"Do you want me to update Solomon? He's at Reynolds', conferring with your dad on what the new security system needs."

"No, don't disturb them until I have something concrete. I'll head over there, circle around, and see if I can find the vehicle. If the lead looks live, I'll call for backup."

"Got it," said Lucas and disconnected.

"You have something," said Lily. She rested her

arms on the bar and looked across at me. "Tell me again Ben Rafferty isn't back in town?"

"According to Maddox, he's not but Lucas does have a lead on our ring thief. Lucas narrowed down where she might be. I'm going to head over there now while there's still a slim chance of catching her." I hopped off my tall stool and grabbed my purse, searching for my wallet so I could pay.

"Save your money," said Lily, already unwrapping her bar apron. "I'll get my purse."

"You're working," I pointed out.

Lily glanced over at Ruby. "Can you cover the bar while I fight crime?" she asked.

"I was born for this," said Ruby. "You go nail that... wait... who are you nailing?"

"No one except our respective husbands," said Lily. "Right?" Under her breath, she added, "Words I never thought I'd say."

"You don't even need to ask! We're going to catch a thief and hopefully nail her to the wall," I said.

"Sounds painful," said Ruby. She pointed to my face, saying, "But if she did that to you, she deserves it."

"Let's go." I waved at Lily to hurry as she dashed to her office, the apron strings flapping in her hand. Less than a minute later, she was back, sliding around the bar, her purse slung over her shoulder, and racing past me to the door. I hightailed it after her, knowing that she wasn't going to get far without the address.

Unfortunately, Lucas had picked the wrong day to send me to Century Street. The rush hour subsiding but traffic was still building up thanks to a crew digging up pipes along three blocks, and a temporary signal system, leaving traffic crawling.

"We need to look out for a silver hatchback anywhere from now," I said as we rolled through a junction.

"You take your side, I'll take my side," said Lily. "And if we don't see it, pull a U-turn and we'll check again."

"This might be a fool's errand. This stretch is a good place to abandon a vehicle and she could call an Uber, hop on a bus, or even walk. Maddox thinks she had an alternate plan in case she had to abandon her safe house."

"Where would she go from here?" Lily's head was turned away as she scanned the parking lot of the strip mall.

"The railway, or a bus station, or to another vehicle. Maddox thinks she might have a backup safe house."

"My money's on that. I bet she's holed up, thinking her plan to throw you down the chute and run away was so awesome—which it was—that no one could track her here."

"That too," I said, liking Lily's optimism. "Except the bit about throwing me down the chute."

"Agreed. We hate her for that. There's a silver hatchback," said Lily, pointing. "Right there! In front of the 7-Eleven!"

I flipped the blinker on and pulled into the parking lot, inching past the vehicle. "Wrong vehicle," I said, my shoulders dropping with disappointment at the older model. I pulled out onto Century Street and resumed our journey.

Three blocks, and two false calls later, we were still rolling when Lily jumped and bounced in her seat. "There!" she squeaked. "That's it!"

I slowed, ignoring the honking from the car behind

me, and stretched my neck. "That could be it!" I said, suddenly thrilled. I'd started to feel the search was a quest that couldn't end but seeing the little, silver car parked between two large SUVs lifted my spirits. I drove to the end of the block, pulled in and circled back, crawling past the car. This section of the street had parking on both sides, as well as a large lot where one could easily lose their vehicle. I drove to the end of the section the hatchback was in before pulling into an empty space.

"The car looked empty," said Lily.

"Unsurprisingly. She could be nearby," I said hopefully as I scanned the buildings. There was a mini-mart, computer repair store, accountant office, dentist, kids' clothes store, Italian diner, and a travel agency. There were also several bus stops, people crowding each one, with destinations that spanned the city. "There," I said, pointing to the motel that took up nearly a third of the block. The L-shaped motel comprised three stories, the doors accessed via open corridors overlooking the street. The side wing occupying the end of the lot had balconies with views of the courtyard behind both wings. "She could be staying there."

"It's not exactly the kind of place a high-end jewel thief would stay," said Lily. She wrinkled her nose. "How many stolen diamonds does it take to pay for a year here?"

"It's exactly the kind of place a jewel thief would stay," I countered. "It's cheap, inconspicuous, and this section of the street is always busy. Plus, it's got easy access links to the rest of town. The motel employees probably don't ask too many questions. Let's check it out. If there's no luck there, we should try the travel agency next. She might have bought tickets to go somewhere else."

Before we headed towards the motel, I insisted on stopping first at the hatchback. The plates were correct and so was the model. I tried the handles on the passenger side, finding they didn't budge, and peered inside. Not a single scrap of litter had been left there. No bags, no leaflets, no packaging. She'd been careful but had she been careful enough? I touched the hood. Cold. She hadn't returned to the vehicle since she parked. Rounding the vehicle, I tested the driver's side and the door opened. I checked inside but all I found were the keys in the footwell, like they'd been dropped and forgotten.

"What are the odds she deliberately left the door unlocked and the keys on the mat?" I wondered.

"Dumb thing to do. This street is known for car thefts. She's lucky she didn't leave her purse."

"I think she wanted the car to be stolen," I said, looking around. Was it sheer luck that car thieves hadn't discovered it during the night? Or was it my luck that we'd gotten here first? Was she brazen enough to drive to her next safe house, assuming the car would be stolen quickly and send us on a wild goose chase tracking it?

"She must be eating somewhere if she's staying here," said Lily, glancing toward the diner. "I don't see any cameras."

"Probably why she picked this area to dump the car. Or even if she *is* staying nearby, she wouldn't eat too close to the car. She could have picked up groceries to keep in the room, especially if this motel has kitchenettes for guests." We moved onto the sidewalk, resuming our path to the motel before we hit the travel agency.

The motel's lobby was sparse but clean with tiled floors, a small seating area with wingback chairs, a large, fake, potted monstera, and a simple, wooden reception desk positioned in front of two doors with small, metal plates. One read "Employees Only" and the other read "Luggage Store". On the counter were two terminals. Plexiglass stands had been set up on each end with neat stacks of pamphlets advertising things to do in town and day trips. A side door led outside onto a paved path with a sign indicating room numbers. A faint lemon scent hung in the air.

"How can I help you?" asked the desk clerk, adjusting her ponytail as she walked through the employee door.

I started to open my mouth, then realized I didn't have a name to ask for. It was unlikely that Cass Temple would check in under her own name and she could reasonably assume her Sally Smith identity was burned.

"I wanted to inquire about room rates," I said. "And availability for tonight."

"You're in luck. We do have some rooms available. We have a queen for eighty dollars and a deluxe room for ninety-five dollars."

"What does the deluxe come with?" asked Lily.

"Two queen beds, a table and two chairs, a kitchenette with hotplate, microwave, mini fridge, and a small sink. Plus, all rooms have their own private bathrooms and showers with hairdryers. Would you like to make a booking?"

"I'm not sure. We were supposed to meet a friend and think she might have checked in yesterday. Perhaps you recognize her? She's around my height and my age..." I stumbled to a stop. I couldn't be sure about her hair or eye color or even the way she dressed. Just how many disguises did Cass Temple have? And how many names?

"Could you be more specific?" asked the clerk.

"Oh, sure. Her name is Sally Smith but she might be using her married name," I added quickly, needing a name to give that I could easily alter.

The clerk didn't reach for the computer keyboard. Instead, she said, "I'm sorry. We can't confirm whether someone is or isn't a guest at the motel. It's against policy."

"But can we leave a message?"

"Why don't you call your friend?" said the clerk, tilting her head. Not quite a challenge but definitely suspicious.

"She hates telephones," said Lily. "She'll leave me hanging for days. She's impossible." Lily wearily shook her head and added, "I have unresolved trauma about rejection. I can't face phoning her."

"I'm sorry," said the clerk, looking anything but.

"That's okay. Thanks for your time," said Lily.

"You can book online if you prefer," said the clerk, the barest wisp of a smile reaching her mouth but not her eyes. "And have a great day!"

"How are we supposed to find her if we can't even find out if she's staying there?" said Lily. We stepped outside and I had to shield my eyes from the sun.

"The clerk didn't say no one checked in yesterday," I decided.

"She didn't even check," pointed out Lily.

"True." I considered that as I pursed my lips in thought. There was no way I could verify a name or even what Cass Temple might have looked like yesterday, or even today but perhaps… I glanced at the hatchback and back toward the hotel, an idea forming in my head. What if the car hadn't been abandoned? Cass might have intended for it to be stolen but what if she really was nearby and planned on using it again? Perhaps I could make her appear on *my* timeline, not hers. And if not… well, I had insurance. "I have an idea. Wait here." I took off at a jog before Lily could ask me, dissuade me, or, even worse… encourage me.

CHAPTER SEVENTEEN

I got into my car and gunned the engine, pulling out and steering towards the hatchback. A spot had opened up next to it. I aimed for it and purposefully cut the corner, deftly smashing the hatchback's headlamp and scratching the silver paint.

I reversed my car, killed the engine, and hopped out. "Oops!" I squeaked for the benefit of the elderly couple strolling past. "Oh no! I better get the insurance details of that car! My bad!"

Hopping back into my car, I pulled into the space, properly this time, and giving the hatchback a wide berth. When I locked up, I examined the smattering of glass on the blacktop and looked around, as if still searching for the owner. Anyone watching me, like the elderly couple who had climbed into their car opposite me and not moved, would think that was exactly what I was doing; but unfortunately for me, no woman dashed across the parking lot to scold me for damaging her vehicle.

Lily, waiting on the sidewalk, frowned at me. "That

looked deliberate," she said when I jogged over to her.

"It was," I whispered. "And now the clerk will be obliged to call down the registered owner. If she checked in to the hotel, she could have asked them to validate her parking," I said, pointing at the sign in the window telling motel guests the rules that exempted them from the same parking lot fees as everyone else. "If she's not there, then I guess we'll have to wait. Come on!" I headed towards the motel as Lily hurried to catch up.

"Hello!" called the receptionist, still smiling like a robot. "How can I help you? Are you checking in?"

"Still no," I said, coming to a stop in front of the desk. "I've had a little accident in the parking lot and damaged another vehicle. Could you check to see if the owner is here so we can exchange insurance details?"

A flicker of a frown then, "Oh, gosh. Yes, of course. Are you okay?"

"Absolutely fine," I assured her. "But I want to do the right thing and get the damage paid for. I have to make sure I hand over my insurance details."

"I can check to see if the vehicle is registered to one of our guests if you give me the license plate."

I made a show of checking the photo I'd taken and reeled off the plate as the clerk typed it into her computer. A moment later, she said, "No, sorry, we don't have any vehicles with that plate registered here."

"Oh no!" I pulled a face.

"Let me see that photo again." She beckoned with her hand and I handed her my phone. "That definitely belongs to one of our guests. I saw the driver when she arrived. She must have forgotten to register the car. I'll call her now."

My heart did a small leap of delight. As the clerk

picked up the phone, Lily and I exchanged subtle but pleased smiles but as the clerk's call lengthened, I felt my resolve waver.

"The owner is on her way," said the clerk. She leaned in, adding, "She didn't sound too mad about it although I explained she might get a fine for not validating her parking. I hope everything gets sorted out amicably."

I thanked her and we moved over to the small seating area by the window, out of the way of the two men entering, pulling large suitcases, and griping about their work.

"Lily, there's a flaw in our plan," I said, my face paling.

"You don't have good insurance?"

"No, Cass Temple knows me. She knows what I look like. There's no way she won't bolt the moment she sees me." I turned to Lily, "But she doesn't know you."

"Oh! I can pretend to be the driver who hit her car."

"Exactly. I just need to hide until you get her on her own. Then I'll spring out and…" I paused.

Instead of sitting on one of the hard chairs, I stood, my hands on my hips, facing the window, watching the world go by as I made a plan. Well, all I could see of the world was an elderly lady walking an equally elderly dog and a youth pushing another youth in a shopping cart. It was only as I scanned the wider area that I noticed a familiar-looking black SUV across the street, parked on the corner and facing the hotel.

"And what?"

I squinted, dropping my purse onto the vacant chair, certain Maddox and Farid were in the front seats of the SUV. Maddox had a straw in his mouth, sipping from a takeout cup. Farid was munching, his hand dipping into a bag of chips. I watched them for a few long seconds before I turned to tell Lily there was another problem with our plan.

Just as I was about to open my mouth, the side door opened and in stepped a woman with shoulder-length, dark blond hair, dressed simply in blue jeans and a cream linen shirt with the sleeves rolled to her elbow, casually elegant. The door closed softly behind her as she made a beeline for the reception, her back to us. I nudged Lily and nodded towards the woman, then turned away, certain she couldn't see my face reflected in the window.

"Is that her?" she asked.

"It could be. She's about the right age. It's hard to tell without getting closer."

"Try and look cool," said Lily, giving herself a little shake. "No, Lexi, not like that."

"I didn't do anything!"

"Then you should definitely try."

"I am cool," I insisted.

"No one who is actually cool says they're cool."

That was a conundrum I didn't know how to deal with so I held back a sigh and waited as the woman walked past the reception and out through the main doors.

"It's not her," said Lily, a note of disappointment in her voice.

I glanced over my shoulder as the woman reached the hatchback and stooped to examine it. "It is," I said, thrilled as she inspected the head lamp and shook her head, then rose, turned, and returned to the motel, apparently not at all distraught at the damage I'd purposefully inflicted.

"I'm going to hide here," I said as I ducked behind the big wing chair, squashing my body between it, the wall, and the large, fake monstera. "We'll confirm and I'll call for backup."

The woman stepped back inside the motel's reception and walked over to the receptionist who was handing keys to the new guests. She glanced around and, through the plastic leaves, I noted the sweetheart face and jawline, unmistakably Cass Temple.

She and the receptionist exchanged a few words and the receptionist pointed to Lily. Cass nodded and moved towards us.

"It doesn't look like there's any serious damage," said Cass, stopping short of Lily as I wedged myself further behind the chair, out of sight. "I don't think we need to get our insurance companies involved with this. There's a mechanic down the road that can probably fix the headlamp."

I reached for my purse to grab my phone and stopped... my purse was on the wing chair, out of reach. If I stuck my hand around, she'd see me and spook.

"I really should go through my insurance. I don't want you out of pocket for my mistake," said Lily, continuing the ruse easily. "Let me take your details. I'm Lily... Lil... uh, Lilian Shu... Schumacher! You are?"

"It's fine, really. You shouldn't have to incur any penalty from your insurance for a little mistake like that."

"I really should pay and we really should exchange details," Lily pressed. I risked popping my head up. Cass was already retreating, Lily on her heels. "I guess

I could write you a check for the mechanic, if you prefer?"

"Really, there's no need. It's a rental and I paid extra for their insurance."

"Oh, gosh, well, great. Should I call the rental company and explain? If you give me your name, I'm sure I can explain what happened and say it wasn't your fault."

"There's no…" Through the plastic leaves, I watched Cass pause, narrowing her eyes and stepping slightly forwards, looking beyond the seating area.

I shot a look over my shoulder, wondering what had grabbed her attention. Across the road, Maddox and Farid had gotten out of their car and were making their way across the street.

"Shit!" hissed the woman. She hardly flashed a look at Lily as she turned on her heel.

"But…"

"Don't worry about the car," said Cass, her back to Lily, speed-walking to the side entrance. She pulled open the door and, with one last look behind her, sprinted.

Across the street, Maddox and Farid began to move faster.

"Let's go," I said, pushing the chair out of the way in my haste to rise and grab my purse. We ran after her, catching the door before it closed. I wrenched it open as the receptionist called out, "Hey!"

"Right behind you!" called Lily as I outpaced her.

Cass Temple took off between the buildings, running at top speed, leaving us no choice but to pound after her while I hooked my purse over my head and shoulder. Across the street, Maddox and Farid's progress had been halted by the flying traffic, leaving them stranded in the middle of the street until the light changed. Whatever questions I had about how they'd managed to also find Cass would have to wait.

Cass rounded the corner and I tore after her, seeing the dead end looming. But instead of turning back, she ran full tilt, leaping to pull down the rickety emergency stairs, and clambering up them with no concern for the noise she made. I grabbed the handrail and turned, skidding on the ground, following. She was almost at the top floor with nowhere to go. I increased my pace, determined to catch her.

Cass was at the end of the walkway, leaning forwards and looking around when I climbed the last few rungs.

"I need to talk to you," I said, stepping out to the open walkway on the third floor. "I think you know what it's about."

Cass glanced back. "No, thanks," she said, far from the friendly demeanor she'd exhibited when coming to my rescue only a couple of weeks ago.

"You stole the ring."

"What ring?" Her impassive face revealed nothing.

"The antique ring from Reynolds'. I know it was you and I think I know why."

"What're you going to do? Arrest me?" she scoffed.

"I'm a PI. I can't do that but I can call the cops. Or you can give me the ring. Or…"

Cass backed up, assessing me as I stepped closer. She was trapped. Maddox and Farid would be here any moment. There was no way out. "Or what?" she challenged.

"Or you can answer to the FBI." I didn't dare glance behind me to see where they were but I was sure they'd followed me. So where were they? And where was Lily? I had to hope that meant Lily had stopped, realizing the value of pointing Maddox and Farid in our direction.

"What makes you think that even if I did steal the ring, I'd still have it?" She fixed me with a challenging look, daring me to share what I knew.

"I know you have it. There's no reason for you to still be in town if you already handed it off so I don't think the delivery has happened yet. That's what you planned to do, isn't it? You stole it to order but you made mistakes," I prodded, relying on guesswork to fill in the blanks.

"What do you think is going on here?" asked Cass. Another backwards step and she was against a room door.

"I think you're cornered and have no way to escape," I said, stepping forwards, my hands up, wary, showing I wasn't armed. Well, I was. I just didn't plan on reaching for my weapon but Cass didn't need to know that. "As for the ring, I think I've been told a story that I'm not sure is true. If you tell me the real story, including who hired you, perhaps I can help."

"How about I tell you about the ring and you tell me how you found me. I know it was you at my safe house," said Cass. "Then you can verify it and bug out of my case."

I thought about it for a fraction of a second. "Okay." Then, "Case? Are you law enforcement?" Maddox had given every indication she was on the opposite side of the law.

"Less law and more enforcement. I'm sure you know by now I find things," she added. "Things like the ring you think I have." She held up her hands, empty. Not that it mattered. I didn't expect her to be wearing it.

"Go ahead." Where were Maddox and Farid? Why was it taking them so long? I needed to stall for time. Cass had no escape, unless she went through me, and I'd already experienced her getting me out of the way. I glanced over the balcony and my heart thumped. Caution was my friend.

"You first," she countered.

"You shouldn't have left your rental car at the retirement village," I said. "It was too easy to pick up on camera and follow. And you took your disguise off too soon."

"That makes sense," said Cass, shaking her head and heaving a huff of exasperation. "Well, I won't make that mistake again."

"Tell me about the ring."

"Hypothetically? Since I don't know what ring you're talking about. Between us girls though, *hypothetically*, the ring belongs to the family that *might* have hired me. They owned a number of jewels that were stolen by the Nazis when their family left Europe during the second World War. They have the purchase receipt, photos, and a letter that mentions the ring. They've been tracking the jewels for decades. This is the only one they found."

"Why not buy it back?" I asked.

"They didn't sell it in the first place!"

"Then why not go to the police?"

"And have it tied up in courts for years while they prove ownership and argue their case for repatriation, hoping someone will right the wrong that they suffered?" Cass pressed her back to the room door and pulled in a breath sharply. "That's enough questions."

"Regardless of what happened, I'm going to need

the ring back. My clients are good people. They did their due diligence and if they were duped, and you can prove everything, I think they'll work with you to return the ring. I also found evidence of the seller's associations so I think my clients will believe you," I said.

Cass looked like she was contemplating that. Then she smiled and said, "I don't think I'll take that risk" before darting through the door she'd been leaning against, and slamming it shut behind her.

CHAPTER EIGHTEEN

I rattled the door knob and banged on the door to no avail. There was only silence. Cass didn't even shout at me to get lost. Frustrated and impeded, I leaned over the railing to observe the path below. Maddox and Farid turned the corner, looking up. I waved to them and turned back to the door.

Maddox arrived first, sprinting up the external stairs just as I was trying to wriggle a slim tool into the door lock.

"Lily said you'd gone this way," said Farid as he stepped off the emergency escape with a rattle of the ladder. "Is it really her?"

"Did you let her go?" yelled Maddox, striding towards me.

"No!" I finally felt the click and the door released. My lock-picking practice had paid off at last! "She must have had a key for this door already. It had to be her backup plan in case she was spotted but I don't imagine she ever thought she'd have to use it. At least, not so soon!" Of course that was why she'd engaged me in

238

conversation; she was simply making time to unlock the door with her hands behind her back.

While that was impressive, I could only imagine how much we'd ruined her day and that made me feel a little bit glad because she was definitely ruining mine.

Maddox ran a hand over his hair and then dashed his hand through the air, almost spinning around. He kicked the railing and it rattled horribly. "Damn Cass Temple and damn her backup plans!" he yelled.

"How did you know she was here at the motel?" I pushed the door, half expecting to find Cass Temple wriggling out the window, her legs flailing behind her so I could grab them. But no, the room was empty except for the three of us crowding the door.

"She's Maddox's nemesis," said Farid as we squashed through. "He spends his days figuring out her next moves and mooning about catching her."

Maddox dropped to his knees and threw back the comforter as he checked under the bed, his gun in hand. From the floor, he muttered, "She's a pain in my ass. A thorn in my side. A…"

"I get the picture," I said. I checked the window opposite, finding it firmly shut. I lifted the latch but it only opened three inches and below was a sheer drop. Unless Cass had vacuum-sucked her body through, there was no way she'd fit through the narrow opening without breaking most of her bones when she landed.

Farid darted to the bathroom, his gun drawn. He slid from view only to return seconds later, shaking his head.

"She definitely came in here. I saw her!" I told them, frowning in confusion. "She walked right through that door!" But where was she now? The room was empty except for the neatly made bed, twin nightstands, and a slim desk under a wall-mounted television.

"Well, she isn't here now so there must be a second exit," said Maddox, getting to his feet and turning around.

"The bathroom window is too small to climb out of," said Farid. "But I'll recheck the room."

"Do that. I'll…"

"Found it," I said, cutting off Maddox as I pulled the closet doors open wide. A small panel had been excised in the rear of the closet, close to the floor, not big enough to walk through, but doable if I crouched and duck walked. The removed panel, the edges neatly cut with a power tool, had been pushed into the adjoining room.

"Let me," said Maddox, nudging me out of the way. He crouched, leading with his gun, attempting to squeeze through the small opening. Halfway, he wedged himself snugly in the hole, and I got a moment of admiring his struggling butt, since I am neither blind, nor dead, nor without humor.

As gently as I could, I placed the sole of my sneaker against his butt and pushed. Maddox toppled forward, grunting. "I hope you didn't enjoy that," he said gruffly.

"Nope," I said, clenching my mouth so I didn't laugh.

"Me neither, partner," said Farid before he covered his mouth and put on a display of coughing to disguise the laugh that seeped out. "After you," he said, waving me courteously towards the hatch.

I stooped and scuttled through on my hands and knees, stretching forwards a little extra so I was out of the closet and quickly rose to find myself in an identical room to the one I'd just left. Farid followed, twisting and grunting to fit through.

Maddox was already rising from checking the bed and after a cursory glance in the bathroom, he darted to the door and pulled it open. Then he ran across the room and wrenched the front door open, bursting onto the walkway we'd stood on just minutes before. He looked down, then smacked his hand on the balustrade. Stepping back into the room, he said, "She's gone."

"Looks like she had this set up in case anyone followed her," said Farid, turning in a small circle to take in the identical room. "I bet she rented both rooms, probably as soon as she got to town, and had it all set up just in case she needed to lure someone to a false room."

"Search them," said Maddox from the doorway. "She must have left something somewhere. We need to know where she's going."

"Why are you after her?" I asked, turning away. The bed covers hadn't been pushed down, the pillows weren't indented. Unless the motel had a particularly sharp daily housekeeping service, she hadn't slept here. Did that mean this motel was a backup for the safe house, or a decoy for a third safe house? No, Cass had been here. I'd seen her with my own eyes, and lost her just as quickly. "Wait… how were you tailing her? Why didn't you call me?"

"We've been tailing her for…" started Farid until Maddox nudged him. In my pocket, my phone vibrated.

"We didn't have a confirmed sighting," said Maddox. "As soon as we did, I would have called."

"Really?" I narrowed my eyes.

Maddox nodded. "Really!"

Somehow, I was skeptical. Maddox might have given me the courtesy to interview her after he'd arrested her, but I was pretty sure he didn't want me in the way. That was just tough luck because *I'd* found her and *I'd* smoked her out.

Fat lot of good that had done. I'd also lost her.

"Why didn't you call me?" he asked.

"I was going to when you spooked her! She spotted you across the road, standing out like a pair of sore thumbs." My phone vibrated saving me from continuing the blame game. Lily had sent a message: *911!!!*

"Guess I'll leave you to it," I said, edging backwards. "Doesn't look like I'm needed here."

"Not so fast!" Maddox blocked my way. "How did you know she was here?"

"Lucas tracked the car she rented and it hadn't left this area," I said. "We drove around until we found it."

"Why didn't you call me then?" he asked.

"We thought she might have dumped the car and used one of the local businesses like the travel agency or caught a bus. When the receptionist refused to confirm if she was here, we needed a sighting to identify her so I created one."

"By crashing into her car," said Farid, nodding now as he glanced at Maddox. "I told you Lexi isn't just a crappy driver."

"You said I was a crappy driver?" My jaw dropped, appalled.

"I said it *could* have been accidental," said Maddox with a scowl aimed at Farid. "But it was good thinking. How did you know she'd come out?"

"We didn't. The keys were in the car so we figured

she hoped it would get stolen and lead us on a merry chase but it didn't. She didn't register the car with the motel either but the receptionist insisted she come out and deal with it." I held up my hands in surrender. "We got lucky."

"Why do you think she's hanging around after stealing from your client?" asked Farid.

"My guess is to make the final delivery. The better question is why does she have so many safe houses in this town?" I asked.

"Well, that's easy, she's..." Maddox's elbow in Farid's ribs quieted him.

"Now she's gone, I guess I'll never know," I said, suspicious of what Farid thought I knew and what Maddox didn't want him to tell me. So much for camaraderie! "Anyway, thanks for scaring her off." I waggled my forefinger at both of them as I circled Maddox, the open door only a few paces away. "Some investigators you are! I spotted you across the street. She saw you almost as soon as she came into the reception area."

"She's got a point," said Farid.

"No, she doesn't!" said Maddox.

"Totally do," I snipped as my phone buzzed again. "That SUV and those suits stand out to anyone up to anything nefarious within a five-mile radius. Anyway, gotta go! Leads to follow! Criminals to apprehend! Toodaloo!" I was out the door, pulling it closed behind me before either man could protest. On the other side of the door, it sounded like something small had been kicked across the room.

Unfortunately, Maddox was right. Sally Smith, Cass Temple, or whatever her name was next week, was gone and I was pretty sure she'd just executed the simplest escape plan in her handbook. All she had to do was lock the door behind her, confident we would waste our time trying to get inside, then slip into the closet, and close the doors behind her as she wiggled through the hole into the adjoining room. Then, while we rushed into the end room, she simply sneaked out the door onto the walkway, jogging away while we chased our tails before we realized what she'd done.

Her backup plan had worked perfectly.

It was as if she'd done it a thousand times before, always ready to outsmart her pursuers.

I kind of liked her!

But I would have liked her more if I'd found the ring.

Now I'd blown my one chance at appealing to her face-to-face and I'd no idea how to find her. There was no way she would return here, not with the Feds buzzing around too, and the car would certainly be abandoned now. If she had another safe house, there was no way she would use it, not after these two were located so quickly. No, she was going to ground.

I jogged down the stairwell, looking around for Lily when I stepped onto the first-floor walkway. She hadn't followed Maddox and Farid so where had she gone to?

"Psst!"

I looked around, in search of the noise.

"Psst!"

It was coming from the walkway between the reception and this wing so I edged forwards, past closed doors and dark windows, the TV flashing in one of them.

"Lexi! In here!" A hand shot out, grabbed my arm, and pulled me inside a room. The drapes were partially drawn but the material was thin, making it light enough to see. Lily grinned at me as she pushed the door closed.

"What are you doing?" I asked, looking around the room she'd pulled me into. The bed covers and drapes were a different color from the motel's top floor and the layout marginally different, but the furnishings were all the same. This room, however, was larger with a kitchenette and a small, circular table with two chairs.

"I figured there was no point in me chasing after you when Maddox and Farid were clearly following you for backup, so I thought I'd check out Cass's room. I knew it was one of these since she got to the reception so quickly after she was called, and she was just tucking a key into her pocket. Since the other two were occupied, I broke into this one." Lily flashed me a pleased smile.

"I broke into a room upstairs!"

"We're so good at this!" squeaked Lily and clapped her hands. "If only we broke into her car too."

"Do you know how?"

"No. You?"

"No."

"Hmm. We should learn," said Lily. "Do you know any car thieves?"

"No."

"No problem. Ruby probably does. If not, Jord definitely does."

"We got lucky that she'd left the car open to be stolen," I decided. "There wasn't anything inside anyway."

"So where did Cass go? Did you catch her?"

"No, she had another escape plan ready. I figure once she realized we were all bearing down on her, her ploy was to get us to follow her upstairs, give us the runaround, and make sure we didn't come back to this room. It makes sense now," I said, taking in the backpack on the chair and the duffel bag on the floor by the bed. A plate, a bowl, and flatware were drying by the sink. "Those rooms were empty but there are things in here. She stayed here, thinking even if we tracked the car, once it was stolen, we'd never check out this location again."

"She didn't figure on us ignoring that plan," said Lily with a pleased smile. "I haven't had a chance to properly go through her things but it's definitely woman stuff. There's a backpack and a weekend bag with a few clothes in it and a lot of cash. I mean *a lot*! Nothing in the bathroom except a disposable toothbrush and a mini tube of toothpaste. She needs a skincare routine!"

"She had really nice skin," I said. She'd been fresh-faced, and pretty without makeup. Her hair looked really good too but I couldn't be sure. Two weeks ago, her hairstyle was a little different. I wondered if anyone knew what she really looked like.

"Probably the result of all that running away from stuff. So much fresh air and blood pumping gave her a healthy glow."

I caught sight of myself in the mirror over the small table. "Do I need to do more running?" I asked, poking at my eye creases. "Do I look healthy?"

"You look tired and bruised. I know it's not all down to late night baby-making because I don't think you'd get bruises from that, although one time when Jord…"

"No! Definitely not and there was no baby-making last night. I didn't even wake up when Solomon came to bed." I peered at the bruise on my cheek. It didn't look any worse and the brief excitement had distracted me from thoughts of my mildly sore but unbroken nose.

"You should definitely be awake for the fun stuff," said Lily. "Anyway, wait until you get a baby and you hurt, and it cries, and you can't sleep. Then you'll think the flu gives you a healthy glow."

"Can't wait." I turned back to her, knowing we needed to act quickly. "You take the bag, I'll take the backpack. We need to hurry. Maddox and Farid are going through the decoy rooms upstairs but I can't be sure they don't know she had this room too. I don't even know how they knew she was here. I'm sure Lucas didn't tip them off about the car."

"The joys of law enforcement means they're tapped into a bigger network with a lot more eyes. You need to polish your informants," said Lily.

"I don't have any informants." I grabbed the backpack from the desk chair and upended it on the bed, taking precisely no care about how I conducted the search. Cass Temple had to know that one of us would figure out where she'd been holed up eventually. There was no point pretending we hadn't found her room.

"Exactly!" Lily pulled open the duffel bag zipper and the contents tumbled out. "Jeans, t-shirts, underwear, socks, three different passports. Hairbrush. Oh!" Lily stopped.

I glanced over, hoping for a revelation. Or, even better, the ring. "What?"

"Moisturizer," said Lily, holding up a small tube to me. "Nice brand. I've been meaning to try it. She travels light. These t-shirts look new and the jeans still have the tags on."

"Pat down the bag in case of secret compartments," I suggested.

"That is so exciting. Do you have secret compartments in your overnight bags?"

"No, but I don't steal stuff."

"I think you'd be good at it."

I frowned. "Thanks... I think?"

While Lily patted the bag carefully, I poked through the backpack's contents I'd dropped in a pile on the bed. A large manila envelope with rental papers for the car made out to, and signed by, Sally Smith. A wad of bills curled into a bundle and secured by a rubber band. A few snacks and a bottled water, and another smaller envelope. I ignored everything in favor of the small envelope and pulled out a sheaf of folded papers and some xeroxed photos. Sitting on the edge of the bed, I opened the loose sheets, scanning them. Cass Temple hadn't lied about her hypothetical client.

"The bag's empty. What have you got there?" asked Lily.

"It looks like a timeline of the ring I'm searching for and copies of a lot of other things, all translated into English. The commission, the date of purchase, the purchaser's name, and the recipients. It appears to have been bought by a man for his wife on her birthday. Events it was worn to with appendix notes. The date it was stolen and by whom. The couple left Poland two days later, in 1938, and arrived first in England and later settled in the United States. There're copies of train and boat tickets and a letter with a translation. I think it's an offer of sponsorship from a relative." I shuffled the papers. "The evidence backs up my suspicions. There's a copy of the letter of the ring's commission, a sketch of the design with a letter from the designer, the receipt, photos. Oh! I think it was an engagement ring, not a birthday gift. Even the boat ticket to the States in their names." I set the papers on my knees, looking up at Lily. Cold shock gripped me. "I think Cass was right. The ring was stolen by Nazis and this couple escaped."

"So how did it get to the people the Reynoldses bought it from?"

"Good question. They had evidence of ownership but… not *this* kind of evidence and not as extensive," I said, showing Lily photocopy after photocopy. "They had evidence of the seller's mother wearing the ring around the time of the occupation and after, and a plausible story why they didn't have receipts. I don't know if they knew who stole it but I did find evidence that they socialized with some very unsavory people. Perhaps they were given it? Or bought it from someone unscrupulous?"

I set the papers on my lap, frustrated by the conundrum that I now held. "If the ring were originally stolen, in what looks like a horrific act of Nazi persecution, then shouldn't the ring be returned to the rightful owners? But also, I don't think the Reynoldses did anything wrong. They didn't know. They stand to lose the money they used to purchase it in good faith. No wonder Cass Temple's clients wanted to bypass the law and reclaim it. They have to be related to this couple."

"It would be more of a problem if you'd found the ring," said Lily. "All this evidence is useless until you have it. For what it's worth though, I think the ring should be returned to its true owners."

"I agree." I stood and arranged the papers on the

bed, taking photos of each one, even though I planned on taking the envelope with me. Whoever Cass really was—and I was starting to doubt her name even was Cass Temple, no matter what Maddox said—I was sure this packet wasn't her only copy. Someone had the originals too, or other copies elsewhere. I set the envelope aside and was considering whether to stuff everything else back inside the backpack or return it when I noticed a small envelope remaining on the bed, forgotten until now. I grabbed it, turned it upside-down, and shook out the small pouch inside. Loosening the ties, I shook it and out tumbled the ring into my open palm.

"*Now* we have a problem," I said, moving towards the door and window to see it in the light the half-drawn drapes allowed. The ring's sapphire illuminated beautifully, the blue brilliant against the diamonds, and I could only imagine how delighted the original recipient had been to receive it along with her proposal.

I could also imagine her pain at losing it to evil.

Had she wondered every day who wore her ring? Who profited from its theft?

"Finding the ring solves the case," pointed out Lily. "If you return it to the Reynoldses, you've done your job. The original owners can go to the police and petition for its return or…"

"Or what?"

"Or you could never find it and let the original owners have it back," she said, fixing me with a determined look. "The Reynoldses can file a claim on their insurance. Everyone gets what rightfully belongs to them."

We both looked at the ring. "I think I have a better idea," I said, holding up the ring and smiling.

"Lexi!" Lily's eyes widened in alarm.

A cool breeze hit the back of my neck, then a creak and a soft footfall sounded behind me. I didn't even have chance to turn.

"I'll take that," said a woman's voice as fingers closed around mine.

CHAPTER NINETEEN

"Let go," commanded Cass. The door shut with a light click and I winced, wondering if I'd been so hasty I forgot to close the door when I'd entered. Had she been just outside, listening to us rummaging through her property, waiting for the right moment to strike?

Probably.

"No way," I replied, clinging onto the band as hard as I could while her fingers twisted around mine. When her other hand joined the fight, I knew I was going to lose the struggle. There was no way I could hang onto something so delicate. Unless... I reached for my purse with my free hand, feeling inside, my fingers wrapping around what I was looking for. "Look down," I said.

"Just give it to... oh." The struggling ceased and she stiffened, holding still.

"Let go or I'll shoot," I said, sounding more confident than I felt as the barrel of my gun nudged Cass's ribs, "and I won't miss."

She let go.

"Now back up. Against the door. Put your hands

up." I took a few steps forwards and turned quickly, keeping my gun trained on Cass. She'd thrown a hoodie over her shirt; the hood was up and she wore a black ball cap but there was no mistaking her. Nor her audacity in returning to the place she'd already escaped from. Except Cass hadn't left and she clearly had no choice. We'd lured her out effectively and once she'd taken us on a wild goose chase, she had no choice but to circle back and retrieve the ring. For all her forward planning, she'd made a stupid mistake that I intended to capitalize on.

"It seems I underestimated you," said Cass, her gaze taking in my bruise as she put her hands up.

"You've only known me for a matter of minutes," I said, including the first brief encounter in my calculation, after waiting for an apology that never came.

"You've known me for a few seconds," said Lily. "Did you underestimate me too?"

"Who are you?" Cass asked, sparing Lily a brief glance before she fixed her gaze on me.

Lily rolled her eyes. "Rude."

"Meet Sally Smith," I said. "Or Cass Temple. Or are you using another name today?"

"Does it matter? We're wasting time."

"I have all the time in the world," I said.

"I don't," said Lily. "I'm paying for childcare. Let's wrap this up so I don't get a fine."

"She has a point," I said, holding up the ring. "I'm working this case and my clients want this ring back. I don't want to add extra days to their bill if I don't need to."

"Then we have a problem because that ring is mine," said Cass. "Give it to me and I'll get out of your hair."

"Not the arrangement I have with my client," I pointed out.

Her gaze darted to the bed where the paperwork lay, obviously rifled through. "You read everything?" she asked.

"We did," I said.

She gave me a disgusted look. "And you *still* want to keep the ring and give it back to your clients?"

I hesitated. "My clients didn't do anything wrong. The fault lies with the sellers."

"But your clients will benefit from the sale. Are they the type of people who want to benefit from the Nazis' crimes?"

My resolve wavered. "I would hope not," I said, unsure of the answer. The Reynoldses didn't seem like those kinds of people, but it wasn't a question I'd directly asked because I hadn't needed to until the case began unraveling. Now that I thought about it, was I benefiting by taking payment for recovering the ring? The idea was so icky, I was tempted to turn the ring over on the spot. But it wasn't my call… or was it? Plus, the vague outline of a plan was whirring in my mind. A plan that would solve everything. A plan that didn't include Cass Temple.

"Then let me have the ring. I can return it to the rightful owners. Tell your clients you couldn't locate it and they should file a claim for the insurance money. Everyone is happy," Cass said, her tone lighter now, gentler, imploring me to do the right thing… according to her. She lowered her arms a fraction. When I didn't react, she lowered them some more so her elbows were at her sides, her fingers still splayed.

"I like that plan," said Lily. "We should do that."

"I have a better idea," I said, my brainstorm becoming clearer. Could it really be so simple? An answer that would make everyone happy?

Well, maybe not Maddox.

"I'm listening."

"But first you have to tell me why the Feds are after you."

"Simple. I steal stuff and they want to catch me," said Cass, the familiar glint back in her eye. "And I don't want that to happen. The latter anyway. I'm cool with the former."

"Stating the obvious," said Lily. "Who are you really? If you want a deal, you should own up to who you truly are!"

"Who's the henchman?" asked Cass, nodding to Lily.

"Hench*lady*, thank you. I'm the one with the cellphone about to call Special Agent Maddox and Special Agent Farid," said Lily. She waggled her phone.

"Long name," quipped Cass and I held back a smile. I was not going to like her! She was causing me problems, professionally, ethically, and probably personally. I had to deal with her quickly and efficiently and not engage in jokes. This was not a girl gang day out.

"Before you make that call," I said to Lily, as she poised her finger over the phone screen. "I want you both to hear my plan."

"Hurry up. If she sticks around any longer, she'll go after our engagement rings too."

Cass raised an eyebrow. "Yours is particularly pretty," she said to Lily.

Lily beamed. "Thank you! Do you want to hear the proposal story?"

"Never mind that," I said before Lily launched into it and Cass ending up stealing my BFF. "Here's what I think should happen." I explained my plan while Cass and Lily listened.

When I finished, Cass smiled. "I like it," she said, "but we just need a little, teeny-weeny addendum to the plan."

I frowned. My plan wasn't flawless but I wasn't sure what I'd missed. "Go ahead."

"I need your help getting out of here. I've escaped the Feds once today and I know they're still around, poking inside my decoy rooms, the steam coming from their ears. I need to make sure they don't get in my way when I get out of here. Can you do that?"

Maddox would be so pissed when he found out.

"I can do that," I agreed, wondering how I could keep this story from ever reaching Maddox's ears. Perhaps I could ensure the future through sheer willpower.

"Maddox is going to be pissed," said Lily, the voice of doom behind me.

"When isn't he?" Cass and I both spoke at once.

"*Interesting*," said Lily, edging forwards to stand at the foot of the bed, looking between us.

"We'll distract Maddox," I said, becoming even more curious as to exactly how well Cass knew Maddox. Ever since I first met her, only a couple of weeks ago, and saw the way they looked at each other, I had the sneaking suspicion their relationship wasn't strictly professional. But were they professionally friendly in their cat and mouse game? Or were they…? I gulped. Did this woman mean something far more to Maddox? Not that I didn't know he dated, and I was sure there were girlfriends here and there, but I'd never come face-to-face with one of his romantic interests.

Was that what I was doing now?

Even worse, was I about to help *her* and potentially screw *him* over at the same time? No, it couldn't be the case. If they were more than professional rivals, then they wouldn't be engaged in these kinds of games, surely? There was too much at stake. Not just Maddox's integrity but his career too. FBI agents climbing the ladder didn't hook up with wily thieves.

It didn't make sense.

Even if I asked, I doubted she would tell me... and I was not going to ask. Although that was partly because I suspected she wouldn't tell me the truth.

"Do you want your stuff?" I asked, indicating the backpack and its contents.

"I'll take the bag with the clothes, the cash, and the passports. Keep the paperwork for your clients. I have copies," said Cass.

"I'll pack for you," said Lily, scooting over to the bed and shoving her things into the bag. She held up a roll of bills. "Is this all real?"

"Very," said Cass, a small smile on her lips.

"And your skincare routine?"

"Lily!" I snapped.

"She has really good skin!" said Lily. "Seriously though, is this moisturizer..."

"Highly recommend it," said Cass.

"We're tracking the rental car and Maddox probably is too," I told her, wanting, no, *needing*, to get us back on track.

"It's a rental. I have no problem abandoning it. I would have already but I had limited options and figured someone around here would steal it here sooner or later."

"Usually it would have been gone in ten minutes. Rough luck."

"Noted. I'll set it on fire next time," she said without a hint of amusement that told me she meant it.

"Where can we take you?" I asked.

"Nowhere," said Cass. "I need a distraction, not a ride. Just make sure the Feds are distracted for the next few minutes and I'll get out of here. So long as the ring makes it to its rightful owners, you won't see me again. Make sure they know I sent you. I'll be watching."

"Literally?" asked Lily. "Isn't that risky?"

"No, it's figurative," snorted Cass. "I'll find out but I'm not going to stalk either of you in person. Plus, if you don't deliver it, I know where the ring will go back to and then I'll just take it again."

Lily tossed the bag at Cass's feet and sidled over to me. "How's that for successfully extracting her backup plan?"

"Brilliant," I said, dryly. "I wouldn't have guessed that was what she'd do."

"You're welcome! And there's no way she can stalk me. She doesn't even know my name."

"Okay, Lily," said Cass.

"Damn it!" squeaked Lily.

"I said it a minute or two ago," I said. "She doesn't know anything else."

"Okay," snorted Cass, and my determination faltered. I couldn't be sure of anything with her.

"How are we supposed to tell anyone anything without your name?" asked Lily. "I'm pretty sure they don't call you Sally Smith or Cass Temple."

"I'm pretty sure they don't know me by *any* name," said Cass. "So you won't need to give one. All you have to do is give them the ring and that doesn't have to be in person. I have a locker set up for the transfer if you need it. The information is in the packet."

"What will you do now?" I wondered.

"With the ring repatriated, my work here is done. I'm leaving town. You won't see me again unless you screw up. In which case, well... you know what happens."

"How do you know we won't just give it back to the Reynoldses?" asked Lily. "I doubt they'd let it get stolen twice."

"Because I think you both have a conscience and you know where that ring rightfully belongs. Before it even crosses your minds, you won't find any links between me and the clients either. Even this meeting is hearsay," said Cass. She rolled her shoulders, all pretense at keeping her hands up gone. "Please don't prove me wrong. I hate it when clients do that. It ruins my week and my billing."

"I still need to run my idea past my clients. How do I get in touch with you?" I asked.

Cass paused a long moment, then said, "I'll give you an email address. For the record, it's untraceable so don't even try, and if you email for anything other than the ring, I'll ignore it. You have forty-eight hours to turn over the ring, then I'll consider our arrangement reneged on. Deal?"

"Deal," I said.

Cass turned and tweaked the drapes, checking outside the room. Apparently satisfied, she picked up the bag Lily had packed and said, "Now help me get out of here, please."

"I need to check where Maddox is," I said, tucking the ring into the pouch before putting it into my jeans pocket. I still held the gun, uncertain if she would make any fast moves. Although I thought we'd reached a deal, she was a thief so she could be a liar too, and I wasn't taking any chances until she'd disappeared. Then I'd explain everything to the Reynoldses and hope they would take my recommended course of action.

"Do it."

I pulled out my phone and called Maddox. He answered quickly with a "What?"

"Are you still at the motel?" I asked.

"Yeah. The rooms are totally clean. It's clearly a decoy that she never even slept in. I'm heading to reception to find out if she has another room number. Where are you?"

"Just hanging out, waiting," I lied. "She hasn't gone back to her car." Which was true.

"I doubt she will now. I'll get it towed. Meet me at the reception desk."

"Give me a couple minutes." I hung up and waited as I held up a forefinger to Cass, silently instructing her to wait. She pulled the drapes closed and I hovered by the door, my eye on the peephole. Less than a couple minutes later, the room dark and silent, Maddox and Farid walked past. I counted to sixty before I opened the door and cautiously stuck my head out, my gun hand behind my back. The two men weren't in sight and the reception door was closing. "They're in reception now but they'll find this room," I said. "You should clear out now."

"Consider me gone. Nice to work with you, Lexi," Cass said as I pulled the door open, wide enough to walk through, and stepped out of the way. Cass paused at the door, then surprised me by leaning in and hugging me. "Don't make me come back," she whispered ominously.

I stepped out, shaking off the weird, overly friendly moment, followed by Cass, and then Lily. Lily, with the packet of photocopies in her hand, pulled the door behind her and it locked automatically. I tucked my gun in my purse and zipped it, turning to check Maddox and Farid weren't about to burst through the door but it remained closed. Turning back, I started to tell Cass she was good to go but she was already rapidly walking away, her hood pulled up, the bag over her shoulder. She rounded the corner of the motel, heading away from her decoy rooms, and a moment later was lost from sight. I wondered what she would do without her vehicle but I figured she probably now had a backup plan for that too, even if it were walking and changing her clothes as she went. Undoubtedly, there was another bag stashed somewhere easy to collect and a passage out of town. Where she went from here would be something I would think about for months to come.

"If you were a criminal, you could be living her life," said Lily as we stood outside the room, watching the empty courtyard. "Although she was wearing sneakers and I don't see you spending your life in sneakers even if you are wearing a cute pair today. Or hoodies. Or old lady blouses. Or putting that sticky, disguise stuff all over your face," she added, waving a hand over her face.

"If the last couple of days are any hint of what her life is like, no thank you." I turned to Lily, something bothering me.

"What's up?" asked Lily.

I shook my head, uncertain I could put a finger on it. I had the ring, Cass was gone, and I had all the evidence I needed to show to my clients, plus, a great plan to save the day.

I should be feeling great.

But... something still niggled me.

"Let's go," I said. "I need to present this case to Solomon and then to the Reynoldses, and put some distance between us and the Feds because I feel guilty."

"We still need to get past them," said Lily, nodding to Maddox who ducked back inside after motioning to us. Then Farid stepped out of the reception, looking around. He saw us and waved, leaving us no choice but to stroll towards him.

"Say nothing," I said through a false smile and gritted teeth.

"The receptionist recognized Temple's photo," Farid said to us, clearly pleased. "Maddox is getting the room number now. She said two women were here asking about her car so I guess that had to be you two."

"It was," said Lily. "You should have tried that."

"That's what I said!" grinned Farid and they high-fived.

When we stepped inside, the receptionist was tapping on her keyboard. Then she handed him a keycard and told him the number of the room we'd just vacated.

"Where did you go?" asked Maddox when he walked over to us.

"I was looking for Lily before we scouted around looking for the thief, but didn't find her," I lied. "I gave up."

"She's in the wind," added Lily, waving her hand through the air.

Maddox narrowed his eyes. "It's not like you to give up so fast."

"I've learned not to waste my time. She could be

anywhere by now." Which was true. I shifted my feet uncomfortably, wishing I were telling him the whole truth but I'd made a deal to help my clients and everyone else involved. I couldn't break it now.

"It's true," said Farid. "Cass Temple's one slippery customer. If you spot her, you can't close your eyes for a second or she'll be gone and the trail will go cold for months."

"Is that how long you've been tracking her?" I asked.

Maddox indicated we should step outside and the four of us formed a circle outside the side door. The more we lingered, the further Cass got away, and my stomach clenched with the discomfort of not revealing the truth. "Longer," he said, "but it's classified."

"Who is Cass Temple really? Is that an alias too?" asked Lily.

"That's her real name," said Maddox. "I know that for a fact but she has access to plenty of other identities so it's useless trying to trace her by that one. But we have her room number now and with any luck, she'll have left her kit behind and holed up nearby until she can reclaim it. Farid and I will search her room and then hang around. I'm sorry if that doesn't help your case."

"Understood," I said. "I guess we'd better let you get to it. Gotta go! Take care!"

Maddox stepped in my way. "What's the hurry?" he asked, suspicion lacing his words as his brows knitted together and his eyes narrowed.

"No hurry. I just learned when to cut my losses." I edged around him and he took two more steps, stopping me. I tried the other direction and he made the same maneuver. It could have been a fun dance, except I wanted to get out of there before he forced a confession from me. Not that he needed to force it out. It was ready to spill from my lips.

"You've never known when to cut your losses. What are you really up to?"

"I've been summoned to the agency. Can't keep my clients waiting!"

"Why are you so keen to get out of here?"

"Because we lost Cass Temple and I need to brief my clients on the case."

"What do you have to tell them?"

"That we know who the thief is and, um…"

"And that you guys scared her off!" Lily jumped in with an accusatory prod of her finger in Maddox's chest. Then she poked Farid's. "You too," she added. "Didn't want to leave you out."

"Thanks, I appreciate it," said Farid. "But…"

"We didn't scare her off. She just evaded capture," said Maddox. "She had this all set up in case her safe house was compromised and we tracked her here."

"Duh," said Lily.

"It's been a rough couple of days," I said. "We found her hideout and lost her again. I'm sure you'll find her without us in the way."

"There's no telling when she'll turn up again." Maddox's shoulders slumped and he lifted his gaze to scan the area, like Cass would be waiting on the next corner for him to spot her. "Maybe we'll find something in her room. It's right over here." He pointed over my shoulder. "Right where you two just… no." He stopped, paling, and when his gaze fell on me, I felt like shrinking. "Tell me you didn't."

"I didn't!" squeaked Lily and I at the same time.

"You. Did. Not!"

"Nope!" I said.

"Did you find her?"

"Does it look like we did?" I asked, spreading my hands.

"I'll find out!"

"Sure, do that," I said. Then I pointed and gasped. "Hey! Is that her?"

Maddox twisted his neck, half turning, falling for my plan.

I grabbed Lily's hand and circled around him, then waved as we put distance between us. He shook his head and sighed, glanced back, then looked at us again. "You better not have helped her," he called as we retreated.

"Would I?" I was jogging sideways, one eye on Maddox, one for obstacles.

"Damn it, Lexi!" Maddox shook his head sorrowfully. "I bet you fell for whatever sob story she gave you."

"As if," I said, then I waved and we turned, jogging for my car. "Do you still have the packet?" I asked Lily.

"Yeah, it's halfway down my pants' leg but it's there."

"Can you extract it?" I asked as I beeped my car unlocked.

"Of course. What if he's right and it *was* a sob story?" Lily asked. She shook out her leg and the packet slipped to the ground. She grabbed it as we climbed in and passed it to me with a flourish. "This is one epic setup if it is."

"It doesn't matter. I have the ring." I smiled at Lily across the car roof and patted my jeans pocket.

The smile began to slip.

I dipped two fingers inside my pocket, searching

265

the small space, but already I knew there was no point.

How could I have been so stupid?

That was no grateful hug from a thief.

Instead, Cass Temple had ignored every step of my plan and deftly stolen the ring right out from my pocket.

And I'd let her go!

CHAPTER TWENTY

My stomach roiled with nausea as I pulled up in the agency's parking lot. Lily had offered to accompany me when I confessed falling for Cass Temple's double-cross, but the idea of injecting my best friend into this mess didn't feel like the smartest one I could come up with, even if I were married to the boss.

No, I had to admit I'd been outsmarted.

Perhaps it was vaguely comforting that I'd been outmaneuvered by a professional thief who remained steps ahead of everyone on her tail. I hadn't even felt her fingers in my pocket, nor the ring when she deftly slipped it out. Cass had been fast and confident in her suspiciously friendly hug, ensuring I wouldn't realize a thing until she was long gone.

She'd probably planned to pickpocket me the moment she saw me slide the ring into the pouch before I put it inside my pocket, readily going along with my brilliant plan until her escape was assured.

She didn't trust me and I'd been a fool to trust her.

Not only had I helped her slip away from the FBI

unnoticed, I'd allowed her to steal from me. Then, after showing her the door myself, I'd blocked Maddox and Farid from finding her as she made her escape.

Even worse, Maddox already suspected I'd aided her and would eventually most likely find out the whole extent. I was cooked.

As I jogged up the stairs to the PI's office, hoping a hole might open up and swallow me, I thought about Cass and her quest for justice. The paperwork she'd suggested we take seemed to back up her story but what if it were just another clever ruse like her decoy rooms, designed to distract and waste our time while she made her next move?

As for the locker information to transfer the ring to her clients? It wasn't in the packet; something we should have known before we'd even left the motel room.

If I hadn't been so pleased with myself for finding the ring, and coming up with a plan to satisfy everyone, I might have taken a moment to check.

I'd been totally bamboozled.

Even worse, I was impressed by Cass's quick thinking under pressure.

No wonder Maddox was furious.

Now I had some serious legwork to do to make up for being conned so easily. And then I needed to think about why that had happened. Was I off my game?

Before I approached Solomon, I stopped by my desk and pulled out my laptop. A few searches later, I had confirmation that the people in Cass's report were legitimate and that she hadn't created a wild ruse in case her motel room was searched.

The Abrams and Mendelson family had been on record talking about their experiences of tracing their ancestors' lives and property with several missing items from artwork to jewelry mentioned. But that didn't mean Cass Temple actually knew them, nor did it mean they'd commissioned her to recover the ring. Without a direct connection between commission and payment, her role couldn't be proven.

Of course, I could go digging for evidence. I could narrow down exactly who the Abrams and Mendelsons were. Then I could scour the family's bank accounts and their finances for loans, secret accountants, or suspicious transactions that could connect them to our thief. I could even comb their social media for calls for help, but I didn't want to...

For once, I didn't want the glaring, finger-pointing evidence.

But I did want the ring.

With it in my possession, and the story verified, I could broker a legal deal between the two parties, leaving no one looking over their shoulder, in exactly the way I'd suggested to Cass back in that dimly lit motel room, right before she plucked the ring from my pocket.

All I had was the packet and once again, I tipped it out, spreading the contents across my desk, searching for information that would further assist me in tracking down the family. A photo in an article, a few years old now, from an antiques magazine gave me pause. Ellie Abrams posed on the steps of her house, a house I'd walked past many times. It was only a few streets away from where I lived. The caption read: *Ellie Abrams continues her search for her grandparents' property.*

I sat back, the photo in my hands. What were the odds on Cass's clients and the ring both finding their way to our east coast town?

Perhaps it was a case of serendipity that the two had ended up in the same small city, and employing Cass to retrieve it neatly closed the circle that had opened when the ring was first stolen.

"You seem worried," said Solomon. I looked up, surprised to see him standing at my desk, looking down at me. I'd been so engrossed in reading that I hadn't noticed him leaving his office. "What happened to your face?"

"Minor incident," I said, touching my cheek.

"Do I need to kill someone?"

I contemplated that. "Not yet."

"Huh." He paused, his face unreadable. "What's going on?

"I screwed up," I said, placing the magazine article on top of the evidence.

He studied me for a moment. "What did you screw up?" he asked. "Yesterday there were clues… the bruise on your face, and a Lily's Bar t-shirt, but you were sleeping soundly. What happened today?" He paused, probably questioning his life choices when he hired me, then said, "Start with the first question."

"The case. I found the thief. I had the ring."

A smile lit up his face. "That's great! When do you plan to tell the Reynoldses?"

I winced. "It was great until Cass Temple stole it right back again and now she's gone," I admitted. Wisely, I thought, I left out the part where I'd been the one to help her escape.

"Ah." Then, "You're sure it's Cass Temple?"

"One hundred percent. She's back."

"I can fill in some of the blanks. You can tell me the rest later."

"I don't know what to say to the Reynoldses. I had

it all worked out. I was going to tell them about the ring's real history—" I said, pointing to the paperwork spread across my desk, "—and suggest it would be great PR to repatriate it to the original owners, who, by the way, might live in town. Everyone would be happy. The ring is returned to its rightful owner's descendants and the Reynoldses get the kind of publicity they can't buy."

"Except they're out the money spent on purchasing the ring and paying our fee," said Solomon who rounded my desk to sift through the contents as he listened.

"I think we should write off their fee."

"Damage control?"

"That, and I don't want to profit on this kind of case. It should be pro bono under the circumstances. Plus, I don't have the ring, which is what we were paid to recover."

"We were paid to identify the thief and patch the hole in their security. You've done the former. I've done the latter. That's two thirds of the case."

"I feel better when you put it like that but I still think I should tell them they aren't getting their ring back and the reason why."

"Let's go together." Solomon beckoned for me to stand and even though I knew he was right, and that I should get it over with, there was a big part of me that wanted to slink away to a mall and shop away my feelings instead. He wrapped me in a hug and I melted, laying my head on his chest. "You can fill me in on the particulars on the way," he said, his words muffled in my hair. "Are you certain the ring is irretrievable?"

"Yes. No. Maybe." Solomon loosened his hold and I stuffed the documents into the envelope and followed him from the office, catching him up on what I'd learned.

As we got into his SUV, I tapped the file in my lap. "The family in the articles have to be the clients. Maybe we should go see them first and listen to what they have to say," I said. "They're involved in this as much as anyone."

"Do you know where they live?"

"The file doesn't list an address but I recognized the house from the photos," I said, pulling out the photocopy I'd placed on top of the other documents. "It makes sense that it's probably their home. I think I'll recognize it if we drive around." I tapped the file again with my forefinger, thinking out loud. "If I can convince them we're not going to call the cops on them, and that we want what's best for them and the Reynoldses, I think I can get them to agree to work with the Reynoldses. I proposed that to Cass Temple... and, well, never mind. At some point, the Abrams-Mendelsons have to receive the ring. It's better for them if they work with us. No one wants to get wrapped up in a lengthy court case."

"It's risky," said Solomon. "They're unlikely to voluntarily implicate themselves in a theft for hire. It's a felony."

"Does a felony depend on whether or not they have the ring?" I asked.

"A mediocre lawyer could argue that it's all fantasy if they don't have it," said Solomon. "There's nothing to say this Ellie Abrams acted unless money changed hands. If they have the ring, a good lawyer will sensationalize the story and they'll win on public sympathy pressure. The DA won't want to touch it. Any reasonable person would want to see a wrong like that righted, and the method to take the ring from the Reynoldses was theft not violence."

"Then the faster we get to them, the better," I decided. "Head to Chilton. I don't remember the street name but if you drive us home, I can direct us from there."

Solomon navigated us home and as we rolled past our house, I called out directions as I remembered them, sending us turning onto several streets before the houses started to look like the same kind of architecture as in the picture. "That's it," I said, pointing to the house as we drove past. "Let's park up here."

"We should observe before we approach," said Solomon. "I'd like to know if they're alone."

"You mean, you want to know if the thief is there or will approach them imminently," I said thinking about Cass's on-the-spot story about anonymous names and locker transfers. I figured since she had the family's background info, the rest of her story was trash… but maybe it wasn't. She was careful to say there were no links between them. An anonymous transfer would ensure that. I gritted my teeth, frustrated at the possibilities.

"Precisely that."

We hunkered down, watching the smart brick townhouse with its neat steps leading up to the stoop and navy blue-painted door for close to an hour but there was no movement outside the house that screamed Cass Temple. Inside, I saw a woman walk past the living room window a couple of times, then retreat further into the house where she vanished from view.

"I think we've waited long enough," I decided. "If

they don't know anything or don't have the ring, we can conduct more surveillance but I think Cass Temple will be wise to that. I can't imagine someone as careful as her, with all her disguises and decoys, just waltzing up to her clients' home when she knows we know who they are."

"I agree. She would set up a meeting elsewhere, or arrange a drop for the money in exchange for the ring's location."

"Maybe she wasn't lying," I said, "but I'm not taking that risk. Also, I don't know where the drop was set up, if it even was."

We hopped out and crossed the road.

The house was a pretty Victorian and in good shape. White gingerbread trim framed the well-maintained brick. The neat front yard featured a mass of pink hydrangeas behind an iron railing, and the driveway off to the right held a mid-priced SUV, hockey sticks and tennis rackets in the back. A couple of Lego pieces were scattered on the porch and a mezuzah was fixed to the door frame. I pressed the doorbell and waited.

The woman who answered was the kind of woman who had the uncanny capacity to neither look old nor young. She was well groomed with ash blond hair, and a good sense of style with her high-waisted, lavender, linen pants and cream, sleeveless blouse, her bare feet in slippers. Lines crinkled the corners of her eyes. Although years had passed, she was definitely the woman in the picture outside this house and the younger woman in the other photos.

"Can I help you?" she asked.

"Ms. Abrams?" I asked in return.

"That's me. That is, I was. Abrams is my maiden

name. I'm Feldman now."

"Mrs. Feldman," I corrected. "We're here to discuss this." I handed her the file, since I could think of no better way to say "we think you commissioned a thief to get your ring back".

She opened the file and her face paled as she leafed through the documents.

Solomon produced a business card and handed it to her. She took it, hardly seeming to register it, as she flipped the pages of the dossier. "What is this?" she asked, passing it to me, pushing her shoulders back as she regained her composure. "Why do you have all these documents?"

"I thought you could tell us," I said.

"I'm the owner of the Solomon Detective Agency," said Solomon, pointing to the card in Mrs. Feldman's hand. "This is my investigator, Lexi Graves-Solomon. My investigator came across this file while researching a case and we'd like to discuss its contents with you."

"May we come in or shall we discuss it here?" I asked when a couple from the neighboring house exited and paused to glance over, taking their time as the woman locked the door.

Mrs. Feldman glanced over.

"Everything okay there, Ellie?" called the neighbor.

"Just thinking of getting some work done," Mrs. Feldman called back, forcing a smile. Then she stepped back while widening the door. "You'd better come in."

CHAPTER TWENTY-ONE

We followed Mrs. Feldman through a parquet-floor entryway into a neat sitting room decorated in powdery colors and she waved us onto the sofa while she took the armchair, sitting rigidly as she folded her hands together.

"Where did you get this?" she asked, unclasping her hands to point to the file that now lay in my lap.

"We're investigating a robbery at Reynolds' jewelry store here in town," I said, figuring I should be upfront. There was no need to try and run rings around her, no pun intended. She knew why we were here and she had to know who also had this information. What I didn't want her to do was become defensive. That wouldn't help either of us.

She laced her fingers together, resting them in her lap. "I see."

"These documents were given to us by the thief we believe was hired to commit the robbery."

"Did you recover the items stolen?" she asked. Despite her efforts to remain impassive, strain

276

glimmered in her eyes and in the tightness of her mouth. There was also a touch of eagerness that was gone as quickly as it appeared.

"The only item stolen was a ring," I said.

She held my gaze. "And where is it now?"

"In a safe place," I said. It was a lie, and yet, it wasn't. The ring almost certainly was in a safe place; I just didn't know where it was. That she'd asked me where it was indicated she didn't have it either.

That was good news for my plan.

"I'm not sure what that has to do with me," Mrs. Feldman said at last. "I don't know anything about your robbery."

"I believe you, or a member of your family, hired the thief to steal the ring on your behalf," I said, holding my hand up as she began to protest. "I can corroborate some of what's in the file from my own research, and I've no doubt I can verify the rest. I also believe the ring was stolen from its original owners, your grandparents. My client wanted me to recover the ring but they were duped and didn't know its provenance. Instead, they were given a history designed to prevent them from looking any further. They haven't done anything wrong. They are also victims here, although of a far different magnitude than your family."

"If you know so much, why haven't you called the police?" she asked.

"We don't see any need to involve them," said Solomon, "and hopefully, you won't either. Lexi has a proposition for you."

"What makes you think I want to hear it?"

"Because it's the best way for you to get your ring back and not face any charges. I think you'll find what

I have to say is fair," I said.

"And your clients?"

"We'll talk to them too," said Solomon. "Lexi and I both think they'll see the value in it."

"And if I protest my innocence in this?" Mrs. Feldman looked between the two of us.

"We won't believe you," I said, "but before you do, hear me out anyway."

Mrs. Feldman threw her hands up slightly, exasperated but willing. "Go ahead," she said.

I laid out what I knew about the ring's sale, the story Madame Michel had given me, and how the Reynolds' purchase had brought it to America. Then I explained how I thought the problem could be solved. Mrs. Feldman listened quietly and when I finished, she remained silent.

"That's a generous offer," she said, her shoulders relaxing. "Let's say, hypothetically, if I agreed that I am the one in search of the ring, you're sure your clients would agree to turning it over?"

"Yes, so long as you stick to your part of the bargain. You participate in the publicity and credit them for the repatriation."

"And you?"

"No credit necessary. I just helped join the dots and make the introductions. I want to try and find a solution for everyone. I want you to have an important part of your family history returned that should never have been stolen from your family."

Mrs. Feldman got up and walked to the window, crossing her arms as she stared out. After a minute, she turned her head and said, "My mother was their first child. She was born just after they escaped to England. Most of their family didn't get that chance. I don't need to tell you what happened to them in the Holocaust.

"When she was a child, my mom was told she would have been given that ring on her engagement. Her mother told her that's what they decided on *her* engagement, that it would go to their first daughter one day, but of course, she never got the opportunity. My mother has only ever seen the ring in photos. My grandparents were together until they passed. They were a very loving family and my grandmother always missed that token of love from her husband."

Mrs. Feldman walked past us and plucked two silver-framed photos from the mantel, passing them to us. The first was a portrait of a couple, standing stiffly in a suit and dress. The second, the same couple older now and far more relaxed, and three children in old-fashioned clothing sat in a garden around a picnic blanket. "This is my grandparents in the 1940s. My mom is the little girl with the ribbons in her hair. The other two children are her sister and brother. They were both born in America."

"They're cute," I said and Mrs. Feldman smiled.

"My grandfather's family had a furniture business and they were quite well to do. They had an affluent life in their home country, Poland. A nice house, good education, nice things. He spoke English fluently. My grandmother didn't speak of her childhood much, but when she did, it was with deep love for her parents. She last saw them when she was twenty. My great-grandfather had negotiated their passage out. He had contacts in England who would sponsor them both. They just had to get there."

She reached for another photo and passed it to me, a staged shot in a studio. The man with his arm draped around Mrs. Feldman was clearly her husband. The teenaged boy and girl, their children. "My daughter, Esther, is nearly twenty now. It made me think a lot about how my grandmother, at only a little older than Esther, newly married, pregnant, and running away from her home country, moving to England, then America with the knowledge that she survived, and her husband and baby survived, but their parents didn't. Aunts, uncles, cousins. Friends. Can you imagine such pain?"

"I'm so sorry," I said because I could not.

"Of course you are! Any normal person would be. You can see in the first photo that my grandmother is wearing the ring. It was their engagement picture."

I angled the frame for the best light, focusing closely on the woman's fingers. It wasn't the clearest of shots, and grainy with age, but it did appear to be the same ring. I passed it to Solomon to peruse.

Mrs. Feldman continued, "When life became increasingly difficult in Poland, my grandparents and their families started making plans to leave. They began to sell their possessions so they had cash. They made arrangements for the younger children, my grandparents' siblings, to go to a relative in England and paid a great deal of money for them to obtain passports and visas to travel. It wasn't easy for them since they were Jewish. It became more imperative that they left when the Nazis came to their house and stole many valuable things but didn't find the cash they'd hidden away. Anything they had left was being taxed until there was almost nothing that remained.

"My grandmother told me she and my grandfather traveled on documents belonging to children that had perished in a fire only a few years before. They were around the same age and could pose as brother and sister. The deaths of those poor children saved the lives of my grandparents. An older sibling and his family were already in the US. Another sibling managed to hide for the duration of the war. Their parents were due to join them as soon as they could. The others, an uncle, had already disappeared.

"When my grandparents left, they didn't know if they would ever see their parents again." Mrs. Feldman returned to sit on the armchair, crossing her ankles. "They each had a small suitcase. That was all their lives had been reduced to.

"Fortunately, my grandparents' families had connections who had smuggled out various paperwork in anticipation that their things would be confiscated. They'd seen it happen to other people they knew. It was supposed to be a security so that they could retrieve things in the future. Quite forward thinking.

"My grandparents and their younger siblings stayed in England for a while and then they all left for the US. By then, two of their younger siblings became of adult age and wanted to emigrate to America. They hoped to start a new life here, far from the horrors of Europe. It was only after the war ended that they were able to find records that their parents had perished in concentration camps.

"It has taken us many years, but we've found several items that were stolen from our family. The houses in Poland were gone, somewhat unsurprisingly, bulldozed long ago. The furniture business ceased operating when my great-grandparents were taken away. Some employees of the business had hidden some things, and some loyal friends too. They got them to my grandparents after the war." Mrs. Feldman paused, fixing her gaze on me again. "My grandmother didn't discuss much about the past but she always talked about this ring, and how delighted she was that day my grandfather asked to marry her. She passed away without knowing what became of it.

"Then I saw it online and found it was here! Of all the places in the world it could end up, it was *here*! It was like it had followed my grandparents. Like it wanted to be found." Mrs. Feldman laughed, surprise and joy lighting her face.

"Why didn't you contact the authorities or Reynolds'?" asked Solomon.

"Because there was no way I could afford the legal fight to have it returned, nor could I afford to purchase the ring. They wouldn't just give it to me. Why would they?"

"So you commissioned its theft," I said. It wasn't a question but a statement.

"I prefer the term repatriation. But let's say I did. What then?"

"How can you be sure it's your ring?" I asked.

"I went to inspect it weeks ago. The band is inscribed with my grandparents' initials, EM and CM. It's fortunate it hasn't been worn much over the decades as the markings are very clearly still there. There is no way it could have been made for anyone else but my great-grandmother."

"How did you find someone to steal it?" I asked. I looked around, assessing her home. She claimed not to have the money for a legal fight but she still lived in a fancy part of town and the home was large and well-maintained. "You don't look like you run with criminals."

Mrs. Feldman smiled and suppressed a laugh. "No, I don't suppose I do. I was recommended to the person we hired. *Hypothetically*, of course."

"*Of course*. By whom?" I pressed.

"By someone else whose family had things stolen during that terrible time in our world's history. Before you ask, no, I'm not giving you their name."

"I'd like to know how you made contact. *Hypothetically*."

"Hypothetically… I sent an email with the particulars of the case. I was contacted at the end of that week with questions about establishing ownership. I sent everything I had, then I was contacted with the terms. A very small sum. Half the money up front, half the money when the job was completed and the ring had been returned to me."

"So you never met?"

"No. I couldn't tell you if the person was a man or a woman. Their age. Their nationality. Their skin color. Nothing." She shrugged. "Hypothetically."

"How did you convey the cash?"

"The email requested a bank transfer. I'm not giving you those details either."

"That's fine," said Solomon, and I knew he'd have those details before the end of the day if he wanted them.

"How is the ring supposed to be delivered to you?"

"I was told to await instructions." She paused. "You do have the ring, don't you? Because, *of course*, I didn't actually commission the repatriation. It was just an exchange of emails. The money was a charitable donation. There's no crime there."

Solomon and I exchanged a look. This was where it could all go horribly wrong. Yet, Mrs. Feldman had trusted us with information. Information we couldn't use and couldn't prove she'd said, all wrapped up in *hypotheticals* and *of courses.* It was only fair we asked her to trust us.

"No," I admitted, "but I expect it will be returned to you very soon."

Mrs. Feldman drew a deep breath. "And what happens then?"

"Then we make a deal with the Reynoldses, and everyone walks away. You will have the ring and you won't risk prosecution. It will be legally yours."

"What if I don't comply? The ring belongs to my family. It never should have been stolen."

"You don't have to comply," I said, "but I think you should. Cases like these are becoming fewer and fewer in terms of success. I think it would help everyone still affected if it's publicized. I know it was a terrible wrong, but we can try to do something right to help you and maybe others too."

"All right then," she said. "I'll agree but only once the ring is in my possession. Until then, all this is a crazy fantasy that no one can prove."

"You'll contact us when you receive the ring?" asked Solomon.

"I will."

Solomon rose. I stood but he didn't make a move for the door. "Thanks for hearing us out," I said, shaking her hand. "And I'm really very sorry about what was done to your family. I hope you know we really do want to help."

"Just help me right the wrong," she said. "We've waited long enough."

CHAPTER TWENTY-TWO

"That's quite the story," said Laura.

The office at the back of Reynolds' Fine Jewelry was stuffy and silent. Both Alan and Laura Reynolds had listened as I repeated the story, as closely as I could to Ellie Feldman and Cass Temple's claims, and explained how the ring had been stolen. Then they exchanged glances and remained silent, their faces indecipherable although I could imagine the whirring of their minds.

With tension hanging in the air between us, all Solomon and I could do was wait for them to make a decision. Behind us waited Dad, stoically silent, listening.

"All right," said Laura, finally. "We'll do it. Alan?"

"It's the right thing to do," said Alan. He ran a hand over his hair and blew out a breath, giving himself a small shake. "Gosh, it really does blow the mind. What a tragedy."

Laura nodded. "It's very different from what we were told but the engraved initials are correct. I didn't put photos of that on the website. That, combined with the documents you showed us, clinches it for me. Oh, I feel just awful that I purchased the ring in the first place. Do you think the Michels knew? Could they have been a party to thefts like that?"

"Madame Michel wouldn't have been born and her mother would have only been a young woman when she came into possession of it, but perhaps? Or her father Jean Dupuis, or their other associates? I found evidence of her parents at a ball with Nazi insignias so it's a strong possibility they supported the regime and profited from it."

"What revolting people," said Laura, distaste etched on the downturn of her mouth. "I don't want the ring back. We couldn't possibly profit from something with that kind of history. No, when it's found, we must return it to the rightful heirs."

"I agree," said Alan. "We'll write off the purchase price somehow. I think we can get the money refunded between our credit card company and the insurers so we won't lose out. The purchase was based on fraud."

"I think that's the end of my vintage purchasing too. I can't risk making a mistake like that again," said Laura with a worried glance at her brother before she turned to me. "I feel like I should have you investigate every last vintage piece we have, just in case. Thankfully, our stock is running low and now I don't intend to purchase more."

"The publicity might help put you at ease," I said. "You would be seen as helping victims, which you want to do anyway, and it should prevent anyone from attempting to sell pieces like that to you in the future. Plus, it will make others more cautious."

"She makes a good point," said Alan, nodding

along. "If it's highly publicized that we value integrity when purchasing items, then no one will want to sell anything dubious to us, and the buyers will be reassured."

"I still don't think I'll take the risk. I'd rather invest in upcoming designers like Jonathan. Do you really think there are more items like the ring around?" asked Laura.

I nodded. "Yes, but as time passes, it'll be harder for survivors and their families to prove ownership and repatriate them. Plus, many of the original owners have passed on and can never truly be avenged or compensated."

"At least we can do something for *this* family," said Laura. "Yes, it's settled. We'll do it. The ring is theirs."

"We'd like to meet them. We'd like to be part of their ring's return. Perhaps we can give them some kind of certification so their ownership is never in question along with a paper trail. It's not much perhaps, but it's something," said Alan. "We can talk it over with them."

"I think they'll appreciate that."

"It's a really good thing you're all doing," said Dad at last.

"Then that's case closed for us," said Laura with a sigh. "But I'd really like to know how we can prevent a theft from happening again."

"We can upgrade all your security but this was a simple case of distraction coupled with sleight of hand," said Solomon. "It's unlikely you can fully prevent a theft like that from occurring again. Steve, do you have an opinion?"

"From my observations, simple preventative measures such as your sales team keeping trays behind a glass partition and only offering one item for prospective buyers to examine at a time would be the simplest method," said Dad. "That, along with the security system upgrades are quick and easy."

"I had a good look at the system and have a plan for the overhaul. We can retrofit an upgraded system with what you already have," said Solomon. "That will come with security monitoring too. If you want to go higher end, we can look at ram raid prevention too but I don't think it's necessary here."

"And the thief? Do you think she'll come back?" asked Laura.

"It's unlikely. Our intel is that she steals for hire and this was a specific case. We don't expect she'll return to your shop," I said, leaning in as I explained. "She doesn't steal for personal gain. Or, at least, not in the way your average thief does." I thought about the diamonds Cass Temple had lifted from under our noses in our last case, and the shell companies and buildings she owned. It was unlikely she even needed the money from her commissions. So what made her do it? Was it the thrill of the job? Or the satisfaction in righting wrongs? How did she really make her money? Perhaps one day she would tell me.

"I'm not sure what that means exactly but I think it's supposed to be reassuring," said Alan.

"Do you have a picture of the thief?" asked Laura.

"Not a clear one but she's a master of disguise so I'm not sure it would help you," said Solomon. He began to rise and the rest of us followed. "The Feldmans are expecting your call," he added.

"One more thing," said Laura, stopping us in the doorway.

"Yes?" I asked, knowing it was going to be the

question I was dreading. The question that everything hinged on.

"Do you have the ring?"

There it was. The question that could bring the whole deal crashing down.

"Not yet," I said.

"Where is it?" asked Alan, confused now. "I got the impression you had it or knew where it was."

"Do you *know* where it is?" pressed Laura.

"I know who has it and I believe it's still here in town but I don't know the exact location. I do believe the Feldmans will receive it."

"There's no point in us calling the Feldmans until the ring turns up," said Laura.

"There's no deal without the ring at all," added Alan. He folded his arms, a touch defensively. "We like your plan but it all hinges on the ring."

"We'll call when we have information," said Solomon. "A little patience will go a long way here."

"We just want what's best for everyone," I said.

"I'll wrap up here," said Dad, giving me a hug. "Well done," he said softly in my ear and squeezed me harder.

We left Reynolds' by the front entrance and walked to the car. "That went better than I expected," I said, still warm from the hug and praise. "But the ring is a problem."

"The Reynoldses are good people," said Solomon. "And you were right that they would be appalled and want to help. Where to now? I can take you back to the office, then I have a site visit. Or do you have a lead to follow?"

"The office works for me. I have a lot of paperwork to do and even more thinking."

"Let's go."

I didn't want to muse any more about the case but when Solomon dropped me outside the office before speeding off and disappearing around the corner, my thoughts were still full of the *what ifs*. I turned, ready to head inside the office and found my way blocked by a pale blue, open-necked shirt, and a red face.

"How could you?" yelled Maddox.

"Pardon?" I said, taking a step backwards, then thinking better of it and stepping forwards again, holding my ground.

"You helped her, didn't you?"

"I help lots of people!"

"Cass Temple! Whatever sob story she told you, it's BS, and whatever she offered you... well, that's BS too!"

"Beef strips?" I asked.

"The other BS."

"Bongo solo?"

"No. BS!"

"Bandit..."

"Bull shit!" yelled Maddox, causing a middle-aged couple to turn and tut.

"Oh, that. Why didn't you say so?" I stepped around him, heading for the sanctity of my office where no one yelled at me without giving a reason first.

Maddox made a strangled, gurgling noise deep in his throat. Perhaps he was swallowing an apology for accosting me in the street?

"You helped my perp escape!"

"No, I didn't!"

Maddox's eyes widened at the lie. "You did! Farid and I saw it on camera at the motel. Cass Temple thought she was being clever taking rooms at a motel with a sketchy camera system but there was one that caught you both. You found her room and you let her go."

I pulled a face. "Technically, Lily found her room."

Maddox made another gurgling noise.

"I wouldn't say I let her go," I said, wincing.

"What would you call it?"

"I... didn't stand in her way."

"You could have told me on the phone. That's why you called to see where I was, wasn't it? I was sheer minutes away, and when I was in the reception area, seconds! I could have apprehended her. What did she promise you?"

"Nothing!"

Maddox narrowed his eyes. "Really?"

"Really! She didn't have to. I already had what I wanted."

"Oh, yeah?"

"Yeah," I sighed and my shoulders dropped. So much for a great day with a great resolution to my case. "Then she stole it right back."

This time, Maddox let out a guffaw. "What else did you expect from a thief?"

"She talked a lot about honor!"

"Amongst thieves?"

"Well, no. Amongst good people doing the right thing."

"And you fell for it." Not a question, a statement.

"Of course not!" I paused... Maddox was right. I'd totally fallen for it but that didn't make her story any less true. Damn it! But what did that matter? She was still going to deliver the ring to the Feldmans. Of that, I was sure. She couldn't justify the theft of the ring without that final step. "What does it matter anyway?

She's gone." Even as I said it, I wasn't so sure. Just why did she have a safe house in a minor city like this? She could have hideouts anywhere… so why here? What drew her *here*?

Then I thought, was the *what* actually a *who* and was he standing right in front of me?

"That's exactly why it does matter. This was my best lead in I don't know how long and you blew it. For all I know, you took a nose dive down that chute just to help her out by distracting me. Thanks a bunch, Lexi."

I'd seen Maddox mad before but never as furious as he was now and I couldn't help feel a teensy bit like I'd made a fatal error. Yet it wasn't my fault that our cases had overlapped and he failed to apprise me about his investigation. If he'd told me what was going on, perhaps I would have done something differently. Instead, he'd stuck to parting with as little information as he could. Despite what he'd said about Cass Temple, she'd stuck around long enough to ensure she delivered the ring to her client, no matter the risk to herself. Only I'd screwed up that plan and now she'd gone to ground.

"I don't suppose you know where she is?" I asked.

Maddox's eyes flashed. "Seriously? You want me to help you?"

"Yes." I nodded emphatically.

"Why would I do that?"

"Because you still need help finding her?"

"Let me get this straight… you want me to help you find her?"

"Yes, please."

"Like you haven't already aided and abetted her escape. I could arrest you for that. I could charge you."

I winced. "I am really sorry," I said.

"You weren't sorry when you weren't caught," he shot back.

"I was and I feel terrible about it now."

"Because she double-crossed you."

"I…"

"Hmm?"

"You're making a lot of good points," I said, "and I am sorry. I didn't mean for any of this to happen. I just wanted a good outcome for the Feldmans."

"And they would be?"

I paused. Now would be a good time to share. Now would be a good time to get back into Maddox's good graces. Plus, I still didn't have any hard evidence implicating Ellie Feldman in the crime. It was all hypothetical, even if my gut knew it all lined up.

"Ellie Feldman commissioned Cass Temple to steal the ring," I said. "Mrs. Feldman lives in Chilton and the ring belonged to her grandparents, the Mendelsons, and it was stolen just before World War II broke out."

"I can guess the rest," said Maddox. "Your clients bought the ring unwittingly and Cass stole it for Mrs. Feldman."

"Yes."

"Anything you can prove?"

"Beyond highly probable but based on circumstantial evidence? No."

"Anything that will stand up in court?"

"Not with a good defense. Plus, my clients don't want to go to court. They're going to give up the ring and transfer ownership to Mrs. Feldman in return for a bucket load of good publicity. I doubt there will be any case against Cass Temple so whatever your case is, you better hope it's watertight because my case is a bucket full of holes."

"Let's get a drink," said Maddox. "All this is giving me a headache and a dry mouth."

"Beer?" I suggested, checking my watch.

"No, it's not that bad that I need to turn to the drink. Plus, I'm still on the clock. How about the café down the street? The one with the striped parasols? You can buy me an iced coffee."

"Deal," I agreed since it was a better offer than his previous suggestion of arresting me. Plus, a few dollars on coffee would go a long way in getting Maddox to open up. Not as much as beer would but I lived in hope.

Maddox refused to be drawn into the topic of Cass Temple as we strolled down the street so instead I told him about the Feldmans and the Reynoldses, and my discoveries about the Michels and Cosette Durand. By the time we sat at a sidewalk table, the last one available, iced coffees dripping beads of water down the glasses, he seemed to have relaxed into a better mood.

"I can't deny you've helped do some good here," said Maddox, which was high praise from him.

"Thank you, but none of it is set in stone until that ring turns up. I'm sure Cass Temple is still in town and I'm sure she'll deliver it."

"I agree but the question is when. She could have left town already with two of her safe houses burned, intending to return at a later date when there's less interest in her." Maddox paused to sip, leaving a sliver of foam on his lip. "I could post a team on the Feldmans' house but there's no way I can get the sign-off to do that indefinitely. It could take weeks or months for Temple to show, if she does at all."

"If she doesn't, she won't get her fee from the Feldmans," I pointed out. On the table next to us, two women were sharing a slice of cake and chattering happily and for a moment, I envied their ease.

Maddox snorted. "Whatever they're paying her, it's chump change. She probably did it for the challenge and the satisfaction, more than the payment. Plus, she could put something like that in the mail and be entirely hands off."

That gave me another thought, a niggling loose end that I thought we'd discounted. "You said you were going to Germany. That was about Cass Temple, right?"

"It was."

"I told you the Reynoldses had a call from Berlin about the ring."

"You did."

"Was that Cass Temple?"

"We have an image of her at the city's main train station a couple of days after that call. So the probability is high but I couldn't confirm it."

That didn't surprise me at all but I was pleased Maddox had answered. I sipped my coffee, finding it perfectly ice cold and sweet. "We're both in agreement she'll hand over the ring. It's just a case of when. Maybe we should smoke her out."

"Sure. How do you plan on doing that?"

"Uh…" I stopped, entirely clueless. Our best leads had been Maddox tracking her safe house—now blown, and Lucas tracking her vehicle—now abandoned. I had no idea where she was, who might be helping her, nor what resources she had beyond that bundle of cash she'd taken. I didn't know nearly enough about her, nor her movements, to have any clue.

But I did have one thing.

I had an email address.

She'd told me I could use it about the case, and nothing else. Which was fine because I wanted to email her about the case… and everything else. But if I did that, she might flee.

So I was back to square one. Or, as I liked to call him, Maddox.

"Thought so," he said.

"You must have something," I said. "There must be something in your research that suggests where she might be."

"There was. I got the safe house right. She was there and she shoved you down a laundry chute."

I touched my cheek gently, finding it tender but not as sore. "Don't remind me." There was a long pause while we sipped. Then, I said, "Really? You don't have anything? How long have you been tracking her?"

"Too long."

"What aren't you telling me?" The words that had been hovering on the edge of my mind finally slipped out.

"I don't know what you mean," he said, the expression on his face so purposefully casual that I knew he knew exactly what I meant.

"Are you supposed to get involved with your targets?" I asked coolly like it was any other innocent question.

Maddox spluttered on the sip he had just taken. "I am not… *what*? You're crazy!"

"Thought so." I gave him my best knowing look, because I'd known him long enough to know the truth could be wrapped in spluttering indignation.

"I don't know what you think but that's not it."

"How do you know that's not it if you don't know what I think?" I fired back.

"I know you're crazy."

"Women are never crazier than when they're right," I said, deciding I needed to get that printed on a mug, a tote bag, and a t-shirt.

Maddox snorted again and checked his shirt for coffee drips. Apparently satisfied there weren't any, he sipped again, then set his tall glass on the table. "We are not together. We are not an item, as your mom would say. We did know each other in our youth, something I'm keeping quiet from my superiors. Only my partner knows, and now you," he said, without needing to add he trusted me to keep that quiet. I would. That was a given.

"How did you know each other?" I asked, the first of approximately seventeen questions to flood my brain all at the same time.

"We just did. I knew her dad too. Then one day, they were just gone and I never heard from her again and life moved on." Maddox paused, raising his glass but not bringing it to his lips. "Then I found her in the middle of one of my cases, put two and two together, and she disappeared again. She's been doing it ever since. I get close and… she's gone."

"That's how you know her real name," I said.

"Yeah, we were teenagers when we met. There was no reason not to use actual names back then. I thought I knew her family well and then years and years after they disappeared, I got wind that her dad was one of the most prolific thieves in the US."

"What's his name?" I asked, reaching for my phone, prepared for the most intense ten minutes of

Googling I might have ever in my life; except for that time Lily and I searched a guy I was about to go on a first date with and found he had nine children, seven baby mamas —none of whom had anything nice to say about him—and a pending court date for petty theft. Which was a shame because he was six-foot-two.

"Don't bother. You won't find anything."

"Why not?"

"Nothing was ever proved and he went dark a long time ago."

"What do you mean 'went dark'?"

"Just that. He disappeared. I'd like to think he's sipping pina coladas on a beach somewhere in South America but the reality is he's probably dead."

"Did you ask Cass?"

"Yes, and she didn't tell me anything. I don't even think she knows."

"This sounds like Ben Rafferty slash Gideon Black all over again."

"I thought that during the case. Part of me wondered if it would be old man Temple uncovered in that shallow grave. I was relieved that it wasn't."

Instead of returning my phone to my pocket, I asked, "What year did you graduate?"

"If you're about to stalk my high school yearbook and as many other years as you feel like searching, don't bother, Cass left town before graduation. She's not in the yearbook. There're traces of her. A birth certificate... a few other things... but officially? Officially, Cass Temple doesn't exist."

CHAPTER TWENTY-THREE

Long after Maddox and I parted company, I fretted about how to smoke Cass Temple out. I researched her identity for two useless, frustrating hours, using the scant information he'd supplied. I set Lucas on the task—without revealing Maddox's connection—and he confessed to not finding anything in the same time frame. Not only that, but he'd hit a wall with the shell corporations and the bank accounts we suspected she used to buy the building Maddox and I had infiltrated.

Maddox was right. Cass Temple was a ghost.

I'd even gone back to the safe house and sat in my car, observing the area closely, noting the occasional person entering and the pedestrians walking past. The penthouse apartment remained empty, no one visible through the broad window panes. Finally, I went to the motel but the silver hatchback was already gone, the space filled by an old sedan. I even thought about heading to Harmony Retirement Village but decided against it. Cass Temple wasn't going to retrace old footsteps. Cass was going forwards.

Ellie Feldman was the future.

She had yet to call me and say the ring had been returned so I had to assume Cass was still biding her time, waiting for the right moment.

By the time I'd written up my report and gone home to eat a light supper, pull on my sleeping dinosaur pajamas, and crawl into bed next to Solomon, I was ready to admit defeat.

Not permanent defeat, but definitely for tonight as I drifted to sleep, my thoughts burdening me.

By the time I awoke, a sliver of sunlight peeking through a chink in the drapes, and the smell of coffee drifting up to the bedroom, I was marginally less pessimistic.

"You were tossing and turning all night," said Solomon when I walked into the kitchen, tucking my sleeveless blouse into my mini skirt. He sat at the kitchen island, newspaper open, coffee in hand. "It was like being in bed with a washing machine."

"Sexy washing machine, thank you," I said, planting a kiss on his cheek as I passed on my way to the coffee pot.

"You seem remarkably perky given how fed up you looked last night."

"It's my superpower." I poured coffee and joined him at the island. "Are you going to Reynolds' today?"

"Yes, one last pass at their recommended security upgrades and then we're installing the hardware. Your dad sent his undercover report already. He had nothing pertinent to report and my assessment of the thief returning to the shop is running at zero percent."

"All that's left is getting the ring back," I said, "until then, there's no deal."

"The ring will turn up."

"The deal might not hold if it doesn't happen quickly. I have an idea how to make that sooner rather than later." While I'd showered, my determination had returned and one option left became clear.

"Oh?"

"It might not work."

"Or it might," countered Solomon. "Do I want to know?"

"It's nothing dangerous."

"Now I don't know whether to believe you. Most people don't start with 'It's nothing dangerous'. They just expect everyone assumes that's the case."

"I thought I was being reassuring!"

"I've met you. Finding you in one piece at the end of the day is reassuring."

I laughed.

Solomon went about putting his breakfast things away and folding the newspaper. He offered it to me but I declined. Instead, I pulled out my phone, made two quick calls that gave me the answers I needed before I clicked on my email app as Solomon's phone rang and he excused himself.

I typed: *Cass, hi. The Reynoldses and Ellie Feldman are both willing to work with each other. Reynolds' will transfer ownership of ring to Mrs. Feldman. No cost. No prosecution. Meeting with both today at the Feldman house at 4PM. Please hand over the ring so the deal can go ahead. Lexi Graves-Solomon.*

Then I inserted the email address Cass had given me.

I read the message four times but I still didn't hit *send*.

Would it be enough to induce her to do what I needed?

I had to hope so. Short of tracking Cass down to her lair—and I was convinced she had one because what was the point of being a globe-trotting thief with a heart of gold, if she didn't get to have a lair?—this would have to do.

I took a deep breath and hit *send*.

But that got me thinking… if Cass were still in town, where would she be?

"I got a call about an incident across town," said Solomon, returning to the kitchen. "I'm going to meet Delgado there. What are your plans?"

"Poke around town a little and then tackle my paperwork. I arranged for the Reynoldses and Feldman to meet later today." I sipped my coffee, feeling quietly pleased at my plan. If Cass didn't agree, I needed to know where she was hiding out.

"Do you want me as backup?"

"I think I have it covered."

"Call if you change your mind," said Solomon.

When the front door clicked shut after him, I called Lily.

"I just dropped Poppy off at daycare and my beer supplier rescheduled their order. Do you want to get breakfast? We don't even have to get it at the bar. We could go anywhere!"

"I want to find Cass Temple before her trail is stone cold. I can't just rely on her to turn up."

"More fun, less nutritious," said Lily. "Pick me up from outside the bar?"

"On my way."

"Bring breakfast!"

I didn't bring breakfast but I did swing through the drive-through for smoothies, which Lily grabbed gratefully when she hopped into the passenger seat.

"Where are we going?" she asked as she pulled the seatbelt across her chest.

"Where would you go if you were a well-resourced, globe-trotting jewel thief with a bag of cash?"

"The mall."

"Why the mall?"

"She needs more clothes than she had in her bag. She only had two days of clean clothes. She doesn't look like she slums it."

"Okay, aside from the mall."

"A really nice hotel with room service."

I gave her side eye. "Really?"

"Being a globe-trotting jewel thief comes with a lot of danger. The opposite of danger is relaxation. Everyone needs balance."

"No, it isn't, it's saf—"

"And relaxation means a bathtub," continued Lily, talking over me. "It means room service dinner on a big tray on the enormous bed. A large glass of wine and dessert. Maybe two desserts. All that running away from the right side of the law would make me hungry."

I had to admit that did sound nice.

"Where's the last place you would go?"

"As a sexy, international, jewel thief?"

"Yeah."

"The scene of the crime."

"Obviously."

"Was it though? You did ask the question."

"Fair point. Where's the other last place you'd go?" I asked, already thinking. Cass Temple wouldn't be foolish enough to go to the safe house she seemed to own through her shell corps, or the motel with her trio of rooms. I wasn't sure if she had access to a new vehicle. I grabbed my phone, quickly typing a message to Lucas to ask if he could find out what happened to the hatchback. That left one place it would be absurd to go to…

"The retirement village!" we both said at the same time.

"She would be nuts to go there," said Lily.

"No, she wouldn't. No one would recognize her. She could pose as an employee, or someone's granddaughter, or a therapist." I bet they get strangers in and out of there all the time.

"And do what? Hang out?"

"There was at least one empty apartment. She could squat in that until she's ready to make her next move." I was already firing up the engine and pulling into traffic before Lily could call me crazy. It was the only idea I had and it was barely a lead.

"Do you think she's sexy?" I wondered.

"Hundred percent smokin'," said Lily and I sighed. "But she's got nothing on us."

"Except the jump," I reminded her.

When we reached Harmony Retirement Village, I pulled over onto the side of the road opposite the bus stop, just as I had that first time Lily directed us here. I'd contemplated driving into the resident parking lot, like Cass had in her old lady disguise, but there was no guarantee we'd see her. If we did, and she took off for the front of the building and my car was in the back, we'd lose precious time retrieving it with no guarantee of picking up the chase.

Plus, I wanted to check my email and my phone had pinged with a message from Lucas that I wanted to read.

"Her vehicle is an official dead end," I said, showing Lily the grainy video Lucas sent me of the vehicle being loaded onto a truck and carted away. "He says the recovery firm is contracted to the FBI. She's definitely not driving it."

"Not after you drove into it. I bet you get an insurance claim. How did your car avoid any damage? I didn't see a scrape on it."

"Luck. I doubt Cass filed a complaint or completed any paperwork," I said as I checked my email. No emails from Cass Temple waited. Damn! "Maybe Maddox called it in. I'd ask but then I'd have to tell him what we're doing and right now, we're at a good place." Not that I wanted to ruin that but I didn't have anything to tell him yet. If I found Cass Temple... then I'd tell him.

"Ask later," said Lily.

We strolled across the road, walked along the driveway and entered the building, thankful for a lack of joyriding elderly citizens intent on mowing us down in their mobility scooters, or geriatric flirts.

Inside, the atmosphere was subdued. Two orderlies were stationed at the reception desk, and another pushed a wheelchair with a chattering resident past us. Then came a crocodile of twelve men and women all moving quickly, and quietly, towards the recreation room.

Lily and I exchanged a glance and followed them.

"Why's it so quiet?" she asked a straggler.

"There was a party last night. Someone brought a keg and set up a martini bar in one of the apartments. Everyone's sleeping it off."

"Is that... is it..." Lily sniffed the air. "Marijuana?"

"What are you? A cop?" snorted the straggler, darting a suspicious look at us before shuffling after the faster movers.

"They're not just sleeping off alcohol," said Lily. "They're all going to have the raging munchies when they wake up. We should have brought snacks."

"Do you have the munchies?"

"No! I'm a responsible grown-up. I meant, we should have brought snacks in case we needed bribes."

"We're just poking around. We don't need bribes."

"You say that now." We walked through the recreation room on the way to the exterior doors. Several bleary-eyed residents were sitting around with plates of cookies and tall glasses of lemonade. One gentleman lay on the couch, his arms around a banana-shaped pillow. He wore a Hawaiian shirt, a straw cowboy hat, and had a cigar wedged between his lips.

"I like this place," said Lily, her eyes widening. "I could see us living here when we're old."

"Everyone here will be dead by then!" I grimaced as the table of ladies next to us gasped and gave me the stink eye. "I thought I said that quietly."

"Top-of-the-line hearing aids, honey," said the lady closest to me. "I can almost hear your thoughts."

"I'm sorry," I said.

"You should be. That stuff is fruity." Her companions hooted as she turned back to them.

"What were you thinking?" asked Lily.

"I know, I should have spoken more quietly."

"No, I mean your thoughts. What did she hear you think?"

"She did not hear me think! She was… oh, never mind." We'd stepped out onto the path that horse-shoed around the garden. One way was Evelyn and Judy, Cass's unwitting accomplices. The other direction was new territory.

"Excuse me," I said to the man with the wheeled

walker coming towards us at a rate of no knots.

"Speak up," he barked, stopping to cup his ear.

"Which apartments are free?" I asked, my voice raised.

"None of them," he barked. "Cost an arm and a leg."

"Hilarious," said Lily between snorts of laughter.

"No, I mean, which are empty?"

He stepped closer, peering at me. "Are you moving in? Well, I'll be damned. Wait 'til the ol' boys hear about this." He winked and shuffled past.

"I'm not but if there're any free apartments, maybe my grandma will and then we'll visit every day," I called after him, which wasn't far, given he'd only moved six inches at the max.

He stopped. "In that case. 1J over there in the corner is empty and 4F is too but your grandma will need to be spritely for 4F since the elevator is forever fizzling out and the stairs get slippery when wet. How're her legs?"

"She's got them," I said.

He nodded appreciatively. "That'll do," he said. "Can't ask for more than that." He shuffled off without a backwards glance.

"Would you want your grandma to live here? She must be close to a hundred by now. You could visit her more often," said Lily.

I recoiled in horror. "You've met Grandma O'Shaughnessy. I want her to live out her days happily in Ireland where I can't hear her curses."

"You're still pissed that she thought I was you and then got disappointed to find out you were her granddaughter."

"She put a curse on me!"

"Fat lot of good that did! Your life turned out just fine," said Lily, then she paused and added, "except for the shooting, stabbing, kidnapping, and getting thrown down a laundry chute."

"I survived them all," I said proudly as my cheek bruise gave a little pulse of alarm. "Grandma's curses will never take me down." Although, even as I said it, I wasn't so sure. Grandma O'Shaughnessy was pretty feisty and seemed to have lived so long that I half-suspected she was brewing her own longevity potions and dancing naked under the full moon. One of those thoughts I could do without.

Apartment 1J was the corner unit and the door was closed. The plants and bushes under the window were as lush as any other in the village but the windows were dark and the door remained unanswered.

I pressed my forehead against the window and squinted. "I don't see anyone inside and nothing to suggest anyone's been there," I said. "Let's check the back and look through the bedroom window."

"I feel like a peeper," said Lily.

"It's never bothered you before," I said as we rounded the corner and headed for the rear.

"True," said Lily, "and I don't think it bothers me now."

We both peered into the large rear window. The bed had a bare mattress and the closet doors stood open. No comforter, no pillows, and definitely no bag full of cash and alternate identities. Not even an empty water bottle. "She's not here," I decided.

"4F?"

"Let's go."

We stepped out of the flower bed, and walked around to the front, looking up for an indication of where 4F might be situated. As I turned my gaze to the left, I grabbed Lily's arm and pulled her back, out of sight behind the corner.

"She's up there!"

"Where?" Lily started to poke her head around the corner but I pulled her back.

"Up! There!" I pointed. "I saw Cass Temple. She was coming out onto the balcony and she had her backpack over her shoulder. She must have stayed the night."

"She stands out like a sore thumb. She's fifty years too young for this place."

"She probably had a story worked out, like us when we go poking around."

"She's so smart," sighed Lily.

"Stop it."

"Are you jealous?"

"What? No? Why would I be jealous?" I snipped, wrinkling my nose in offense.

"Because she's so smart."

"I'm smart!"

"*Okay*," said Lily.

"I am!" I insisted.

"Not 'international criminal who gets away with it' smart."

"I'm 'gonna catch her' smart," I said. "If the elevator is working, I need you to engage it and wedge something in the doors so she can't use it. I'm going to take the stairs and cut her off."

"On it," said Lily and saluted me.

I peeked around the corner. Cass Temple's head and shoulders were visible above the balcony wall as she started in the direction of both the elevator and the stairs. We needed to cut her off—now! "Ready? Go!"

We took off along the pathway, hugging the building as closely as we could and hoping our target didn't look down. When we reached the elevator, Lily punched the lift button, which flashed that it was opening.

Lily grabbed a nearby lawn chair and brandished it as the doors slid open. "I'll stick this in the doors," she said.

I gave her the thumbs up and began to ascend the stairs, knowing that at any moment I would come face-to-face with Cass. I didn't know which of us had the upper hand. Me because I knew what I was walking towards, or her because she was descending and had velocity behind her if she chose to take me out like a bowling ball.

I rounded the first turn. No Cass.

The second, and I paused, my back to the wall as I heard footsteps.

Then she was there, in front of me, and her eyes widened a smidge. "How did you find me?" she asked, stopping dead still.

"I'll never tell." Damn it. I would lie awake at night and think of fifteen better responses, all infinitely cooler than that.

"Okay, sure," Cass said as she glanced over her shoulder.

"You're surrounded."

"By octogenarians," she fired back.

"Did you get my email?"

"I got it."

"I only want the ring, then you're free to go."

"What makes you think I still have it?"

"Ellie Feldman doesn't have it and neither do the Reynoldses. They've made a deal. If you don't hand it over, the deal's off."

"I didn't make a deal with you," she said, pointing to me.

"It doesn't matter. I'm trying to help you out here. The Reynoldses will relinquish the ring. Ellie Feldman will get it back, and both of them can stir up some publicity to help others in the same position. It's a win for everyone."

"And you get to wrap the case up nicely. Is there a bonus in it for you?"

"No. We're writing off the fee for the ring investigation. I just want to do the right thing." I held out my hand, palm open, waiting. All she had to do was reach forwards and drop it in my hand.

"What about me?"

From the corner of my eye, I saw Lily edging around the corner of the stairwell.

At that moment, Cass turned and leaped onto the top of the balcony. Her backpack slipped from her shoulder and she caught it with her hand before it dropped away. I darted forwards and grabbed the other strap just as she jumped. As she fell, I pulled hard with both hands, throwing myself backwards, and jerked it out of her hands. Scrambling to my feet, I rushed to the edge and looked over.

Cass had landed on the ground, and was rolling before springing to her feet.

"Drop the backpack," she called, waving for me to throw it.

I unzipped it, checking inside. The cash and the identities remained but the ring wasn't inside. "Four PM at the Feldmans'," I said, hoping Cass wanted the contents enough for me to use the backpack as leverage. "Return the ring and I'll give you the backpack."

She looked at me long and hard, then nodded and sprinted away.

"C'mon," I said to Lily as we watched her disappear once again. "We've got work to do."

~

"Are you sure this is going to fly?" asked Lily.

"You look more nervous than the Feldmans and the Reynoldses," I said, casting a glance at the huddle of people in the Feldmans' living room. Solomon and my dad had arrived only minutes ago, the muscle if we needed it. Not that I thought a fight would break out but tensions were high and the excitement palpable.

"I'm very invested in this. I got you the big lead to find your thief and I want to see her get her just desserts, although I'm not sure what those should be. Did she really do the wrong thing?"

I looked between the Reynoldses and the Feldman family, all chatting away without any hint of awkwardness. I had no idea what the answer was so I said, "I'll make sure you get credit in my report."

"Thanks, and I'll send you my fee."

"Sure! You can have ten percent of mine."

Lily's eyebrows rose in surprise. "Really?"

"Sure. Let me see what ten percent works out to be," I said, counting on my fingers. "Hmm, one hundred percent of zero, minus ninety percent, equals... zero!" I closed my fingers into a fist and dropped my hand.

"Yay! I'll take that in cash." Lily laughed, not at all perturbed at her cut.

"Here," I said, brushing my palm rapidly like I was dispensing dollar bills.

Lily mimed tucking the phantom bills into her back pocket. "Pleasure doing business with you."

It was exactly three fifty PM and we were standing in the window of Ellie Feldman's townhouse. Behind us were Alan Reynolds, Laura Reynolds, Ellie and her husband, Danny, and Ellie's mom, Ruth Abrams, formerly Mendelson. Ellie had put out homemade cookies and tall, ice-filled jugs of lemonade like we were having a book club meeting, not waiting to repatriate stolen jewelry.

The meeting, so far, had been smooth, not awkward. The Reynoldses had arrived armed with all their documentation and a dozen fascinating stories of how they acquired jewelry for the vintage arm of their business. Laura reddened as she told the gathering how it hadn't occurred to her to ask about Madame Michel's war era affiliations, and how the Frenchwoman had been indignant when she'd called, refusing to speak further. The Feldmans, in return, had been warm and welcoming, keen to share their own documents and tales. Not one of them had shot an accusation at the other, which was good because I'd been concerned about tensions rising.

Ellie Feldman had technically commissioned a crime, but the Reynoldses had decided to take the bigger view. The ring had been stolen from Ruth's parents, and the Reynoldses could help right a terrible wrong.

Now, Ruth was telling everyone a story about her early years in America and the others were laughing and Ellie was passing Alan old photos, pointing out the jewelry worn, asking for his and Laura's expert opinions and thoughts.

I glanced at my watch, three fifty-five.

Five minutes to go.

Then I glanced at my feet where Cass Temple's

backpack slumped. Once Cass had run from us again, Lily and I had taken the backpack to the agency and turned it upside-down and inside out, patting it down to ensure it was empty. I'd catalogued the contents, xeroxed the IDs and counted the cash before returning everything to the backpack.

Now I was toying with the idea of leaving the backpack on the stoop for Cass to collect because I couldn't fathom her not delivering the ring somehow. But would it be in person? Or would she send an intermediary? Or lead me on another chase?

The latter was the worst possible outcome because, so far, Cass had won every chase. I might have found her each time—partially thanks to Lily—but she'd also outsmarted me.

Only this time, I had leverage.

I had something she wanted and I was pretty sure it was the passports, her face accompanied by a different name on each one.

Three fifty-eight.

I scanned the street, noting the two women walking past, deep in conversation, a dog on a leash. On the other side of the street, a man jogged. Two cars passed.

Just when I was about to turn away, I saw her.

She was just standing there.

On the other side of the road, a Red Sox cap pulled low over her eyes, long blonde hair sweeping to her elbows, her sweetheart face undeniably familiar despite the large sunglasses. She wore a t-shirt, cut-off jeans, and sneakers, every inch a woman in summer. Her hands were thrust inside her pockets.

She lifted one hand and tapped her forefinger in the air, towards me.

"Lexi, look at this," called Laura. "I'd love to know

what you... oh!"

I grabbed the backpack, darting around Laura as she approached me, ignoring Ellie Feldman's gasp, and wrenched open the front door as a large truck trundled past. When it cleared, the street was empty.

Cass had disappeared.

At my feet, on the brick stoop, was a small, black box.

I squatted to pick it up, snapping the lid open and smiled.

The ring had come home.

Underneath it was a scrap of folded paper. I unfolded it: *Drop the backpack over the side and close the door.*

Without looking, I dropped the backpack over the railing where it landed with a small thump. I turned away, closing the door behind me. Not just on the street and the backpack, but on Cass and the case.

"Is that...?" Ellie started as I rested my back against the door. Everyone had grouped into the entrance to the hallway, expectant expressions on their faces. I smiled. "Mom?" Ellie stepped away, letting her mother come forward, slow but steady with her cane.

"I think this is yours," I said, and offered her the open ring box.

Ruth's jaw trembled as she took the box in her shaky hand and gazed at the ring. "You don't know what this means," she said, her eyes filling with tears. "This is the only piece I have of my parents beside photos. Oh, look everyone, look!" She turned, showing them all the ring as they crowded around her, voices chorusing at once.

The commotion was suddenly interrupted by the wail of a siren close by and then it was receding into the distance, the voices picking up again.

"Was that Maddox's SUV?" asked Lily, her hand shielding her eyes as she peered through the window panes surrounding the door.

I grinned. "Gosh, was it?"

"What about honor amongst thieves?"

"I'm not a thief," I said and winked. Cass Temple might have upheld her part of the bargain, but I had my own relationship to mend with Maddox. Keeping him informed was the least I could do. The most was dropping a small tile tracker into the backpack I'd given her and passing the details onto him.

Whether he caught her or not, well, that was between them.

CHAPTER TWENTY-FOUR

"Operation: Sapphire" read Lily, over Dad's shoulder. She was perched on the edge of his armchair in the living room a week later, attempting to read the front page article after he'd raced inside, brandishing the newspaper, and plopped into the easy chair. "I like it. We should have called it that from the beginning."

"I'll read it out for everyone," said Dad as he held up the newspaper, obscuring every part of his head except for a tuft of his almost gray hair. From behind the pages, he continued in his best newsreader voice, "'In a remarkable feat of serendipity, Alan Reynolds and Laura Reynolds of Reynolds' Fine Jewelry were able to identify and assist in the return of an engagement ring stolen from the Mendelsons, a Jewish family, prior to their escape from Poland in the run-up to World War II. The Reynoldses returned the stunning sapphire and diamond ring to its rightful owner, the Mendelsons' daughter, Ruth Abrams, also a Montgomery resident. Investigators from the Solomon Detective Agency assisted in the effort.' Well! What a story!" Dad collapsed the paper, his smile a mile wide. "I am so proud of you, honey!"

"Thanks, Dad!" I returned his grin with one of my own. "It was a team effort."

"Serendipity is such a lovely word," sighed Mom. "Perhaps we should have called Serena that."

"Then we could call her Aunt Dippy," said my nephew, Sam. "Except everyone will think she's a Diplodocus." He snorted. "Like a dinosaur because she's so old!"

"Can't you make your children behave? Ever?" asked Serena, giving the stink eye to Garrett and Traci who were both suddenly very interested in an apparently missing button on Garrett's shirt. "When you have a baby, I hope yours will behave better," she added, turning her attention to me.

Everyone's eyes landed on me. It was like the air had been suddenly sucked out of the room.

"But I doubt it," Serena added, returning her focus to her little girl, Victoria, who was busily stacking blocks and smashing them with her little, chubby fist, then clapping gleefully as they tumbled to the floor.

"Are... are you..." stammered Mom, her eyes widening as her gaze went from my face to my stomach.

I sucked it in and rolled my eyes. "I'm not pregnant."

"I thought you'd have seven children by now," said Serena, her gaze returning to me. "It constantly surprises me that you waited until marriage and you're still not pregnant."

I restrained my hands behind my back, fighting my desire to flip her off. Well, not the desire, just the action. The desire to flip her off remained.

"Oh." Mom's shoulders sagged. "I hoped for a double whammy of good news. The icing on this case would have been another grandbaby."

"There's plenty of time for babies," said Dad, putting the newspaper aside, dislodging one of his grandchildren from climbing into his lap, and standing to wrap his arm around me. "This is a fascinating case. I'm so glad I got to be part of it."

"Couldn't have done it without you, Dad," I said, leaning into his hug.

"Or me," said Lily, flashing her hands like I could forget her.

"Or Lily," I agreed. "You were both excellent consultants on the case."

"That's right," agreed Lily, nodding sagely. "And I did it out of the goodness of my heart for no fee."

"Because you were bored and nosy and there *was* no fee," I corrected.

"That too," she agreed.

"Your dad was also bored and nosy," said Mom. "Thankfully I'm never either of those things."

"Thankfully," I deadpanned.

"I have neither the time nor the inclination," continued Mom.

"Absolutely."

"I'm a very busy woman."

"Yup."

Her phone trilled and she checked the screen as her eyes widened. "The new class program at the Adult Ed Center has just been announced!" she said, thrilled. She nudged my dad. "There's a two-for-one offer on so many of them."

"Is that right?" said Dad, collapsing back into his chair to bury his face in the sports section.

I was spared from saving Dad and his imminent sign-up to a class he had no idea he wanted to take by Solomon walking into the room, arriving so stealthily, I hadn't heard the front door open or close.

"Hi," I said as he wrapped his arm around me and kissed the top of my head. "I wondered when you'd get here."

"What's happening?" he asked.

"We're reading about the case," Dad said, waving the newspaper and pointing to the headline. "It's a great resolution."

"I just wish the ring had never been stolen in the first place," I said. "But I'm glad Ellie and Ruth and the Reynoldses are teaming up to raise awareness. Perhaps there are others who can still be helped."

"Whatever happened to that woman who stole the ring?" Dad wanted to know. "Did Maddox catch her?"

"No, he said they caught sight of her outside the Feldmans' and she had the backpack, but she disappeared pretty quickly. They eventually found the empty backpack on a bus heading downtown but the thief was long gone. I assume she had several exit routes planned before she even approached the Feldmans' house with the ring."

"She's a wily thing," said Mom, looking at her phone. "Do you think she does parkour? There's a Parkour for Seniors class here. What do you think? Two-for-one?" She looked at my dad and a ripple of fear spanned his face.

"I doubt it was parkour," I said. "She probably had disguises stashed in every direction and a vehicle to circle back to. There was no way she would trust me."

"She does seem very untrusting. Not a way to live," decided Mom.

"To be fair, Lexi did double-cross her," said Lily.

"I didn't double-cross her! I just alerted Maddox to the plan should he happen to be in the area," I said. "And the tracker in her bag was simply a precaution."

Lily snorted.

"That sounds like a double-cross," said Mom, looking up from her phone. "Your dad said she was an honorable thief. A real life Robin Hood."

"She stole diamonds from under our noses in our last case," Garrett reminded them. "She might do some good deeds but she stole gems that didn't belong to her."

"Exactly," I agreed.

"And nearly got me fired," Garrett added.

"She's so smart," said Lily. "Imagine putting one over a seasoned detective."

"Gave you the slip too," said Garrett.

"I'm strictly an amateur," replied Lily. "I can't be blamed."

"There isn't any blame to be had," I said. "Cass Temple isn't just a professional thief, she's a formidable opponent. She's perfected her craft over many years and she has a lot of resources. She plans all of her heists very meticulously."

"I am not allowing Victoria to listen to any of this," said Serena, scooping up her daughter and striding from the room. She paused at the door. "You don't all have to talk shop at home, you know."

"Now who's a fangirl?" said Lily, ignoring Serena's huffy fit entirely. Serena huffed again and stomped into the kitchen. Then to my mother, Lily said, "You should try the parkour. Cass Temple jumped off a balcony to get away from Lexi."

"I've felt like that," said Mom. "Do you want to

take the two-for-one offer?"

"Absolutely, so long as it fits in between Poppy's daycare, my shifts at the bar, and Jord's shifts at work."

"I'll request the course information and put you down as a maybe," said Mom, already enthusiastically tapping the screen.

"If she breaks a hip, it's on you," said Dad, pointing a warning finger at Lily. Then to me, "So you've no idea where this Temple woman is now?"

"None. Maddox figures she left town that same day. He said the building we tracked her to, which we think she owns through various shell corporations, was put up for sale yesterday so his guess is she won't be back."

"That'll make your life easier," said Dad. "It's better for your case completion rate to work against amateurs."

Next to me, Solomon laughed.

I frowned, uncertain if my dad were casting doubt at my abilities or considering Cass Temple's formidable ones. Regardless, he was right. Life would be a lot easier without Cass Temple outsmarting me. Not only that, but she had the knack for looking good while she was doing it. It was infuriating and admirable. Not for the first time, I wondered if we'd be friends in another life.

"Who's that?" called Dad when the front door opened.

"It's me, Tara," replied my cousin, walking in, hand-in-hand with Special Agent Sadiq Farid. She brandished a large box of chocolates, which she handed to my mother and they hugged. "Thanks for inviting us to dinner," she said.

"And me," said Maddox, walking in after them.

"How's my favorite Graves?" he said, embracing my mom while she blushed pink. "You're not my favorite," he said pointedly to me. "You lost my thief."

I threw my hands in the air, exasperated.

"Lexi handed Temple to you on a platter," said Solomon. "You lost her all by yourself."

"Not true," said Farid. "I was next to him in the car."

"We have a lead on her," said Maddox. "She was spotted in Buenos Aires two days ago."

"What's she doing there?" I asked.

"My guess is either she's taking a much needed vacation or she's targeting a yacht that got into port that same day. It's owned by a Russian billionaire with a taste for fine art and stolen Far East antiquities. One doesn't want to assume she's planning a heist," he added with a shrug that wasn't nearly as nonchalant as he intended, "but she probably is."

"We're hoping to head down there," said Farid. "I've got my bag packed in anticipation. Just waiting for the okay from the big boss."

"It's a hard life," said Maddox, "but someone has to do the tough jobs like these."

"Say hi from us," said Lily.

"Send us a postcard," said Dad.

"I'll bring you a treat," said Maddox to my mom. She giggled and fanned herself.

"We could go salsa dancing at the Adult Ed Center," said Mom, preening now.

"Nothing would make me happier than whisking you around the dance floor," said Maddox smoothly.

"Hands off," said Dad, folding the corner of his newspaper to fix Maddox with a stern look. "I might be retired but I'm still a crack shot."

"If Grandpa dies, you can marry Gran and then you'll be my grandad," said Sam and Maddox paled.

"Yeah," snorted Dad, retreating behind his newspaper once more to laugh.

"No one is dying, and no one is getting married," said Mom. "But there might be babies." She shot a pointed look at me.

"Are you..." Maddox trailed off as he gazed at my abdomen.

I sucked it in once more. "No!" Before I could say anything else, a movement caught my eye from outside the house. A brown-haired woman had been walking past but now she stooped, perhaps tying a shoelace or picking up something she dropped. She'd looked directly into the window, then disappeared out of sight, yet for a few seconds I'd had a full, clear view of her sweetheart face.

I glanced around me to see if anyone else had noticed the passerby but everyone was engaged in conversation. Solomon with my mom, Maddox and Farid were inquiring about some sporting event from my dad, Traci was reprimanding the children as they raced around, and Garrett was attempting to extract his foot from the Lego cage Sam had built around it. Only Lily, still perched on the arm of the armchair, was giving me a quizzical look.

The woman hadn't arisen. I beckoned Lily to follow as I took a long, careful step over two nieces and narrowly avoided collision with a nephew, to stand at the window overlooking the street.

Slowly, the woman arose, pulling a hat over her brunette bob, one hand on the top as if to keep it from flying away in the breeze. She wore a pretty, green summer dress, a small, cream purse slung across her shoulders. Instead of continuing her walk, she turned and looked directly at us.

"Is that…" started Lily softly.

"It can't be," I said, equally surprised.

The woman smiled warmly and waved her free hand, giving us a little finger flutter, before she turned and strolled away.

"We've got to tell—" Lily began to turn but I caught her arm.

"It can't possibly be her! You heard Maddox. She was sighted in Buenos Aires only two days ago," I said softly so only she could hear.

"She could have turned right around and got back here before they even confirmed she was ever in Buenos Aires. A wild goose chase to convince everyone she was thousands of miles away," said Lily. "Her air mile points must be astronomical!"

"Surely not," I muttered, but I wasn't sure if I were replying to Lily or considering whether Cass Temple had just waved to me outside my parents' house.

If she had, was she challenging me? Or warning me? Telling me that she knew where my parents lived? That she could come here any time? It was eerie and disconcerting, yet I'd never considered Cass a creep. Formidable, wily, conscientious, all of those things… but taking the time to send a vaguely threatening message didn't strike me as something she would do.

That left one option.

She was actually saying goodbye.

Not to the Reynoldses, nor to the Feldmans, nor to Maddox, but to me.

She could have done that in a number of different ways: a message through the detective agency's website, a postcard in the mail, even a note on my windshield. But no, she knew where I was and when, and she made sure I saw her.

"We should…"

"No," I cut in, deciding it was too ludicrous to be real. "It can't be her. It was just someone who looked like her. A neighbor or someone who knows my parents. That's why she waved. She was just being friendly. We're seeing things that aren't there."

"Yeah," snorted Lily, "That was Cass Temple and she had chutzpah."

I glanced back at the crowded room, the detectives, the FBI agents, and the PIs. I could have a full-scale search underway in minutes and we still wouldn't catch her.

"She's gone," I said. "Whoever it was."

"If she came earlier, she could have had dinner," said Lily, patting her stomach.

"In handcuffs," I said, smiling now.

"Yeah. Maybe you're right. Maybe it wasn't her."

"Maybe," I said, as we turned back to the chaos that was my family squashed into my parents' living room. "Maybe we'll never know."

Poppy toddled over to Lily at that moment and cried out for her, distracting her. I left them to their comfort cuddles, circling back to Solomon.

"What do you say we get out of here?" asked Solomon softly.

"I say yes. Where do you want to go?"

"Home."

We paused as the kids dived into the toy box my parents kept for them and emerged triumphantly, and loudly, with foam swords and light sabers.

"In need of a quiet night?"

"Not really."

"Huh?"

"I thought we'd get back to our side project."

I frowned. What hadn't I remembered, what paperwork hadn't I completed? Then... "Oh!" I smiled and lowered my voice. "Oh! That side project. Project Baby?"

"Exactly that. It's time we got this show on the road."

I glanced at my family, all occupied, all happy with the families they'd made, and extended family we'd created. I wanted to make mine. I wanted it so badly, I couldn't imagine not having what they had. I couldn't imagine not having what we wanted.

"Let's go," I said, and took his hand as we headed for the front door. "Perhaps you could square a long weekend away with the boss soon?"

"I can do that. Where do you want to go? Somewhere special?" asked Solomon as we slipped away, not wanting to suffer through any lingering goodbyes.

"Yes. Home." That was the most special place I could think of and I was lucky to have one. To never have to roam. To always have a base that welcomed me. We'd made that together.

I pulled the door shut behind me and we took a step towards our future.

Lexi Graves will return!

Love mysteries? Get *Deadlines*, a gripping, fast-paced, Hollywood whodunit, out now in paperback and ebook!

Shayne Winter thought she had it all: a dream job at the *LA Chronicle*, a sleek new apartment, and a picture-perfect LA lifestyle. But day one is a disaster—her apartment is a wreck with a roguishly handsome squatter, and her new job as chief reporter has been reduced to writing obituaries after her predecessor, Ben Kosina, waltzes back in.

When her first assignment—the accidental death of washed-up child star Chucky Barnard—takes a twist, Shayne sees her shot at redemption. Chucky's sister insists it was murder, and Shayne is determined to uncover the truth. But with a stubborn detective, a cutthroat Ben, and a killer watching her every move, she's in over her head. To save her career and her life, Shayne must crack the case—before the killer sets her final deadline.

Love mysteries? Get *Murder in the Library*, a standalone cozy mystery, out now in paperback, audiobook, and ebook!

Sara Cutler loves her job as head librarian in the charming mountain town of Calendar, where life revolves around books and quirky patrons. But her peaceful world is shattered when she discovers a body in the rare books section, threatening not only her quiet life but the library's very survival.

To save it, Sara vows to solve the murder, even if it means clashing with Jason Rees, the dashing developer determined to demolish the library. Sparks fly as their rivalry deepens, especially when the victim is revealed to be a jewel thief—and her stolen treasure is still missing.

With the whole town abuzz and danger closing in, Sara must solve the case, recover the jewels, and avoid falling for the one man who could ruin everything.

Made in the USA
Columbia, SC
13 July 2025

60684511R00202